SUPERNATURAL™

CHILDREN OF ANUBIS

ALSO AVAILABLE FROM TITAN BOOKS:

SUPERNATURAL™
CHILDREN OF ANUBIS

TIM WAGGONER

SUPERNATURAL created by Eric Kripke

TITAN BOOKS

Supernatural: Children of Anubis
Print edition ISBN: 9781785653261
E-book edition ISBN: 9781785653285

Published by Titan Books
A division of Titan Publishing Group Ltd
144 Southwark St, London SE1 0UP

First edition: April 2019
10 9 8 7 6 5 4 3 2 1

To receive advance information, news, competitions, and exclusive
offers online, please sign up for the Titan newsletter on our website:
www.titanbooks.com

A CIP catalogue record for this title is available from the British Library.
Printed and bound in the United States.

This one's for D.J. Qualls. Party on!

HISTORIAN'S NOTE
This novel is set after the Season 12 episode
"The One You've Been Waiting For."

ONE

Clay Fuller ran through the dark woods, arms raised before him to protect his face. Branches slapped against his bare forearms, stinging and drawing blood. He barely registered the pain. He was too focused on surviving the next few minutes.

His heart pounded in his ears like thunder. The only other thing he could hear was the thrashing of leaves as he dodged tree trunks and tried not to get his feet tangled in the underbrush. If he tripped and fell, he was a dead man. But if he slowed down, even a little, he would also die.

Damned if you do, damned if you don't, he thought. It was far from a comforting observation.

It was only early November in Indiana, but the night air felt winter-cold. The trees around him formed a canopy that blocked much of the moonlight. His body shook, but whether from cold, terror, both, he didn't know. Something else he didn't know: which direction he was running in. He could be running *deeper* into the woods, and if that was the case, he was well and truly screwed.

He kept running, but the adrenaline was beginning to wear off, and his legs felt like heavy iron weights. Each step became an effort. Despite his determination, he started to slow down.

No! he thought. *No, no, no, no!*

He couldn't hear them coming after him, but he could *feel* them. The back of his neck tingled, as if someone—many someones—were watching him. He caught glimpses of swift movements at the edges of his vision. But whenever he turned to look he saw nothing.

He realized then that the going was becoming easier. The trees were fewer and farther apart here, and the underbrush was sparser. He was coming to the edge of the woods. The relief was so strong that it nearly brought him to his knees. He pushed on, no longer feeling weary. He was exhilarated, and his body now seemed light as the air itself. He was going to make it! All he had to do was get out of the woods, and it would all be over. He'd be free, and more importantly, alive.

The ground sloped upward, and he could see an edge of black asphalt lining the ridge at the top of the hill. A road. He had no idea which one, but it didn't matter. Out of the woods was out of the woods. He'd be safe once he reached the road, and he'd pick a direction and start walking. Someone had to come by eventually.

He was halfway up the hill when the first one attacked. He caught a dark blur of motion out of the corner of his left eye, and then he felt a hard impact on his left shoulder. The blow staggered him, but he managed to remain on his feet. An instant later the pain hit him, a white-hot agony that made him clench his teeth and draw in a hissing, pained breath. He took a quick glance at his shoulder and saw his shirt had been shredded, and blood poured from a series of deep cuts in his flesh. There was no sign of the creature that had tagged him. It seemed to have disappeared, but he knew it was still there, along with the others. They could bring him down at any time, so why were…

Then he understood. They were playing with him.

Terror brought with it a fresh burst of adrenaline. He attacked the slope with grim determination. This was his last chance. He saw nothing this time, but he felt an impact on his right calf, and the leg crumpled beneath him. He landed hard, the impact knocking the breath from his lungs. Fire blazed to life in his calf. He didn't want to look down and see what had been done to his leg. Besides, he didn't need to look to know how serious the wound was, given the amount of blood that had already filled his sneaker. The wound would be deep, skin torn, the muscle exposed, shredded.

His surge of energy waned as quickly as it came, leaving him weak and shaky. He wanted nothing more than to close his eyes and rest. But if he did, he'd never open them again. He gritted his teeth and began crawling. He had almost reached the road when he heard growling. Soft at first, but quickly growing louder. It came from multiple directions—his right, his left, behind him—and he knew the hunt was over.

They stepped into his view then. There were three: two males, one female. At first glance they appeared human, but then he noticed their bestial teeth, curved claws, and animalistic eyes—eyes that shone with savage anticipation.

Their posture was an eerie blend of human and animal. They stood on two legs, but they were hunched over, heads thrust forward, nostrils flaring as they scented the air. They held their claws at the ready, fingers twitching.

Clay had never been a religious person. He'd never thought much about what, if anything, might lie beyond this life. He'd figured that if there was any sort of afterlife, he'd find out about it after he died. But now, looking up at these three monsters—their snarling mouths dripping with frothy saliva—he hoped there wasn't any life after death. If there was a Heaven and Hell, he had a good idea which one he was going to end up in.

The trio of monsters rushed toward him. When he screamed, the sound could be heard for miles.

Amos Boyd rumbled down Brewer Road in his pickup, the words *Boyd Fix-It* painted on the doors along with a smiling cartoon fish wearing a baseball cap and holding a wrench. He was a rail-thin man in his sixties—a widower these last three years—and he spent most of his time working. It kept him busy, so he didn't think about how much he missed his Emily. And, if he was being honest with himself, he still took on handyman work and odd jobs mostly so he had people to talk to. It could get lonely in his little house on the outskirts of Bridge Valley.

Amos had just finished dinner at Biddie's diner and was headed to the neighboring town of Cradock to install a new sink for a client. He didn't mind working late. He liked to keep busy, and besides, what the hell else did he have to do?

Instead of taking the highway, he'd opted to take Brewer Road. Brewer ran through a large stretch of woods, and he took this route whenever he could, especially in fall, when the leaves became a riot of oranges, reds, and browns. He drove with the driver's window partially down, enjoying the cool night breeze. Emily had loved the outdoors. He always felt close to her again when he drove through here, almost as if she was sitting in the passenger seat, smiling at the beauty surrounding them.

He was thinking about his wife and hoping that wherever she was, she was thinking about him too, when a man flew out of the woods and landed on the road in front of him. Amos jammed his foot down on the brake and gripped the steering wheel tighter as his truck skidded to a stop.

"What the *hell*?"

Amos wasn't aware that he'd spoken. His nerves were jangling from shock and he couldn't think clearly. He didn't immediately question why the man had come flying out of the woods as if shot from a catapult. Nor did he wonder why the man didn't stand up but instead lay on his back, looking up at the sky, eyes wide, mouth opening and closing as if he were trying to speak but couldn't manage to get any words out. He *did* notice the man's clothes were torn to shreds and that he was covered from head to toe in some kind of thick red paint, but Amos had no idea where the man had found so much paint in the woods, let alone how he'd gotten it all over himself.

His brain kicked into gear then, and he realized he was looking at a severely injured man that had jumped—no, had been *thrown*—from the woods onto the road. He was about to dial 911 when three figures darted out of the woods.

They moved with a swift grace, and at first Amos thought they were some kind of large animals: wolves or mountain lions. But when the three gathered around the fallen man and were illuminated in the wash of headlights, Amos saw that they were people. Sort of. Blood dripped from fangs and long claws—the man's blood, no doubt—and they stood like animals prepared to attack. They fixed their gazes on Amos, beast eyes gleaming, lips drawn back to more fully display their teeth. They growled low in their throats, a deep, dangerous warning. *This is our prey. Keep your distance.*

Amos dropped his phone on the seat next to him, opened the glove box, and removed his Smith & Wesson revolver. He opened the driver's side door and climbed out so he could get a better shot at his targets. He stepped to the front of his vehicle and raised his weapon.

"Get the hell away from him!"

Amos's mouth and throat were dry. His words came out as more of a croak than a command, but since he was the one holding the gun, he figured it didn't matter.

The three lunatics continued growling, but while the men remained still, the woman started walking toward him. No, not walking, *slinking*, moving with the fluid grace of an animal. Amos was about to warn her to stay back or he'd shoot, but then he saw her fangs and claws—*really* saw them this time—and her inhuman, hungry eyes fixed on him.

Without thinking, he fired three rounds in quick succession. One in the shoulder, one in the stomach, and one in the chest. She made small *oof* sounds as each round slammed into her, but while blood blossomed from each wound, there wasn't as much as there should've been.

The woman's bestial smile was hideous, and she made a snuffling canine sound that Amos realized was laughter. She continued toward him, but one of the males let out a growl and she stopped. She gnashed her sharp teeth, her claws clicking together as her hands clenched and opened, clenched and opened, as if it was taking all her will not to rip out his throat.

They stood like that for a while longer—the woman snarling, Amos aiming his gun at her—and then he fired once more. The round missed the woman, and then, moving faster than his eyes could track, she spun around and raced back to her companions. She plunged a clawed hand into the wounded man's chest—causing him to cry out one final time—and removed his still-beating heart in a thick spray of blood. And then the woman and the two men disappeared into the woods, leaving Amos standing on the road, gun still raised, body trembling, a fresh corpse lying only a few feet away.

TWO

"Dude, I *still* can't believe I killed Hitler!"

Sam took a quick look around the small diner to see if anyone had overheard Dean. There were six other people present—a mother and her two young children, a couple in their seventies, and a brown-uniformed delivery driver—but only the mother glanced in their direction. Sam gave her a sheepish smile and shrugged. She frowned then turned away.

"Inside voice," Sam said to his brother, but Dean only grinned, still hyped from the case they'd just finished. Or maybe he was excited about the slice of pie sitting on the table before him. It was something called Razzleberry Delight, a multi-layered fruit-filled, cream-topped dessert that looked like a diabetic's worst nightmare. The other customers were all eating slices of pie too, from traditional favorites like apple and coconut cream to more… *interesting* creations like candied bacon and jalapeno or cotton candy and butterscotch swirl. Sky-High Pies supposedly served the best pies for a thousand miles—at least, that's what their slogan claimed. Sam had opted for a safer choice—pecan—and he had to admit it was damn good. Maybe the best he'd ever had. Everyone seemed to be enjoying their desserts, especially Dean, who was already on his second piece of what Sam thought of as death in a pie tin.

After dealing with the Thule in Columbus, Dean had insisted they celebrate their victory over the Nazi necromancers by visiting Sky-High Pies, and while Sam had been reluctant to come here at first, he was glad they had, if for no other reason than it was nice to do something normal after their last case.

They continued eating in silence for a time. Dean put the last forkful of Razzleberry Delight into his mouth, closing his eyes and sighing.

"So what's the verdict?" Sam asked. A few bites of his pie were still left, but he wasn't sure he could finish them. If he couldn't get them down, Dean would.

Without opening his eyes, Dean held up a finger. He finished chewing, swallowed, then opened his eyes and smiled.

"Best. Pie. *Ever*."

"Better than Biggerson's?"

Dean's smile fell away and his expression became reflective.

"That's a tough one." He thought for a moment, and then said, "Sky-High Pies is better."

Dean glanced down at the remaining pecan pie on Sam's plate. Without asking, he began eating.

Sam smiled. Their lives were often chaotic—if not downright insane—and it was little things like Dean's love of pie that helped counter some of the craziness. It was such a small, normal thing, but that was what made it so comforting, especially after a case like the last one. It was important that they paused to appreciate everyday pleasures, like a good piece of pie.

"You know what would go good after this pie?" Dean asked.

"More pie?" Sam asked.

Dean grinned. "You aren't wrong, but I was thinking about a cup of coffee. There's a little diner about thirty miles from here called Josephine's, which is supposed to have the best coffee in the state. Maybe we could swing by there and—"

Sam's phone buzzed, cutting Dean off. He had an email alert. Sam had set up search engines to alert him whenever a news item fitting the right parameters was posted somewhere. This message was one such alert.

Dean's expression became serious. Time to get back to work. "What is it? Another case?"

"Maybe," Sam said. "It's a news story from Bridge Valley, Indiana."

Sam went on to tell Dean about how several days ago a truck driver came across the scene of a mutilation murder involving three people who "acted like animals" *and* who'd taken their victim's heart. "The local sheriff said he suspects it might be the work of some kind of cult," Sam said.

"The sheriff's an idiot," Dean said. "If you're talking animal people who steal hearts, you're talking werewolves. And it sounds like it might be a pack."

"Sure does," Sam said. He slipped his phone into the pocket of his jeans. "Looks like that coffee is going to have to wait."

"How far away from here is Bridge Valley?"

"I don't know. A few hours, I guess," Sam said.

Dean stood. "Well, if we're hitting the road, I'm getting some pie to go."

"I'm not sure I'm ready for this, Grandfather."

Fifteen-year-old Greg Monsour stood next to a wooden table on which a tall, lean figure lay. His head was shaped like a canine's, with a long snout and high pointed ears. The man—although Greg had trouble thinking of him as such— was wrapped in graying strips of cloth from head to toe. This was fine with Greg. He had no desire to see what was beneath the bandages.

His grandfather and grandmother stood at the foot of the table, both smiling encouragement. Nathan and Muriel Monsour were both in their early sixties and short—Nathan only an inch over five feet, Muriel a couple inches under. Their hair was so white it almost glowed, especially when compared to the brown skin of their Egyptian heritage. They were both thin, almost to the point of looking unhealthy, but that was a family trait, as was their height—or lack of it.

"Our people always look hungry to remind us of where we came from," Nathan had once told him. Greg wasn't sure what he'd meant by that, but he'd never worked up the courage to ask. His family was big on tradition—it was practically a religion with them—and one thing you didn't do was question tradition. Elders must be shown respect and their wishes obeyed in all matters, the family must remain separate from the world of humans as much as possible, and the rituals that sustained Anubis must be performed with

absolute precision, lest something go horribly wrong. Greg didn't see any harm in asking questions, though. How else were you supposed to learn? But the Monsour way was simple: keep your mouth shut, listen, and do what you were told. It drove him nuts sometimes, and he couldn't wait until the day he was an Elder. Maybe then he'd be able to change the rules, or at least loosen them a little.

Nathan wore a long-sleeved white button shirt, khaki slacks, and black shoes. He always kept his shirt collar buttoned as a nod to formality. Greg thought he'd be happier wearing a suit and tie all the time—if Muriel would allow it. She wore a flannel shirt, jeans, and sandals, and she kept her hair back in a ponytail. She was less rigid about tradition than Nathan, at least in some things—like how the family dressed—but not, however, on what they were about to do. What *he* was about do.

"Your mind is wandering," Muriel said. Her voice was gently chiding, but a stern look had come into her eyes. Greg broke off his musings and forced himself to concentrate.

The three of them stood in a small room that, aside from the table, contained shelves of stone containers, all of which were labeled with hieroglyphics. Greg's ancient Egyptian wasn't as good as his grandparents would've liked, but he knew enough to identify what was inside the jars. More or less. A stone column was located in a corner of the room, well away from the table and its occupant. A small fire burned in a recessed area atop the column, heating beneath a copper bowl containing a bubbling mixture. The room already smelled of age—mildew and wood rot—and the brazier added a miasma of exotic spices that made Greg think of a funky little shop where old hippies sold "all-natural" health supplements. He was familiar with the smell. Normally, the entire family attended the Rite of Renewal, and Greg had done so since he was an infant. But today was different. Today he was conducting the rite all by himself for the first time, which was why Nathan and Muriel—his teachers—were in attendance. This was partly to keep him from becoming too nervous, but it was also a precaution. No need for the rest of the family to be endangered. If he screwed up, only the three of them would die.

No pressure, he thought.

"Is the amaranthine prepared?" Nathan asked, intoning the words in a solemn voice.

Greg resisted the urge to glance toward the brazier and double-check. He was supposed to show confidence.

"I have to add the final ingredient."

He was so nervous his voice cracked on the last word, but his grandparents acted like they didn't notice.

"Then do so," Muriel said. Her tone was more encouraging than Nathan's, but her gaze was just as serious.

"Yes, Grandmother."

Greg thought of his first lesson in conducting the rite, delivered by his grandparents when he was fourteen.

"Why do I have to learn the rite?" he'd asked. *"Everyone else knows how to do it."*

Too late, he'd feared his question would offend Nathan's sense of tradition, but he'd only smiled and said, *"Everyone in the family must know how to perform the rite. What if some of us are incapacitated? What about when we die? No matter what, the rite must be performed, once a month, during the cycle of the full moon. It is the jakkals' sacred duty and our great honor."*

Greg walked to the shelves and opened a polished wooden box. Inside, a bronze dagger lay on black velvet. Hieroglyphs were etched into the metal, and although the light in the storeroom wasn't especially strong, the symbols seemed to glimmer. He removed the Blade of Life Everlasting, gripped the handle with both hands, and pressed it flat against his heart, point upward. He then crossed to the brazier, taking ten measured steps. Why it had to be ten, he didn't know. Would the rite fail if he took nine steps or eleven? It seemed like such a small detail, but his grandparents had drilled into him the importance of getting every single detail of the rite correct. He did not want to disappoint them.

When he reached the brazier, he stopped and held the blade over the bubbling amaranthine with his right hand, keeping the left pressed over his heart. He spoke a series of words in ancient Egyptian, doing his best to pronounce each distinctly.

"We praise you, Great Anubis, son of Nephthys and Set, Lord of the Sacred Land, Protector of the Dead, Guardian of Eternal Shadow. You, who inhabit the borderland between life and death, darkness and light, dreams and waking. We brew for you this holy elixir so that you might drink deep and continue your long slumber until such time as your people once more have need of your guidance, strength, and savagery. We pray you find our offering worthy, Dread Lord, that your eyes remain closed, your heart silent, your limbs still, until the next cycle begins."

Despite his determination to conduct the rite properly,

he feared he rushed the words. His grandparents didn't say anything. He held his left hand over the amaranthine, then pressed the edge of the knife to his palm.

This was going to hurt.

He gritted his teeth—which, without his being aware of it, had sharpened—and drew the blade slowly across his palm, slicing through skin and deep into the muscle beneath. He made a fist and let his blood run down into the amaranthine. The mixture turned black, and a coppery tang mingled with the smell of weird spices.

The blood streaming from his fist slowed to a trickle and then stopped altogether. He opened his hand. There was no sign of the wound, and no blood on his hand either. His body had reabsorbed it as he healed. Pleased and relieved that he hadn't messed up anything yet, he returned the Blade of Life Everlasting to its case. There was no blood on the dagger. He wasn't sure if his body had reabsorbed it or if the blade had drunk it as payment for its service. He wasn't sure he wanted to know. Then he returned to the brazier and lifted the copper bowl containing the now-completed amaranthine. He felt his flesh burn, but he forced himself to ignore the sensation. Pushing through pain was part of the ritual, and he would heal soon enough. All he wanted to do now was finish the last part and get this over with.

He carried the amaranthine to the table. There was an imperceptible gap between the cloth strips over the figure's mouth. He lifted the bowl to the gap and slowly poured the mixture into the mummy's mouth. Anubis remained still as death, but Greg—with his people's enhanced hearing—

could detect the soft sounds of swallowing. When the last of the amaranthine was gone, Greg let out a relieved sigh, but then crimson light began to glow through the bandages covering Anubis's eyes. The sight terrified Greg. During all his lessons in attending to Anubis, he'd never seen the god do anything like this. Something was wrong. "Grandfather, Grandmother, what's happening?" he cried.

"Step away from the table," Nathan said. He spoke softly, and for the first time in Greg's life, he heard fear in his grandfather's voice. "Before Anubis—"

Nathan's eyes went wide, his mouth fell open, and he transformed. His teeth became fangs, his fingers lengthened into claws, his ears grew pointed, and short golden fur sprouted on his cheeks and chin. But his eyes—which normally would have been a bright amber—glowed with a strange crimson light. There was no sign of Greg's grandfather in those eyes.

Nathan rushed to Greg's side, moving fast as lightning, and grabbed the boy's wrist in a grip like iron. Startled, Greg let go of the empty bowl. It hit the mummy's chest and fell to the floor. Greg tried to pull free, but his grandfather's grip was too strong. His touch was so cold, it burned. The pain intensified, becoming so bad that Greg was tempted to transform and gnaw off his hand. Maybe he'd grow a new hand, maybe he wouldn't. So long as the pain stopped, he didn't care one way or another.

Greg began to transform out of reflex, but his change came slower to him. Despite Greg's youth, his grandfather was an Elder, and far more powerful. Jakkals could heal almost any wound, except those caused by gold, but injuries inflicted by one of their own people took far longer to heal. There was no way he could survive an attack by Nathan, and he knew it. At first he couldn't understand why Nathan had suddenly become a mindless, vicious animal, but then he realized what must have happened. He was no longer looking into his grandfather's eyes, but rather those of Anubis. He'd done something wrong during the Rite of Renewal, and Anubis had partially awakened. The god had possessed Nathan and was using the Elder to defend himself against what, in his dreamlike state, he viewed as an attack.

Nathan raised his free hand, his claws still lengthening, but before he could strike Greg, Muriel was suddenly there. She backhanded her husband so hard that his jaw broke with a sharp crack. His head snapped back, and he collapsed to the floor, stunned.

Muriel quickly moved past Greg and lowered her head, placing her mouth close to Anubis's ear. She then spoke in ancient Egyptian.

"*Great Dark One, return to your slumber. All is well.*"

Greg looked at Anubis's cloth-wrapped body. The crimson light emanating from the god's eyes dimmed, and his chest ceased its rise and fall. His eyes went dark once more, and his lungs stopped working. With a shaking hand, Greg touched the god's bandaged wrist, but he felt no pulse. Anubis had returned to his slumber.

Now that Greg was free of Nathan's grasp, he inspected the flesh where his grandfather had grabbed him. The skin on his wrist was dry and leathery, almost as if he had aged in the place where Nathan—or rather, Anubis—had touched him. He expected to see the skin return to normal as his body's supernatural healing capabilities went to work, but seconds passed and his wrist looked no better. *This isn't good,* he thought, fighting to keep a surge of panic at bay.

"Don't worry," Muriel said. "Anubis was not fully awakened, and so was not at his full strength. Your wrist will heal, although more slowly than you're used to. You'll be fine."

His grandmother's words reassured him.

A moment later, Nathan groaned and rose stiffly to his feet. His features were human once again, and his eyes no longer glowed crimson. His lower jaw tilted too far to the right. He reached up and put it back into place with a sickening *click*. He opened and closed his mouth experimentally, and then smiled.

"I'm all right," he said.

Muriel stepped to his side, and he put his arms on her waist.

"We're lucky Anubis didn't fully awaken," she said. "Otherwise, he might've taken full control of you, and if that happened—"

"You wouldn't have been able to knock me out so easily," Nathan said, smiling.

Muriel smiled back, but Greg could feel the tension between them. They'd all just had a very close call, and they knew it.

Anubis existed in a twilight state, neither fully alive nor fully dead, and when he was awakened, the god himself didn't rise to fight. Instead, he possessed a vessel, and when the time came, the jakkals willingly, even joyfully, consented to be used by their god. But no one could resist the ancient one's power, and he could take control of anyone he wished, regardless of whether they gave him permission. Anubis could've just as easily possessed him or Muriel as he had Nathan, and there was nothing they could've done to stop him. Greg wondered what it would be like to have the god's spirit take over his body. He'd been taught that serving the god as a vessel was the greatest honor a jakkal could hope for, but Greg found the idea terrifying. Did you lose consciousness when Anubis took over, or were you instead aware the entire time, a passive presence in your own body, able to do no more than observe? Either way sounded awful.

"I'm so sorry, Grandfather," Greg said. "I didn't know that could happen."

"Don't be too hard on yourself," Nathan said. "Mistakes happen. It likely occurred because you mispronounced a word or two of the invocation."

"Or you didn't let the amaranthine brew long enough," Muriel said. "The Rite of Renewal is more art than science. But you did well enough for your first try."

"That's right." Nathan clapped Greg on the shoulder. "You'll get it right next time."

Greg knew his grandparents were trying to make him feel better, but it wasn't working. He looked down at the slumbering form of his people's god and feared that the next time he tried to conduct the rite by himself, it would go even worse.

THREE

As the Impala cruised past the WELCOME TO BRIDGE VALLEY sign, Dean turned off the radio—a classic rock station, naturally—and sat up a bit straighter in the driver's seat. Regardless of what they suspected was happening in a given case, they needed to be hyper-aware of their surroundings. When you were a hunter, you had to be ready to shift gear at a moment's notice. If you couldn't do that, you wouldn't last very long. So while the news report *sounded* like they had a werewolf pack on their hands, they had to remain open to other possibilities—which meant paying attention.

They'd stopped at a rest area a few miles outside town and changed into what Dean thought of as their monkey suits. Even after all this time using their FBI-agents-investigating-a-mysterious-death bit, Dean still hadn't gotten used to wearing these clothes. The shirt collar always itched, and the pants felt a little tight. He wondered if they'd shrunken a little the last time they'd been dry-cleaned. Without realizing it, he removed one hand from the steering wheel and tugged at his pants, as if trying to loosen them.

Sam smiled. "What's wrong? All that pie catching up to you?"

Dean put his hand back on the steering wheel and gave Sam a look. "Very funny."

Bridge Valley looked much like any other small Midwestern town that the brothers had visited over the years: modest suburban neighborhoods, strips malls, fast-food and chain restaurants—even a Biggerson's. The one place of interest, an amusement park called Happyland, was closed and long deserted. The farther into town they drove, the more rundown the houses became, and the more unkempt the properties. More than a few houses had boarded-up windows, but none of them had For Sale sign in the yards.

"Looks like this town's fallen on hard times," Dean said.

"I think I know why."

Sam nodded to a small office building up ahead with a sign above the entrance that read FRESH START: DRUG AND ALCOHOL ABUSE CLINIC.

Dean sighed. There were all kinds of monsters that preyed on people, and not all of them had fangs and claws.

Downtown looked as if it hadn't changed much since the mid-twentieth century. Three-story brick buildings, old-fashioned street lights, wooden benches for pedestrians who wanted to sit and watch the traffic go by. There were signs proclaiming the area to be a historic district, and Dean thought if that meant old and boring, then it was an excellent description. There were a few promising places—a donut shop, a pizza joint, and a bar called The Whistle Stop. The latter was located next to the office of the local newspaper, *The Bridge Valley Independent*.

Convenient for the staff, Dean thought. *After a long day of writing stories about cows and cornfields, who wouldn't want to throw one back?* Then he remembered the clinic they'd passed, and he felt guilty. From what they'd seen so far, booze and drugs were nothing to joke about in Bridge Valley.

The sheriff's office was located in the city building, which looked more like an old-timey courthouse: all white marble, thick columns, and wide stone steps. From the moment they pulled into the parking lot, the brothers were "on." The key to getting people to buy into their FBI disguise wasn't so much to look the part, although that was important, but to project an aura of detached, professional confidence. That meant looking slightly bored, presenting themselves with an air of authority, and above all, no smiling or making jokes. FBI agents did *not* have a sense of humor. Not while working, anyway.

They walked up the stone steps, continued through a pair of chrome-and-glass doors, and flashed their fake IDs at the security guard on duty. The Winchesters had put on this act dozens of times, but Dean always felt a tightening in his gut as he prepared to meet the local law. Maybe this would be the time their fake IDs didn't work, and if that happened, they'd have to find a way to get out of here without hurting anyone. That, or get ready for an extended stay in a place where the rooms had bars instead of doors. As usual, Dean marked the exits. A certain amount of perpetual paranoia had become second nature to the brothers over the years.

A few minutes later, they reached the sheriff's department,

and—after showing their IDs again—a deputy ushered them into the sheriff's office.

Sheriff Alan Crowder was a fit-looking man in his early fifties, clean-shaven, his silver hair cut in a military style. He didn't rise from his desk to greet them as they entered, and he regarded them with a cold, level gaze that told Dean they weren't welcome here.

Crowder's office was professional and impersonal: a desk with a computer and office phone, chairs, an American flag on a stand in one corner, and framed certificates detailing the man's accomplishments on the walls. The one personal touch was a large photograph hanging on the wall of the sheriff and his family—wife, sons, daughter. They were all smiling, showing perfect white teeth. Crowder's smile looked as if it didn't come naturally to him.

There were two chairs in front of the sheriff's desk, but he didn't invite them to sit. Dean figured the man was doing this on purpose to let them know this was *his* territory. He didn't take it personally. They had run into more than their fair share of local cops who wanted to play Mine's Bigger Than Yours. Let the big bad sheriff play his power games. All the Winchester brothers cared about was getting the information they needed to work their case.

"Sheriff Crowder," Sam said. "I'm Agent Curtis, and this is Agent Olson."

Dean kept his expression neutral as Sam introduced them, but inside he was irritated. Sam thought he had been getting too reckless with their fake names. They'd been on a case not long ago, and one of the officers they'd worked with believed

Dean was related to the famous singer whose last name he'd "borrowed" and kept asking Dean if he could get an autograph from his "cousin." *"Not for me,"* the cop had said, embarrassed. *"For my kid."* So Sam had taken to jumping in and introducing them before Dean could speak, using generic cover names. He figured Sam was probably right, but that didn't mean he had to like it.

"What can I do for you?" Crowder asked, an edge in his voice that told Dean the man was more than a little irked by their presence.

"We'd like to talk to you about Clay Fuller," Sam said.

Crowder's eyes narrowed. "Now why would a couple of federal agents be interested in a small-time drug dealer like him?"

"We aren't at liberty to discuss the details," Sam said, "but the murder shares some… similarities with other cases we've worked on in the past."

Cases featuring some very toothy, very hungry wolf-people, Dean thought.

"I don't see what's so special about a drug pusher getting killed," Crowder said. "Pretty run-of-the-mill stuff, if you ask me."

"The reports we've seen said Mr. Fuller was mutilated," Sam said, "and his heart was removed. Not exactly 'run-of-the-mill.'"

"And the killers were described as animal-like," Dean added.

Crowder let out a snort of a laugh. "You boys getting your news from the tabloids? I know that's what Amos Boyd said. He's a nice guy and all, but he's starting to get up there, plus he's been known to take a drink now and again, if you know what I mean. But putting all that aside, you know eyewitness testimony is unreliable. When people find themselves in stressful, traumatic situations, their perceptions go all to hell. I have no doubt Amos witnessed Fuller's murder—the end of it, at least. Hell, he was the one who called it in, and he was on the scene when one of my deputies got there. But I think when he saw the savagery with which Fuller was attacked, and when he saw the blood... Fear and imagination did the rest. I think Fuller's murder was ordered by a rival drug pusher or maybe someone he owed money to. But he sure as hell wasn't killed by animal-people."

These were all reasonable things to say, and yet Dean's bullcrap detector was going off like crazy.

"What about removing the heart?" Dean asked.

Crowder shrugged. "Maybe it was some kind of cult thing."

"Not to dispute your account," Sam said, "but if my partner and I are going to do our due diligence on this case, we'll need to take a look at the body."

"I'm afraid you're too late," Crowder said, not quite smiling. "Fuller didn't have any relatives, so once the coroner released the body, it was cremated."

Sam asked Crowder if there had been similar attacks in the area, and the sheriff said, "You mean druggies killing each other, or are you asking about attacks of the heart-stealing variety? Either way, it's a yes on one and a no on the other."

They asked a few more questions after that, but Crowder's answers were no more helpful. Afterward, the sheriff stood for the first time since they entered and leaned forward, hands palm-down on his desk. He drew his lips back from his teeth in what Dean supposed was meant to be a smile, but which had all the warmth of winter in Antarctica.

"If there's nothing else I can do for you boys, I really should get back to work. Bridge Valley may be a small town, but there's still plenty to do around here."

"I guess so," Dean said, "what with citizens getting killed on the side of your roads and all."

Crowder's smile, such as it was, didn't falter. But his eyes—which were a deep forest green—flashed with momentary anger. But then it was gone, as quickly as it had come.

"One of my deputies will show you out," the sheriff said. "You boys have a nice day."

"That guy's a mega-douche," Dean said.

The brothers stood in the city building's parking lot next to the Impala as they talked.

"Yeah," Sam said. "Awfully convenient that Clay Fuller's body was cremated."

"I thought the same thing. How much you want to bet that if we spoke to the coroner, we'd hear the same story that Crowder gave us? That Fuller was killed by regular humans?"

"No bet," Sam said. He and Dean would check with the coroner just to cover their bases, though.

"You think Crowder's got something to do with Fuller's death?" Dean asked.

"I suppose it's possible, but we've encountered local law enforcement that were reluctant to cooperate with the FBI before. And we've run into authorities who can't admit that something really weird is going on in their town and conceal the truth while they try to figure out what the hell to do. Crowder could fit into both of those categories."

Once in a while it was more effective to come right out and tell people that their real job was to protect them from supernatural threats. Sam doubted this approach would work in this case, though. Crowder didn't strike him as the most open-minded person.

"Okay," Dean said. "Crowder's a jerk, but that might be as far as it goes. We should talk to the guy driving the pickup—"

"Amos Boyd," Sam put in.

"Yeah, him. It'll be interesting to see if he sticks to the story he told reporters or if the sheriff's gotten him to change his tune."

"Speaking of reporters," Sam said, "I think we should stop by the local newspaper office. Maybe somebody there can tell us more about Amos—if he's a credible witness, where he lives…"

"Good idea. And hopefully they can tell us if there have been other strange deaths or disappearances in the area. Let's just hope the sheriff hasn't told them not to talk to out-of-towners."

Sam supposed that was a possibility, but in his experience, reporters—even small-town ones—were dedicated to informing their readers about any potential danger they might face. And reporters did not respond well to being told what news they could and couldn't report. The trick with reporters was getting them to talk without answering whatever questions they might ask in return. And they *always* asked questions.

"Look on the bright side," Sam said. "There's a bar next door to the paper, right? If we don't learn anything useful, we can stop in there, ask a few questions, maybe get an early dinner. I'm sure they serve something deep-fried, greasy, and thoroughly unhealthy."

"You had me at deep-fried," Dean said.

* * *

After the two agents departed, Crowder sat down at his desk once more, leaned back in his chair, and stared up at the ceiling. He didn't believe the agents had told him the truth—at least not all of it—about why they'd come to Bridge Valley. He supposed it was possible the FBI was investigating mutilation murders where the victim's heart had been torn out. Murders other than Clay Fuller's, that is, but he hadn't gotten wind of any outside Bridge Valley. There was something about the agents' interest in Fuller that rubbed Crowder the wrong way. They had seemed professional enough, at least in terms of their attitude. Their suits could've used a good pressing, and he doubted their haircuts were regulation. But they'd projected alert, calm confidence, which said they weren't easily intimidated. They'd resisted his attempts to stir them up. Although he had started to irritate the square-jawed one toward the end. The questions they'd asked had been normal enough, but there'd been something about the *way* they'd asked them that bothered him. An intensity, as if his answers mattered to them. Mattered a *lot*.

His instincts told him he'd have to keep close watch on them while they were in his town—and his instincts were *always* right. Whatever their agenda was, the last thing he needed was for a couple of feds to start causing trouble in Bridge Valley. He lowered his gaze to the family photograph hanging on the wall. This town was more than just the place where he lived—it was his *territory*, and he intended to defend it, no matter what.

FOUR

Nathan—nursing a lingering headache from being possessed by Anubis—sat in a black vinyl chair and sipped a cup of coffee, also black. Like most of their belongings, the chair had been reclaimed, which in this case meant it had been found on the side of the road, waiting for garbage collectors to pick it up. It held a faint odor of mildew. He found it rather pleasant. Jakkals liked things that were *well-seasoned*, to put it politely. He didn't like the way the chair leaned to the right, however. Seasoned was one thing. On the verge of falling to pieces was another. At his age, he preferred comfort over thriftiness, but he would never confess this to anyone in the family, even his beloved Muriel. As an Elder, it was his duty to uphold their traditions, and scavenging was one of their oldest practices. But he could at least admit to himself, if only privately, that tradition could sometimes be a pain in the ass. He shifted his weight on the lopsided seat in a futile attempt to get more comfortable.

Sometimes literally, he thought.

Aside from the vinyl chair, there was an orange couch, several plastic milk crates that served as end tables, and a soiled throw rug that might once have been white but which now was a mottled gray. There was no television in the room, for the building had no cable or satellite connection. Their people lived off the grid as much as possible, and when they wanted to watch movies or listen to music, they had DVDs and CDs to play on the communal laptop they shared.

Muriel entered the room from their small kitchen. Their current quarters were somewhat cramped—a handful of rooms that had once served as office space—but Nathan was used to living in close quarters. When you moved around as much as their family did, you made do with whatever living spaces you could scrounge up.

Muriel carried in hot tea in a chipped mug, and she took a seat opposite him on the couch, which had been repaired in numerous places with duct tape. It might have been functional, but it was one of the ugliest pieces of furniture Nathan had ever seen.

"How's Greg doing?" he asked.

"How's your *head* doing?" Muriel countered.

He could hear the worry in her voice. While they'd done their best to reassure Greg that what had happened with Anubis wasn't anything to be concerned about, Nathan had never experienced anything like it. Nathan had seen their god stir unexpectedly before, but he'd only witnessed a twitch of a hand, a turning of the head. Nothing compared to the god forcibly taking over Nathan's body as if he had no more free will than a puppet. There had been almost no warning, only a sudden tingling sensation on the back of his skull, and then his very *self* had been shoved roughly aside. Anubis's mind—or at least a portion of it—had taken over, forcing his body to change before attacking his grandson. If Muriel hadn't managed to convince the god that he was safe, Nathan didn't know what might've happened. Would Anubis have used his claws and his teeth to kill Greg? If one jakkal wounded another badly enough, they could die. The thought sickened Nathan. He'd been aware the entire time Anubis had possessed him, unable to do anything but watch as the god went after Greg. If Greg had died, Anubis would've been the one who'd done the killing, but Nathan would've been there every second, helpless. He took a sip of coffee, hoping it would settle his stomach, but it stung his throat and hit his gut like caffeine-infused lava. His head throbbed harder, and he winced.

"Don't worry. My head's still attached." He tried smiling, but it came out as a grimace. "Greg?" he prompted.

Muriel sipped her drink, which smelled of pungent spices. The tea's recipe had been passed down through the millennia, and its scent was as familiar to Nathan as his own. He wouldn't have been surprised if Muriel had brewed it for that very reason.

"His wrist is starting to heal, but the process is far slower than it should be. I believe he will make a full recovery, but it will take some time."

Muriel didn't sound as sure of herself as Nathan would've liked, but then how could she be? As far as he knew, nothing like this had ever happened before.

"Where is he now?"

"He's having his lessons with Marta," Muriel said.

Given how often the Monsours moved, and more importantly, to protect their family's secret, the children were homeschooled. Greg would be in one of the bedrooms with his mother, going over educational material on the laptop, although for their kind, the word *bedroom* meant the place where they laid out their sleeping bags. He was glad Marta was keeping the boy busy. Hopefully, it would prevent him from dwelling on what had happened during the Rite of Renewal. And just as importantly, while Greg was occupied, Nathan and Muriel could speak plainly without hurting their grandson's feelings. They didn't have to worry about anyone else in the family overhearing. Greg's father and older sisters were out on a scavenging run and wouldn't be back until later.

"Do you have any idea what went wrong?" Muriel asked.

Nathan started to shake his head. The motion set off a fresh wave of pain and he instantly regretted it. "None whatsoever. You?"

"No. I paid close attention to Greg's every word and action—as I know you did, my love—and as near as I could tell, he performed the rite perfectly."

"That was my assessment as well."

He took another sip of coffee, Muriel drank more tea, and the two of them sat in silence for a time as they thought.

"Perhaps the ingredients for the amaranthine—" Muriel began.

"They were fine," Nathan said. "We both inspected them

beforehand. Their scent and texture were in acceptable condition."

"Then perhaps there is something wrong with this place," she ventured. "This *was* the first time we attempted the rite since moving here."

Attempted being the operative word. Greg had completed all the steps of the rite before Anubis had stirred, but Nathan didn't know if the rite had worked. If it had, Anubis's sleep should've remained undisturbed. But it hadn't. Did that mean the rite needed to be conducted again? If so, they couldn't afford to wait. The cycle of the full moon lasted three days. The day of the full moon itself, and the days before and after. The rite worked at any time during the cycle, regardless of whether the sun was high above or if it was the dead of night. Tonight was the actual full moon. They still had some time left, but not much.

As far as Nathan knew, the rite had never been conducted twice during a single cycle. He didn't know what effect it might have on their god. It could ensure his slumber or it could wake him, and Nathan didn't want to chance that.

"A thought occurs to me," Muriel began. "One so terrible that I don't wish to speak it."

Muriel was not prone to exaggeration, and if she spoke these words, she meant them.

"Go on," he said, unsure if he wanted to hear what she had to say but knowing he must listen. It was his duty.

"How old do you think Anubis is?" she asked.

The question took him by surprise.

"I…" He trailed off and thought for a moment. "Our

family history goes back almost four thousand years, and our people were guarding our sleeping god even then. There is no way to know how long we have been his keepers as well as his worshippers."

"All we know is he is *old*. Immeasurably so."

"Yes."

"He *is* a god, and time does not affect him the same way it does us. But it *does* affect him. We must change his cerements from time to time, and even the need for the Rite of Renewal proves that time passes for him. If it did not, there would be no need to help him sleep."

Nathan didn't know where Muriel was going with this line of reasoning, but it did not seem productive to him. Still, he continued listening.

"So what does old *mean* for a being such as him? Is he so old that his power is not what it once was? Is he so old that his body—perhaps even his mind—has aged to the point where the Rite of Renewal is losing its effectiveness?"

He understood what she was driving at then, and the knowledge caused the hair on the back of his neck to rise in alarm, and his teeth and fingernails to grow sharper, as if he suddenly found himself in danger.

If what Muriel was suggesting was true—if after all these long millennia Anubis was finally growing old—they might not be able to keep him sleeping much longer. And if he woke and refused to listen to the family's guidance, it was impossible to say how much damage he might do. Nathan thought of Anubis as a powerful protector of the jakkals on those rare occasions when his great strength was needed and they were forced to wake him. But if Muriel's theory turned out to be correct, their god had become a ticking time bomb that could go off any moment, threatening the family's survival.

"What are we to do?" Muriel asked in a plaintive voice, but Nathan had no answer for her. One thing was certain, though: they couldn't pray for divine guidance, not when their god was the problem that needed to be solved.

FIVE

Amos Boyd pulled into the driveway of his ranch house in the early afternoon. He parked, but instead of getting out of his pickup right away, he sat there awhile, thinking.

He'd left around six a.m. and had already put in almost a full day's work, and he was tired and hungry. He parked in the driveway because the garage door opener was broken. He worked as a handyman these days, but he never seemed to find the time to take care of the jobs that needed doing in his own home. It was like that old saying: *The cobbler's children always go barefoot.*

It was one thing to do work for others and get paid for it, and another to work for yourself for free. Especially when you were tired, which he was all too often these days. He didn't think of himself as an old man—all right, not *very* old—but he ran out of energy earlier in the day than he used to. In his mind, he was still in his thirties, but his body was more than twice that, and it had its own ideas about when to work and when to rest. He'd started the morning fixing Louisa Hudson's drier which only blew cold air, and he'd finished by mending a leaf blower for eighty-nine-year-old Tom Munoz, and he'd stuck around afterward to clear the leaves off the man's yard at no extra charge. And in between he'd worked several more jobs. He was exhausted, and all he wanted to do now was eat lunch, sit in his favorite chair and watch TV the rest of the afternoon. And if he dozed off, so much the better. He needed the rest after everything that had happened.

He'd wanted to stay busy this morning, wanted—no, *needed*—to work in order to keep his mind off the terrible thing he'd witnessed. He'd seen the mutilation and murder of a young man, and he hadn't been able to prevent it. He'd been having trouble sleeping ever since, and when he'd finally drifted off last night, he had nightmares of being surrounded by fanged, snarling people who advanced toward him step by step, curved claws ready to tear into him. He'd woken up abruptly, momentarily disoriented. He thought he'd heard someone scream and realized that it must've been him. He'd started early today and worked hard all morning, hoping to tire himself out so he wouldn't experience a repeat of last night.

And as bad as seeing that young man murdered by those three crazy people—or whatever they were—the aftermath hadn't been much more pleasant for him. Reporters from both Bridge Valley and neighboring towns had gotten wind of what had happened, and before long the sheriff's office had reporters and news vans parked outside. A fair number of looky-loos showed up as well, most likely having heard the report on their police scanners or via social media. All those people looking at him, shouting questions… It had been too much for him, and when the sheriff finally turned him loose, he was more than ready to go home and try to forget about what he'd seen.

As if that were possible.

He'd done his best not to dwell on the murder today, but while he was repairing a machine or plastering a hole in the wall, images came to him—yellow eyes, blood-slick teeth and claws—accompanied by sounds and smells. Growling, the primitive scent of excited animals, the wet tearing of flesh, the crack of ribs…

It hadn't helped that he'd been getting calls from representatives of one media outlet or another, wanting him to appear on camera and talk about the "grisly crime" he'd witnessed. But worst of all was the knowledge that the police didn't believe his story, that crazy people with fangs and claws killed a young man and stole his heart. Sheriff Crowder had kept a stony face the whole time he'd interviewed Amos, but it was clear the man hadn't credited his story. Some of his deputies hadn't bothered to hide their disbelief and exchanged smirking glances with each other when they thought he wasn't looking.

He was starting to doubt his own memories. Everything had happened so fast. Was it possible he'd only imagined the killers had possessed animalistic traits? Maybe they'd looked like beasts to him because they'd *acted* like beasts? And maybe he'd only *thought* he'd hit the woman when he'd shot at her. It was dark, and he had been scared and confused. Hard to aim in those circumstances. Sheriff Crowder had suggested all these things, and maybe the man had been right. Amos didn't know.

He got out of his pickup and entered his house. As soon as he set foot inside, he felt better. Coming home wasn't the same without Emily here, but they'd lived in this house for close to fifty years, and her presence still suffused the place, and that was a comfort to him.

He walked through the foyer and into the kitchen. Although he'd been looking forward to lunch, now that he was here, he wasn't hungry. He *was* thirsty, however. He got a bottle of beer from the refrigerator and took a long, satisfying drink. When he lowered the bottle, he realized something was wrong.

Rusty.

Rusty was an old tabby cat that he'd picked up from an animal shelter a few weeks after Emily passed. He'd thought having a pet around the house would be good for him, and he figured a cat would be fairly low maintenance. He'd planned on getting a younger animal, but when he saw Rusty, grizzled old thing that he was, he felt he'd found a kindred spirit. Rusty wasn't overly affectionate, which suited Amos fine, but the cat liked to be in the same room as his owner, and he always came to greet Amos when he got home and meow for a treat. Amos would give him a pinch of lunch meat—roast beef was his favorite—and then they'd settle down for a quiet evening of watching TV.

But there was no Rusty.

Amos supposed he could be down in the basement using his litterbox, but Rusty had *never* failed to greet him at the door. Not once.

He felt a cold prickle on the back of his neck, as if someone was watching him. He put his beer down on the kitchen counter and turned around quickly, but no one was there.

Getting paranoid in your old age, Amos. But on the other hand, he hadn't reached his current age by not listening to his gut instincts. He told himself he should call 911, but he'd dealt with the sheriff and his deputies plenty yesterday. They already thought he was a few bricks shy of a load, and if he *was* letting his imagination run away with him, he didn't want them to come out here, find nothing, and have another reason to laugh at him. No, whatever this was, he'd handle it alone. He went back outside to get his revolver from his pickup, and then returned to the house.

Holding his gun with the barrel pointed toward the ceiling, like he'd seen cops in police shows do, he began slowly moving through the house, doing his best to make as little sound as possible. If there was someone else inside here with him, they'd have heard him come in, but he didn't want them to know his exact location. He'd already been in the kitchen, so he checked the living room. As he entered, he was prepared to see an intruder—maybe holding a weapon of their own—standing in the middle of the room. But no one was there. He quickly checked behind the couch and the easy chairs on either side of it, but he found nothing other than a few dust bunnies.

He turned back around and headed for the hallway that led to the bedrooms. The hall, like the living room, was empty. There were five doors in the hallway leading to three bedrooms, one bathroom, and a linen closet. He stood in the middle of the hall, listening for the slightest sound—a scrape of movement, a sigh of breath—but he heard nothing, save the nervous pounding of his heart. He flipped a mental coin and chose to investigate the bathroom first.

If this was a movie, the hero would kick the door open, level his weapon, and shout, *Freeze or I'll shoot!* This wasn't a movie, though, and he opened the door the usual way, but he stepped to the side, in case someone was in there. But the bathroom was empty. Starting to feel a bit foolish now, he checked the bedroom across from the bathroom. This room had belonged to Amos and Emily's only child, Traci. She was in her thirties and lived with her wife in Portland, so now it served as a guest room, which meant it stayed empty most of the year, except for Thanksgiving and Christmas, when Traci and Rebecca came to visit.

It was empty, too.

He continued down the hall, passing the linen closet on the way. There wasn't enough room for anyone to hide in there—too many towels, sheets, and blankets—so he didn't bother checking it. The last two rooms were located at the end of the hall, on opposite sides. The one on the right was his and Emily's bedroom. He still thought of it as being hers too. The one on the left was nominally a home office—a desk for a computer, a filing cabinet for important papers—but over the years it had become an unofficial storage room. There were cardboard boxes filled with Traci's childhood toys, clothes which Emily had never had the heart to get rid of, holiday decorations, and boxes of paperback westerns that Amos had read over the years and thought he might get around to rereading someday. It was as empty as the rest of the house. He closed the door to the office, stepped to the master bedroom, and then—expecting to find nothing—opened the door.

Cool air wafted over him, and when he turned on the light, he saw the window over the bed had been broken, the curtains torn down and shredded on the floor. Glass shards covered the comforter, and standing nearby, slowly slicing her palm with a piece of glass—was the woman who'd ripped out the young man's heart.

She didn't look at him at first. She watched blood flow from the wounds she'd created on her palm, almost hypnotized by it. Amos knew he had to be mistaken, but it looked as if the cuts healed almost as soon as she made them.

She wore the same clothes she'd had on yesterday, only now they were stained with stiff patches of blood, and her eyes, teeth, and claws were those of a beast.

My god, he thought. *My nightmare from last night… it's coming true.*

He'd lowered the revolver to his side when he'd stepped into the room, but now he raised it, took aim at the beast-woman, and fired. Once he started, he didn't stop until he'd emptied his weapon. Amos was frightened, so his hand wasn't as steady as it could be, but he still managed to put four of the revolver's six rounds into the woman. One hit her left shoulder, one entered her lower left abdomen—drilling a hole through one of her kidneys, he thought—one struck the meat of her left thigh and passed right through, but one slammed into her chest, a few inches to the right of her heart. But while the woman's body jerked with the impact of each bullet and she let out soft grunts of pain, she did not go down. Blood soaked her clothes with fresh gore, but she didn't take her gaze from her palm, which she still slowly cut with the glass shard. After a moment, she looked at him and smiled, displaying fangs. She turned her wounded palm to him. Now there were no cuts or scars, no indication the skin had been marred at all.

He understood why she did this. Just as her hand had healed the damage she'd inflicted upon it, so too had the bullet wounds he'd caused. His revolver might as well have been a pea-shooter for all the effect it had on her.

The woman's hand blurred. Fiery pain exploded in the space between the first and second fingers of his right hand. The woman had thrown the shard like a shuriken, and it had sunk deep into his flesh. He cried out in pain, and his hand sprang open reflexively. The revolver dropped to the floor with a heavy *thunk*. Not that the loss of the weapon mattered. He didn't have any more ammunition on him, and even if he had, those bullets would've had no more effect than the first ones. Blood pattered to the floor like thick crimson rain. It was difficult to read expressions on the woman's inhuman face, but he thought she was amused at the current situation. Amused, and excited.

How had she found his home? Could she have tracked his scent? Before last night, he would've found the thought ridiculous, but now…

He made no conscious decision to flee. One instant he was looking at the woman, and the next he was running down the hallway. He ran wildly, slamming his shoulders against the walls, leaving a trail of blood behind him.

As he passed by the linen closet, the door flew open and one of the men who he'd seen with the woman yesterday leaped out, snarling. He swung his hand at Amos's retreating back, and Amos cried out as claws tore through his shirt and ravaged the flesh underneath. The man was *strong*, much more so than he looked, and the strike nearly knocked Amos down. But he managed to remain on his feet and kept going, now bleeding from his back as well as his hand.

How had the man squeezed himself into the linen closet? There was no way he should've fit. But the detail was not important right now, not when there was a pair of monsters in his home, eager to kill a… a…

Witness, he thought. *I saw what they did—what they are—and they want to make sure I never speak about it again.*

He ran down the hallway, intending to make for the front door so he could get in his pickup. But he heard footsteps behind him, accompanied by animalistic growls, and he knew that if he did manage to get out of the house—and that was a huge *if* right now—he'd never make it to his vehicle. The door to the basement was in the kitchen and if he could reach it… He veered toward the kitchen, ran to the basement door and slammed it shut behind him. The door had a lock on the inside, but before he could engage it, one of them slammed into the door and knocked him backward. He tumbled down the wooden stairs into darkness and hit his head on the concrete floor. The impact caused him to see a momentary flash of light behind his eyes, but the darkness quickly returned. He thought he'd lost consciousness—

which at this point would come as a relief—but then he heard a *click*. Fluorescent light, *real* light, flooded his eyes.

The basement was filled with more junk from his life with Emily and Traci that he'd never been able to part with. Traci's first two-wheel bike—her *big-girl bike*, she'd called it. Emily's workbench covered with crafting supplies—hot glue gun, scraps of paper, containers filled with beads and sequins. Plastic tubs filled with neatly folded old clothes. A long cardboard box containing the artificial Christmas tree he'd put up every year since Traci had been a baby. All of the things down here were remnants of his time on Earth, memories of what had been a life well lived. His only regret was how hard Traci would take his death. But she had Rebecca to comfort her. She'd be all right.

He thought of Emily, thought of her loving smile, and it brought one of his own.

See you soon, sweetie.

The woman began descending the stairs, and the man followed behind her. They came slowly now he had nowhere to go. Amos put his hand out, intending to push himself to his feet so he could try to put up some kind of fight before he died. As he did, his hand touched something furry and wet, and when he looked to see what it was, he learned what had happened to poor Rusty.

He heard movement behind him, and he turned his head to see the third man—fanged and clawed like the others— standing behind him. Or was it a different man? He looked so much like the other that they could be… Of course. Twins. Resting on the floor next to the man was a pile of towels, sheets, and blankets, along with some wooden shelves. He understood then how the other man had fit into the closet, and he had time to think it was a pretty clever trick before the three fell upon him, biting and clawing.

Six

Greg stood next to his mother as she looked over the bananas. Most of them were green, a few were yellow, but none of them was to her liking. Normally he hated going shopping with her because she was so picky, but after screwing up the Rite of Renewal so badly this morning, he was relieved to be away from Nathan and Muriel. Neither of them had said or done anything to make him feel bad. They'd gone out of their way to reassure him that he'd do better next time. But he couldn't forget the fury in his grandfather's crimson eyes as their god used him as a weapon. So when Greg's lessons were finished for the day, and his mother asked if he'd like to help her with the grocery shopping, he'd jumped at the chance. Anything to get away from the site of his failure.

Marta Monsour picked up a bunch of ripe bananas and held them to her son's face.

"Do these smell like they're starting to go bad?"

Marta was in her late forties, short and thin, black-haired and brown-skinned, like most of their people. Like

Muriel, she believed it was more important to fit in with her environment than adhere to tradition when she was in public, and she blended into the crowd in a red Indiana Hoosiers sweatshirt and jeans. She tugged at her sleeves as if the cloth irritated her skin. Perhaps it did. His people did possess heightened senses, after all, touch included.

And speaking of heightened senses…

"Go on," she urged. "Smell them."

Greg knew his mother wouldn't be satisfied until he did as she wanted. While a jakkal's senses remained strong when they were in human form, his were especially acute. He glanced around to make sure no one was looking, then closed his eyes and inhaled deeply.

"Sorry. They're still fresh." So much so that the smell nauseated him a little. Their people not only worshipped a god associated with death, but like the animals they were related to, they were carrion-eaters. They preferred their food to be at least on the verge of spoiling, if not rotting.

Marta sighed and put the bananas in their cart. "We'll just have to leave them out and wait until they're ready," she said. She gave him a smile. "Let's go see if we can find some wilted lettuce."

She pushed the cart toward the lettuce, and Greg followed dutifully behind her. Maybe he'd made a bad choice accompanying her. Right now, stewing in his own shame at home sounded better than being a living rot detector for his mom. At least it wouldn't have been as boring.

He was tempted to put his earbuds in and listen to some music, but while his mom didn't dress traditionally in public, she was still plenty traditional when it came to her expectations of his behavior. He knew she'd view his attempt to lose himself in music as disrespectful to her. So his phone would have to remain in his pocket, leaving him to listen to the tinny pop music playing over the grocery's sound system.

Sometimes being a monster really blew.

Morgan—sixteen, tall, lean, short brown hair—walked behind her mother. Sylvia pushed a cart filled with groceries—mostly meat—toward the produce section. Morgan carried her brother Joshua on her hip. He was a year old and capable of riding in the cart, but he fussed if someone didn't carry him. Especially these days. He was teething again, and while the process was painful enough for human children, for their kind it was doubly so. A human mother might've given her baby a topical anesthetic for the pain, but medicines had no more effect on werewolves than poisons did. Luckily, Joshua's gums would heal soon after his new teeth finished whatever amount of growth they were going to do this time, but until then, the poor little guy would just have to tough it out.

Sylvia had showed Morgan how to soothe Joshua by massaging his sore gums with the tip of her finger. She'd tried it, and it worked—kind of—but when one of Joshua's new teeth turned wolf-sharp and he bit her, that was the last time she'd tried to soothe him that way. Now she bounced him gently on her hip and hummed along with the music playing on the store's sound system. Joshua still fussed now and again, but not nearly as much as he could have, and Morgan took that as a win.

Sylvia was in her forties, although she looked ten years younger. Morgan hoped she looked like her mom when she reached the same age. Sylvia was nearly six feet tall and didn't have an ounce of fat on her, with well-defined muscles and rich chestnut-brown hair. She wasn't simply pretty; she was striking, and not for the first time, Morgan thought she'd have made a fantastic model. But their people didn't like to stand out. They believed in hiding in plain sight. Why else were they capable of assuming human form? But there was a difference between plain sight and turning a spotlight on yourself. Maintaining a relatively low profile was important for their people's survival. But sometimes this frustrated her. She was in high school, and she would've loved to try out for extracurricular activities like drama club, band, cheerleading, basketball, track... anything really, just as long as she got to do *something*. But her parents wouldn't allow it. Not only would she attract undue attention, her Pureblood speed and strength would give her an unfair advantage over humans. The last time she'd tried to convince her parents they'd said no, and she asked her dad why *he* didn't maintain a low profile. His eyes had flashed with anger, and he'd begun growling softly. That was the last time she brought up the subject.

She dressed plainly, in accordance with her parents' wishes. Today she wore a T-shirt featuring one of her favorite anime characters, a gray cardigan, jeans, and black boots. Sylvia, however, wore jeans that were a bit too tight, makeup that was a bit too heavy, and a blouse that was cut a bit too low. Not exactly a low-profile look, but then she figured parents— werewolf or human—often went by the motto *Do as I say, not as I do*. She couldn't help smiling. Who would've thought parental hypocrisy would be a defining trait of both species?

Later, Morgan would realize that she was aware of the boy's presence before she saw him. Partly it was his scent, so much like that of her people but with tantalizing differences: unknown spices combined with the sweet-rank odor of decay. But it was more than that. She felt a thrill of recognition, as if she were approaching an important, maybe pivotal event in her life. An awareness of something big moving behind the scenery of the universe.

And then she reached the produce section and she saw him. She supposed another girl might not have considered him handsome. He was skinny and short, and she was taller than him by at least a foot. But he had a kind face, with gentle brown eyes, and thick black hair that almost but didn't quite curl. He wore a navy-blue hoodie with frayed cuffs, a black T-shirt, threadbare jeans, and old tennis shoes. She liked the way he dressed. He looked comfortable. She wasn't supposed to dress up, but her father wouldn't allow her to leave the house grungy either. *"We have a certain reputation to maintain in this town,"* he'd say. Sometimes she just wanted to be free to make her own choices.

She thought the boy was handsome. She wasn't sure of his age, but she figured he was close to hers. One thing she was certain of: she'd never seen him before. He was probably new in town. So if she went over to say hi, she'd just be being neighborly, right? Sometimes her dad said she was too aggressive for her own good. Maybe so, but growing up a Pureblood had taught her that if you wanted something in this life, you had to go out and get it. And she wanted to talk to this boy.

She glanced at her mother. Sylvia was checking out a display of oranges, inhaling their scent, her eyes closed. It was as good a time as any for Morgan to make her getaway. Still holding onto her baby brother, she started toward the boy with the almost-curly hair. His mother was holding up a head of lettuce and peering at it closely. The boy stood several feet away from her, looking bored. Morgan knew how he felt. He looked up as she approached, and she smiled and gave a small wave. The boy looked startled and suddenly wary, as if she'd drawn a weapon instead of making a friendly overture.

Maybe he's not used to take-charge girls, she thought. Or maybe he simply didn't expect anyone his age to be friendly to him. New kids always had it tough when they moved to Bridge Valley. The majority of families had been here for generations, and besides, this was the kind of town people moved away *from*, not *to*. Newcomers weren't common. Most Bridge Valley citizens were suspicious of anyone not born in town and kept their distance.

Good thing I'm not like most people, she thought.

As she drew near the boy, he took a quick look at his mother. She was still engrossed in her lettuce inspection. With an uncertain smile, he started toward Morgan. She was surprised to find herself feeling suddenly self-conscious. She felt a desperate need to check her reflection. She was certain her hair was a rat's nest, and she wished she had some breath mints. And what about Joshua? He was calm now, but he could start fussing again at any moment—and how embarrassing would *that* be? For the first time in her life, she wanted to retreat from an uncomfortable situation, but before she could do so, she and the boy were standing in front of one another.

Now that she was in close proximity to him, his strangely alluring scent of spices and rot was much stronger. She found it almost intoxicating. Her upper and lower incisors sharpened a touch, pressing against her tongue. Her body had never reacted this way in the presence of a boy, and she concentrated on making her teeth return to their human shape.

The boy drew in a deep breath through his nostrils. He was inhaling her scent. Up until this moment, it hadn't occurred to her that he wasn't human. But now she realized that he was like her only… not. This realization didn't frighten her. Rather, it relaxed her. It told her that this was someone she could be herself—her *true* self—with.

"Hi," she said. "I'm Morgan." She nodded to her brother. "This is Joshua."

"I'm… Greg." He paused before giving his name, almost as if he wasn't sure it was a good idea. But then he smiled and Morgan was reassured. At least he was friendly.

Morgan glanced at her mother then turned back to Greg.

"Let's move to another aisle," she said. "That way we can talk in private."

Greg looked doubtful for a moment, but then he nodded. They left the produce section and went into the next aisle where the shelves were filled with breakfast cereals.

"I haven't seen you at school," Morgan said. "You must be new to town."

"Yeah, but that's not the reason you haven't seen me. I'm homeschooled."

"Oh. That's cool."

She could smell his clothes, too, and she knew they were secondhand. She wondered if his family was poor. Not that she'd judge him for that. Her family wasn't wealthy, but they didn't want for anything either. Her father's people had lived in Bridge Valley for generations, but her mother had told of how her old pack had been forced to relocate several times because hunters had tracked them down. Her pack had abandoned their houses and possessions and started over again from nothing. So while Morgan had never been deprived, she felt a certain amount of kinship with anyone who was.

"I…" Greg broke off and frowned, as if he wanted to say something but wasn't sure of the best way to go about it. Finally, he blurted out, "Are you what I think you are?"

She grinned. "If you think I'm awesome, then the answer's yes."

He grinned back. "I do think that. But there's something else."

She knew her dad would be furious with her, but she couldn't stop herself. All of her instincts told her she could trust Greg, and the words came tumbling out.

"I'm a werewolf. A Pureblood."

His eyes widened, and as they did, the brown of his irises became bright amber for an instant. "I'm a jakkal," he said.

She frowned. "I've never heard of jakkals before."

He shrugged. "We try to stay off people's radar, you know?"

"My family does the same." She tried to think of something else to say, but the best she could come up with was, "How do you like Bridge Valley so far?" *God, how lame!*

"It's all right. It's worse than some places my family has been, but it's better than others." He paused, and then added, "We move around a lot."

He tugged self-consciously on his right sleeve, the motion drawing her gaze. She saw the flesh on his wrist was dry and wrinkled. "Are you okay?"

He tugged his sleeve down even farther. "It's nothing. I had a little accident earlier, that's all. It'll heal soon."

She couldn't think of anything to say to that, so she simply nodded. She didn't know how much longer her mother would be distracted, so she decided to make a bold move while she could.

"Do you have a phone?" she asked. "Let's exchange numbers."

He looked at her in surprise, and she thought he was going to say no, which of course would be the sensible thing to do. Who was foolish enough to swap phone numbers with someone they've just met? But he removed his phone from his pocket with a smile and they quickly exchanged numbers.

"It's better if you text me," Morgan said. "My family doesn't like me talking on the phone to people they don't know."

He nodded. "Texting will work fine."

After that, they stood in silence, smiling at each other. There was nothing awkward about this silence, though. It felt good, as if they didn't need words. Just being in each other's presence was enough.

Morgan felt a sudden rush of air, and then her mother was there, her eyes glowing yellow.

"Get away from him," Sylvia said. "He's a filthy carrion-eater, and he stinks of death and decay."

Sylvia's voice had become guttural, and her words were difficult to understand. Her tone of absolute loathing was unmistakable though, and that set Joshua to crying. Sylvia didn't turn toward her son though. She continued facing Greg, eyes blazing, as if she expected him to attack them at any moment.

Then in the blink of an eye, Greg's mother arrived and inserted herself between Sylvia and her son. Her eyes were amber, and she bared teeth that were pointed, although not as prominent as those of a werewolf. Her ears tapered to subtle points, and her nails were long. Whatever a jakkal was, it seemed to be related to a werewolf, at least as far as Morgan could see and smell.

"Back away from my child." Greg's mother sounded as bestial as Sylvia. While she was a good deal shorter than Morgan's mother, she did not seem intimidated in the slightest. "You know what the bite of my people can do."

The women started growling at each other, and Sylvia began to transform too. Morgan feared they would start fighting right here in the grocery store. She exchanged a horrified glance with Greg, and then they each took hold of one of their mother's arms and tugged her backward.

"Mom!" Morgan said forcefully. "We're in public!"

At the same time, Greg said, "Stop this before someone sees!"

So far they'd all been lucky. They were the only ones in the aisle, but didn't the grocery have security cameras stationed around the store? If their mothers began fighting, their battle might be recorded. So much for the low profile her parents always warned her to maintain.

At first, neither woman listened to her child. Morgan thought they were going to begin biting and clawing each other, but then they stopped growling and—although it seemed to take an effort for them both—they returned to their human forms. Sylvia pulled free of Morgan's grip and scowled darkly at Greg and his mother.

"This is *our* territory, *scavenger*." She practically spat this last word. "Leave town now, while you're still alive to crawl away with your tail tucked between your legs."

Greg's mother's eyes flashed amber one last time, then she turned and stalked off, leaving her cart behind. Greg gave Morgan one last apologetic look, then he turned and hurried after his mother. Joshua was still crying, but Sylvia didn't seem to notice.

"What were you doing talking to one of *them*?"

There was more than a hint of snarl in her mother's voice, and Morgan knew that whatever had happened between the two women, this wasn't the end of it.

SEVEN

The Bridge Valley Independent's office looked small from the outside: a single window with business hours written on a sign in the corner, and a narrow door with the name of the paper painted on the front. The brothers parked on the street and got out of the Impala.

"Not exactly *The New York Times*, is it?" Dean said.

They stepped inside. There was a single main room with several smaller ones branching off from it. In the middle was a single antique desk that looked at least a century old, on top of which rested a laptop and printer. The lights were soft and yellow and the floor was made from dark wood boards that creaked beneath the brothers' feet.

A woman in her late twenties sat behind the desk. She had short black hair and wore a long-sleeved purple-and-white blouse with black slacks, and hoop earrings in the shape of hearts. A scarecrow-thin man sat in front of her. He had straight black hair that looked as if he'd applied too much hair gel and it hadn't had time to dry. He wore a gray suit jacket over a black dress shirt, jeans, and somewhat grubby sneakers. He held a small notebook in one hand and a pen in the other.

Both the woman and the man turned to look at them, and Sam was stunned to see that the man was none other than their old friend Garth Fitzgerald IV, retired hunter and werewolf. Garth broke into a wide grin when he saw them. He opened his mouth to say something, but then he glanced at the woman, dropped the smile, and assumed a neutral expression.

"Can I help you gentlemen?" the woman asked.

Sam and Dean identified themselves as FBI agents and showed their IDs.

"Are you guys really FBI agents?" Garth said. "That's awesome!" He gave the brothers a wink.

Sam knew that Garth—in his own awkward, overly enthusiastic way—was trying to help sell their cover story, but it was the kind of help they didn't need. A big part of making their cover work was getting past the introductory stage as quickly as possible, so people didn't have time to question their credentials. And it was even more important that they get past this stage when dealing with someone whose job it was to ask questions. Someone like a reporter, for example.

"Sorry for the interruption," Sam said, "but my partner and I are investigating the murder that took place outside town several nights ago."

"You mean the gory one where the guy's heart was ripped out?" Garth asked. "That's why I'm here too. I'm working on a book about mysterious murders in the Midwest, and when I got word of what happened here, I hightailed it to Bridge Valley."

Sam and Dean exchanged a quick glance. As cover stories went, Garth's wasn't bad. It might not have the authority and intimidation factor of claiming to be an FBI agent, but it explained why he would want to ask questions about any strange killings. But why did Garth need his own cover story at all? He'd suggested teaming up with them on a permanent basis, but Sam and Dean had urged him to remain retired. Garth had found a place for himself with his wife and her extended family. So what if they were all werewolves? Family was family, and so long as they remained peaceful and fed only on animal hearts, it was all good as far as Sam and Dean were concerned. Weird, but good.

Had Garth changed his mind and started hunting again? Sam hoped not. Hunters' lives contained more than their fair share of violence, and while Garth had been used to that as a human, being around violence—and the darker emotions it could stir—wouldn't be good for him now that he was a werewolf. Fighting and killing could make the animal half of him stronger and harder to control. His pack strived to live in harmony with their wolf selves, but it was a delicate balance. If Garth was going to maintain that balance, he needed to live a normal life. And yet, here he was.

A terrible thought occurred to Sam then. Garth had joined a peaceful pack that didn't believe in preying on humans, but the Winchesters were here investigating a murder committed by what sure as hell sounded like a trio of werewolves. Could Garth have been one of them?

Sam felt guilty for thinking this. He told himself that Garth would never do anything like what had been done to Clay Fuller. But both Sam and Dean knew that the dark powers of the supernatural world could be difficult—if not impossible—to resist.

From the frown on Dean's face, Sam knew his brother's thoughts were running along the same line. They would have to speak to Garth about their concerns, as uncomfortable as that might be, later.

"We'd like to ask you a few questions," Dean said. He looked at Garth. "If Mr...."

"Thrash," Garth said. "Raleigh Thrash."

Dean raised an eyebrow.

"If Mr. *Thrash* doesn't mind us taking you away from him for a few minutes?"

Garth waved a hand in a "No big deal" gesture. "Fine with me, as long as I get to listen in. Totally off the record, of course."

Dean knew a real FBI agent wouldn't permit this, but since Garth was working the same case they were, letting him listen made sense.

"Sure," Dean said. "Knock yourself out." He turned to the woman. "Okay with you, Ms...."

"Melody Diaz. Editor, office manager, and head reporter." She shook their hands. "I'm happy to help in any way I can. You two want to pull up a couple chairs? My sports guy is out covering a middle-school football game, so you can borrow the chairs from his desk."

She pointed toward an ancient office chair and a simple wooden chair in front of an old metal desk. Neither looked particularly comfortable.

"Thanks, but we're fine," Sam said.

"I don't blame you for passing on them," Melody said as she sat back down. "As you can see, we put the *small* in small-town newspaper. We can barely afford the necessities, let alone upgraded office furniture."

"I hope you don't take this the wrong way," Sam said, "but I'd think things would be more… lively in here right now. A murder like Clay Fuller's would be news anywhere, but in a small town—"

"It should be the story of the century, right?" Melody said. "I've got another of my people out looking into Fuller's background. But, honestly, a story like this gets so much coverage from larger papers and television stations that we end up just covering the basics and trying to add a more local angle, like highlighting the problems our community's been having with substance abuse. That kind of thing."

Sam understood exactly what she meant. The cases he and Dean investigated were usually grisly and baffling, and because of this they attracted a good deal of media attention. This was one of the reasons why they tended to ditch their suits as soon as they could when working a case—so reporters wouldn't recognize them as FBI agents and try to interview them.

"I take it you've already spoken with the sheriff?" she asked.

"He's not exactly forthcoming, is he?" Sam added.

Melody laughed. "That's one way to put it. You ever heard the phrase 'Trying to get blood from a stone'? Well. That's a hell of a lot easier than trying to get Alan Crowder to tell you anything useful."

"The sheriff did confirm that Mr. Fuller's heart was removed from his body," Sam said.

"*Removed* is too neat a word," Dean said. "How about *ripped out*?"

"Did he confirm the part about heart-stealing monsters too?" Garth asked. "I mean, whoever heard of anything more laughable?" He gave a too-loud and entirely unconvincing laugh.

Says the werewolf, Sam thought.

"I reported that aspect of Amos's account because it was news," Melody said, "and I figured his story would get out to the public sooner or later. I did my best to avoid sensationalizing it though. Unlike some media outlets in the area." She scowled. "Damn ratings-chasing vultures."

"Do you believe him?" Dean asked. "Or do you think he's a couple toys shy of a kid's meal?"

"We'd never met before I interviewed him." When the three men looked at her, she said, "What? You think because we live in a small town everyone knows everybody else? Bridge Valley isn't *that* minuscule. He seemed shook up by what he'd witnessed, but otherwise he appeared clear-minded. His story seems crazy, but *he* doesn't. But still, heart-stealing wolf people?" She shook her head at the idea.

"Were you able to look at the body before it was cremated?" Sam said.

"I asked, but the sheriff told me I couldn't see it until Fuller's next of kin were notified. As near as I can tell, he *has* no kin in town, and the body was cremated before I could pester the sheriff again about letting me see it."

"Do you have an address for Mr. Boyd?" Sam asked.

"Sure." She pulled her phone from her pocket and consulted

the notes app. "He lives outside town, twenty-four Edgewood Road. I've got his phone number too, if you want it."

She read it out, and Sam dutifully wrote it down.

"Have there been any other strange deaths in town lately?" Sam asked.

"Real weird ones," Dean added. "Mutilated corpses, severed limbs, heads torn off—that kind of thing."

Melody looked at Dean as if he might secretly be a serial killer. "No, nothing like that," she said.

"But there *have* been disappearances, yes?" Garth asked.

"It's true," she admitted. "We did a story on that last summer. Bridge Valley has a higher rate of disappearances than is average for a town our size. The sheriff says our drug problem is most likely to blame. People might leave town to avoid paying off debts they owe to suppliers. Some might be suppliers who end up in disputes with their competitors— disputes which turn deadly, and the bodies are buried in unmarked graves."

"Sounds reasonable," Dean said, his tone neutral.

"*Sounds* is the operative word," Melody said. "I believe there are too many disappearances to simply explain away. And there's a definite pattern to when the majority of them have occurred."

Garth glanced at Sam and Dean, eyebrows raised, smiling, as if to say, *Wait for it…*

"Around the time of the full moon," she finished.

"Could be coincidence," Sam said.

Melody sighed. "I know. But something about the whole situation feels hinky, you know?"

"We do have some experience with hinkiness," Dean said.

EiGHT

Near Seattle, Washington. 1992

"I'm bored."

Nine-year-old Sam Winchester sat cross-legged on one of the two beds in the small motel room. His brother Dean—thirteen—sat in a vinyl-covered chair in the corner, feet propped up on the other bed. The TV was turned to what network executives liked to call a "daytime drama," but which their father always referred to as a soap opera. Sam thought the name was weird. He knew what an opera was—a play where people in costume sang loud songs in another language—but no one sang in these shows, and he had absolutely no clue where soap came in.

He'd seen this particular one before—it was called *Heartbreak Hospital*—but he could never keep track of the various storylines. Characters cheated on their lovers with other characters—Sam wasn't exactly sure what *cheating* entailed, but it seemed to have something to do with kissing—and they experienced different medical conditions, everything from unexplained pregnancies to amnesia. Currently, a man who was a doctor was in his office embracing a woman lawyer who, up until a week ago, had been his mortal enemy. They were both married to other people who were, ironically, at that exact same moment lying in bed with each other in a house on the other side of town.

Dean hadn't responded, so Sam turned to face his brother and tried again. "Can we see if something else is on? I don't like it when they start kissing."

Dean didn't take his gaze from the screen as he answered. "You will when you're older. Now shut up. I want to see if Dr. Martin realizes he's really with Alexis's evil twin Anika." He grinned. "Anika is *so* much hotter than Alexis."

Sam frowned. Weren't the characters played by the same actress? How could one be hotter than the other? Sighing, Sam faced the screen once more. Dean loved to watch TV. It didn't much matter what was on, just as long as it had a story to it. Once he started watching something, he was practically hypnotized until it concluded. Sam was the complete opposite. He liked to watch shows he could learn from, like quiz shows or science programs. He hated this mushy junk.

They were in Pennington, Washington, a small town not far from Seattle. Although really, they could have been pretty much anywhere. The inside of one cheap motel room looked the same as any other to Sam. Their father had brought them here because he'd gotten a lead on a warlock living in Vancouver who supposedly had a mystic artifact that could track demons. John Winchester hoped to use it to track the yellow-eyed demon that had killed their mother. Finding and killing the yellow-eyed demon was an obsession with their dad, and Sam sometimes thought there was nothing more important to him in the whole wide world—including his sons. He'd never say this out loud, especially around Dean. Dean was always trying to explain why their dad left them alone so often and how the work he was doing saved people's lives. Sam knew this was true, but he still couldn't help missing their father, and sometimes—a lot of times—feeling abandoned by him.

At least he hadn't left them alone this time.

There was a series of knocks on the door—three slow, three fast—then the sound of a key in the lock. The door opened and Bobby Singer stepped inside. He wore his usual baseball cap and khaki army jacket, both of which were wet, and he carried a pair of plastic bags full of snacks and soda. He kicked the door closed then put the bags on top of the dresser.

"Seems like it's always raining in this state," Bobby said.

Bobby locked the door, then went into the bathroom to dry off his face and hands. Dean got up to check out what Bobby had brought them. He pulled out a jar of peanuts, popped a handful into his mouth, and then offered the jar to Sam. Sam took a few, and as he was chewing, Dean took two bottles of pop from the second bag and handed one to Sam.

Bobby came out of the bathroom, tossed his wet cap on the small desk and hung his equally wet jacket on the knob of the door. He sat down and glanced at the TV. Dr. Martin and Anika were kissing so fiercely it looked like they were trying to eat each other's faces.

"Is that Anika?" Bobby asked.

"Oh, yeah," Dean said, grinning.

"Well, I hate to interrupt your afternoon Sex Ed., but I need you to turn off the TV," Bobby said.

Dean's grin fell away. He snatched up the remote and did as Bobby asked. Normally, Sam would've been thrilled to not have to watch any more of that show, but the tone of Bobby's voice told him that something important had happened. Both boys put their pop bottles down on the nightstand and looked at Bobby expectantly.

Sam didn't want to ask *The Question*, as he'd come to think of it, but he couldn't stop himself.

"Is Dad okay?"

Bobby smiled. "Far as I know, he's fine. He called the front desk and left a message for me earlier. He said he's still working on the warlock case but he's making good progress. He told me to tell you he loves you both, and he hopes to get back soon."

Dean smiled. He always loved hearing from Dad, even if the message was passed along by someone else. Sam was relieved. It was hard knowing that whenever Dad went on a hunt, he might not come back, and if he did, he might not be altogether human. But Sam wasn't sure that Dad had actually told Bobby to say the other part. Sam figured Bobby added the "Dad loves you" part whenever he passed along a message from their father, but he appreciated it. Bobby was like a second father to them, and when he told them their dad loved them, it was like he was saying it too.

"What I have to tell you boys is that I'm going to have to work tonight. Maybe all night. Will you be all right if I do?"

"Sure," Dean said. "I've watched Sammy by myself lots of times. We'll just watch TV until you get back."

"And eat a ton of junk food while I'm gone," Bobby said.

Dean smiled but didn't say anything. Sam clenched his teeth. He didn't like it when Dean called him *Sammy*.

"What are you going to do, Bobby?" Sam asked. He always worried when Dad was on a case, and he worried just as much—if not more—when Bobby was too.

Bobby looked back and forth between the brothers, as if trying to decide how much to tell them. Bobby once said he believed it was better to face an ugly truth than believe a pretty lie. Sam wasn't exactly sure what that meant, but it sounded cool.

"The clerk at the convenience store told me about a murder that happened last night. Might not be anything supernatural…"

"But?" Dean prompted.

"Could be the work of a werewolf," Bobby said. "The attack occurred in the parking lot of the local hospital. The police think it was the work of a serial killer. They might be right."

"But you don't think so," Sam said.

"Whenever you come across a corpse that's been torn to hell and is missing a heart, you've got to check it out."

"Especially if the murder happened during the cycle of the full moon," Dean said.

"Bingo."

Dean grinned as if he were in class and had just given a teacher the right answer.

"I'm going to stake out the hospital parking lot tonight.

Werewolves are creatures of habit, like any animal. They return to the same hunting grounds as long as the food supply holds out."

The thought of Bobby out there in the night, alone, with a werewolf lurking somewhere nearby, frightened Sam. Bobby gave him a smile.

"Don't worry. I'll have my gun, and I got plenty of silver bullets. I'll be all right."

Bobby's words reassured Sam somewhat, but they didn't relieve all his anxiety. Still, he gave Bobby a brave smile.

Bobby pulled a twenty-dollar bill from his wallet and handed it to Dean. "For dinner. There's a pizza joint not far from here that delivers. Number's in the phone book. I circled it earlier. You boys take care of each other while I'm gone, you hear?"

Sam nodded, and Dean said, "We always do."

Bobby sighed and his shoulders sagged. He grabbed his cap and jacket—neither of which had dried much during the few minutes he'd spoken to them—and left. Once the door was closed, he turned the knob to make sure it had locked behind him.

Dean turned the TV back on, but *Heartbreak Hospital* was over—luckily—and he started surfing through the channels. Sam lay back on the bed and got comfortable. It looked like it was going to be a long night.

Finally, Dean found something that caught his attention. "Awesome!" he said.

At first Sam didn't know what he was looking at. A woman in a thin floor-length nightgown was running barefoot across hilly terrain. It was night, and a full moon hung in the sky, casting the world in an eerie glow. The woman looked absolutely terrified—mouth open in a silent scream, tears falling from eyes wild with fear.

"What is this?" Sam asked.

"It's a movie. I haven't seen it since… well when I was around your age. It's called *Night of the Blood Moon*. It's a classic, one of a series of Italian horror films starring Paolo Mansetti. As far as I'm concerned, he played the best werewolf ever!"

Dean loved all kinds of movies—even mushy romance ones so long as they had pretty women in them. But his absolute favorite kind of movie was horror. He lived for scary movies, and he knew all about them. When they were made, who directed and starred in them, whether they were originals or remakes… Sam had never been able to figure out why. Given what Dad and Bobby did for a living, Sam would've thought Dean would get his fill of spooky stuff in real life. Dad had even taken them with him sometimes. Dad said he wanted to prepare both of them.

Sam knew Dean intended to follow in their father's footsteps. It was obvious. Dean practically worshipped their father. If their Dad had remained a mechanic, Dean probably would've started fixing cars. But Sam wasn't like their dad at all. He loved the man but sometimes found him a complete mystery. Sam wasn't mechanically inclined or good with his hands. He liked to be by himself sometimes so he could read or just think. And he liked to plan things out instead of stumbling through a situation and hoping everything would work out in the end. He was more like Bobby than Dad or Dean.

Dad didn't like horror movies as much as Dean, but they did watch them together on those rare occasions when John was at home. Dad and Dean would laugh at the on-screen monsters, and Dad would complain about how unrealistic horror movies were. Sam always tried to watch scary movies with them, but he *hated* horror movies. He always got scared watching them, and the thought that his father actually hunted things like the ones on the screen frightened him even more than the films themselves. Dad and Dean might laugh at a walking skeleton that was really a big puppet hanging from wires, but all he could think about was that his dad fought *real* ghosts—ones that were angry and could kill you.

But *this* movie, *Night of the Blood Moon*, bothered him more than usual. This movie was about a werewolf, the same kind of monster that Bobby had just left to hunt. Sam really didn't want to watch the film, but Dean did. And Dean was older and bigger and in charge of the remote. Plus, he had the pizza money Bobby had given him. Sam wanted to stay on his brother's good side. So he sat and watched the nightgowned woman run through the darkness. But when a wolf howl emitted from the TV's speaker, he couldn't help jumping. He was glad that Dean was too absorbed in the movie to notice.

"Watch this, Sammy. This is our first good look at the so-called monster."

A man—or at least a creature shaped like a man—leaped in front of the woman. Terrified by his sudden appearance, she tripped and fell. She looked up into his eyes and screamed.

The camera moved in for a close-up of the monster, and

Sam gasped in fright. The werewolf's face and hands were covered with wiry black fur. The creature's nose was an elongated canine snout filled with sharp teeth. The fangs were especially prominent, so large Sam didn't know how the thing could close its mouth. A terrible, hungry intelligence blazed in its bloodshot eyes, and it raised hands with wickedly curved claws as it snarled and lunged toward the woman. She screamed again, louder and higher this time, and Sam imagined that instead of attacking the woman, the werewolf was attacking Bobby or Dad.

That was enough for him. He ran into the bathroom, slammed the door shut and locked it. Then he sat on the floor with his back against the tub, closed his eyes and pressed his hands against his ears so he wouldn't have to listen to the woman's screams anymore.

A few moments later, he heard a knock at the door.

"Sammy? You okay?"

Sam opened his eyes and lowered his hands. He didn't say anything, though.

"Come on, don't be such a baby! It wasn't *that* scary!"

Still Sam didn't respond.

After another minute, Dean spoke again, this time in a softer voice.

"I turned off the TV. It's okay to come out."

Sam sat there for several more moments before finally rising to his feet. He walked to the door, unlocked it, and Dean opened it.

"Sorry," Dean said. "I guess a werewolf movie wasn't a good choice, what with Bobby going off to hunt one."

Sam nodded.

Dean turned away and headed back to the chair he'd been sitting in. Sam followed and sat cross-legged on the bed close to his brother. Dean made no move to turn the TV on again, and Sam was grateful. The boys sat in silence for a time before Dean began talking.

"You know how Dad says that one of the greatest weapons monsters and ghosts and stuff has is fear?"

Sam was unsure where Dean was going with this, but he nodded.

"Those things are dangerous, and you have to respect that, but if you let yourself be scared by them, you'll hesitate when you see one, and then it'll get you before you can defend yourself. That's why it's important to learn to control your fear—so it doesn't control *you*."

Their father had told them this numerous times. It didn't make complete sense to Sam. Didn't people have the option of *not* confronting monsters? Didn't fear prevent them from putting themselves in situations where really bad things could happen to them? Not everyone was a hunter, after all, or wanted to *be* a hunter. Sam had never brought up these questions with their dad, and he wasn't going to bring them up now. He wasn't sure Dean would understand, and he didn't want to disappoint his big brother more than he already had today.

Dean continued. "Werewolves are like any other monster. They're a threat, but if you understand it, then you'll be ready to face that threat. And you can beat it."

Sam nodded, although he wasn't sure he believed it.

"Good. Let's dig into the snacks Bobby brought, and we'll

find something to watch on TV—something we both like. Sound good?"

Sam forced a smile. "Yeah."

But no matter what they ended up watching, Sam knew he'd still be thinking about the werewolf from *Night of the Blood Moon*, and the way the woman screamed and screamed.

NINE

Present Day

The Winchesters thanked Melody for her time, apologized to Mr. "Thrash" for interrupting his conversation with the reporter, and then headed next door to The Whistle Stop. It was small, but the layout was familiar: bar, countertop, stools, TV hanging on a wall with a sports channel playing, and a scattering of patrons who looked as if they might've come in for a quick one at lunch and lost track of the time—or how much they'd been drinking. The brothers had chosen a table near the kitchen because no one was seated nearby, and they could talk without being overheard. They ordered three beers, took a table in the back, and waited. It didn't take long.

Garth entered the bar and immediately wrinkled his nose in disgust. Then he headed straight for Dean and Sam, sat down at the table, and took a drink.

"Man, everything tastes *amazing* when you're a werewolf!" He wrinkled his nose again. "The bad thing is that everything smells a hundred times stronger, and there are some people in here who not only need to shower more often, they should consider seeing a digestive specialist."

Dean envied Garth's enhanced senses, but not the price he had to pay for them. Always fighting to control violent, aggressive impulses… He knew what that was like from the time he'd carried the Mark of Cain. He never wanted to return to living like that. Then again, Garth had always possessed a certain goofy optimism. Maybe that counterbalanced the animal within him.

"Let's get this out of the way first," Dean said.

Garth jumped in before Dean could finish. "I had nothing to do with Clay Fuller's death. It's still strictly animal hearts for this boy." He held up a hand with his first three fingers pointed upward. "Lycanthrope's honor."

"You know we had to ask," Dean said.

"Sure. No hard feelings."

"It's good to see you," Sam said.

"Same here," Garth said. "Damn, I missed you guys!" He got up from his seat and, with a big grin on his face, went in for a hug. Dean wasn't big on physical displays of affection— especially when it was dude to dude—but Garth was a hugger, and the best thing to do was get it over with as fast as possible. Besides, Garth was like a particularly persistent fungus: he grew on you.

"How's Bess?" Sam asked.

"She's great. She's still in Grantsburg with the rest of the pack, holding down the fort."

"The two of you have any puppies yet?" Dean asked. He was surprised to see Garth blush.

"Not yet. Maybe one day. Purebloods don't produce children as often as humans do. That's why there aren't as many of us. Well… that's one reason."

An uncomfortable silence fell between them. Hunters had been responsible for the decrease in the Pureblood population. Dean had mixed feelings about this. He didn't want any harm to come to Garth or Bess—or to the other members of their peaceful pack, which he thought of as vegan-wolves. But he and Sam had never encountered any other packs like Garth's, and they *had* encountered plenty of Purebloods who were just as dangerous as any other kind of monster. More so, since they possessed their full intelligence when they transformed.

The longer Dean was a hunter, the more complicated and confusing the job became. Sometimes he longed for the days when all he had to worry about was protecting people and trying not to get killed.

"So you're here for the same reason we are," Dean said.

Garth nodded and took another drink of beer. "Yeah. I'm still retired from hunting overall, but after the last time we talked, I realized that I'm in a unique position: I'm a hunter *and* a lycanthrope. So I decided to use my abilities—natural *and* supernatural—to help others of my kind. I search for strange occurrences which might be lycanthrope-related, and when I find one I check it out. If I encounter a Pureblood, I tell him or her about my pack and how we live, and I offer them a place with us—*if* they're willing to live by our rules."

"And if they're not?" Sam asked.

"It's time to bring out the silver," Garth said, his tone grim.

Dean frowned. "I thought werewolves couldn't handle silver, not without it hurting like hell."

"I wear industrial-strength rubber gloves to handle silver bullets. I don't need them to hold my gun or a blade—as long as the handle isn't silver. Having my flesh so close to silver hurts, but it's not too bad."

"What do you do if you encounter any regular werewolves?" Sam asked.

"I make them the same offer. They lose their intelligence when they transform, but my pack chains them up and locks them in cages before they change. Keeps them out of trouble."

"How do you manage to convince them they're werewolves?" Dean asked. "They have no memory of changing."

"Once I track them down, I chain them up and take video of them transforming. The next morning, I show it to them when they're human again, and then I transform to prove I'm legit. Sometimes they accept my offer, sometimes they don't."

Dean didn't have to ask what happened in the latter case. It was silver bullet time.

"'Are we human?'" Garth said. "'Are we animal? We are both, and we must make peace between the two if we are to truly be one.'" He spoke as if he were intoning a piece of great wisdom that had been passed down through generations.

"What is that?" Dean asked. "It sounds like something you'd find inside a werewolf fortune cookie."

"Is it from a book that werewolves hold sacred?" Sam asked, clearly intrigued. "An ancient text that the Maw of Fenris uses?"

"Nothing like that," Garth said. "Lycanthropes didn't write

much down over the centuries. They're more about actions than words, you know? So I decided to write a book of my own." He grinned. "Which means I only half-lied to Melody. I *am* writing, just not about weird murders."

Dean exchanged a quick look with Sam.

"So you're writing a… what?" Sam asked. "A book of werewolf wisdom?"

"Something like that," Garth said. "I call it *The Way of the Fang*. Catchy title, right?"

"Uh, yeah. Sure," Dean said.

"I won't be able to publish it, of course. Got to protect the pack's secrets. But when I'm finished, future generations of lycanthropes will be able to pass it around and read it. Who knows? Maybe it'll convince some of them to live peacefully, like my pack."

At first it had seemed to Dean that Garth was writing some kind of self-help book for werewolves. But now it sounded more like he was composing a werewolf bible. Dean had a hard time imagining Garth as some kind of prophet, but Sam and he had encountered stranger things during their careers.

Garth had a way of reinventing himself periodically. So his becoming a werewolf who hunted other werewolves, as well as author of *The Way of the Fang*, seemed only natural to Dean. The next step in his personal evolution, what Dean had come to think of as the Garthening.

"So you're doing werewolf rehab now," Dean said. "That's cool… I guess."

"It's more than that," Garth said. "I save people who rogue lycanthropes might prey on, and by taking out the bad ones on my own, I prevent hunters from doing it. Less chance anyone will get bitten and turned like I did. Don't get me wrong; I *love* being a lycanthrope, but I know this gig isn't for everyone."

"And by keeping werewolves off hunters' radars," Sam said, "you're more likely to protect your pack because fewer hunters will be looking for werewolves in the first place."

Garth nodded. "That's the idea."

Dean was impressed. Garth might be a little weird—okay, maybe more than a little—but his natural optimism had helped him adjust to what would've been a lousy situation for any other hunter. Hell, more than a few hunters would've put a silver bullet through their own skulls rather than live life as a monster, Dean included. But Garth had always possessed a go-with-the-flow attitude, and it seemed to have served him well in this case.

"Do you think we're dealing with rogue werewolves here?" Sam asked.

"Sure sounds like it. Hard to tell without a body to examine, though. I'd have known after one good sniff, but cremation obviously destroyed any scent of Fuller's killers. Along with the body itself, of course."

A thought occurred to Dean. "Could you pick up a scent trail at the location where Fuller died?"

"If I can find it. I tried to set up an interview with the sheriff, but he wouldn't talk to me. Said he didn't want to have anything to do with, and I quote, 'A muck-raking hack writer.' Maybe you guys can get him to tell us where the murder scene is."

"I doubt it," Dean said. "He's not exactly the talkative type."

Dean realized that despite no one saying anything about it,

Garth was going to be joining them on this hunt. Or maybe they were going to be joining him. Good. Garth had proved himself on more than one occasion, and his special abilities would come in handy. *I just hope he doesn't have fleas,* Dean thought.

"We need to talk to Amos Boyd," Sam said. "He can tell us where the murder took place. He might even be willing to take us there."

Which meant they had to keep their monkey suits on a little longer. *Fantastic.* Without realizing it, Dean tugged at his shirt collar.

"You guys going to finish those?" Garth nodded to their beers. Dean's was two-thirds empty, and Sam's was only half empty.

Dean exchanged a look with Sam, and then said, "Not if we're going back to work."

Garth finished their beers, one after the other, then smacked his lips. When he noticed the brothers looking at him, he said, "I can drink as much as I want without it affecting me." He patted his flat stomach. "Lycanthrope metabolism makes me immune to poisons, alcohol included. Let's go."

Garth started toward the door without waiting to see if they'd follow. He was more assertive than he had been before becoming a werewolf. More confident too. He almost made being a werewolf seem appealing. Except for the part about alcohol. What was the point of drinking if you couldn't feel its effects? You might as well be drinking water all the time. Dean shuddered at the thought, and then he and Sam followed their friend.

* * *

Where are they going?

Melody stood in The Whistle Stop's small kitchen, keeping the door cracked so she could watch the two FBI agents and the writer.

She'd become suspicious of the three men early on during the agents' questioning of her. They made a point to avoid looking at each other, and during the few times they interacted, she couldn't escape the feeling that they already knew one another. If pressed, she wouldn't have been able to explain why, but even an editor-slash-reporter for a small-town newspaper knew the importance of following up on a hunch. So when the writer left, she waited for a few seconds before peeking outside to see where he was going. She was not surprised to see him turn into The Whistle Stop. Maybe he just wanted a drink, but her intuition told her it was more than that. So once he'd gone inside, she locked up her office and hurried down the alley between the two buildings. She entered the bar through the back door and hid by the restrooms until she could catch the bartender's attention. He owed her a favor. He snuck her into the kitchen, and she watched the three men through the crack in the door.

She felt more than a little foolish, but she couldn't deny that playing spy was fun.

She couldn't hear what they were saying, but from the way they interacted she quickly became certain they knew each other. The two agents didn't act stiff and professional now. They were more relaxed and casual, and the cute one—Who was she kidding? They were both cute—tugged at his collar now and again, as if he wasn't used to wearing a suit. And if the three men knew each other, why had they pretended not to? Especially since they were all interested in Clay Fuller's death. It didn't make sense, and she *hated* that.

When the three men left the bar—as a group—she hurried out of the kitchen and saw them going down the sidewalk, talking as they went.

She had a decision to make, and she had to make it fast. Should she follow them on foot or should she assume that wherever they were going, they'd end up driving there? Then it hit her: Amos Boyd. The agents had wanted to know where he lived. That was where they were going. It had to be. She darted out of the bar and ran toward her four-by-four.

Time to do some tailing. God, she loved her job!

TEN

Morgan sat in the front passenger seat of the SUV, next to her mother. Joshua was strapped into his car seat in the back, sleeping. Morgan envied her brother's ability to fall asleep anywhere. It would be great to unplug and escape reality whenever you wanted.

Sylvia had one hand on the wheel of the vehicle, and she held her phone with the other. She was upset and driving too fast, but Morgan wasn't going to say anything. She didn't want to become the focus of her mother's anger—any more than she already was, that is.

"Yes, I'm sure it was one of *them*." Pause. "Because I could *smell* it on them! Just because there haven't been any around here since we were kids doesn't mean anything. They're here *now*!"

Sylvia listened for several moments, brow furrowed and lips tight. Finally, she said, "I understand." Then she ended the call and dropped the phone. She didn't slow down. If anything, she sped up a little more. She kept her gaze fixed on the road ahead as she spoke.

"Be thankful I didn't tell your father that I caught you talking with one of them. You were close to the boy long enough to get his stink all over you, so if you don't want your father detecting it later, you'd better take a long, extremely thorough shower when we get home. I'll take your clothes out back and burn them."

At first Morgan thought she hadn't heard right. "Burn my clothes?"

"I'd have to use too much bleach to get the carrion-eater's stink out, and that would end up ruining them. Easier to just burn them."

"Mom, aren't you being a little too…" She wanted to say *dramatic*, but she knew that would only anger her mother, and she might end up getting cuffed on the face for mouthing off. The claw wounds would heal eventually, sure, but better not to get hit in the first place.

"Cautious?" she finished.

Sylvia shot her a sideways look and then surprised her by laughing.

"Jakkals aren't a *threat*, dear. They aren't as strong and fast as we are, and since they're carrion-eaters, they don't compete with us for food. There's nothing they can do to harm a strong pack like ours."

After Greg and his mother had left the store, Sylvia had refused to answer Morgan's questions. Now it seemed Sylvia was willing to talk, and Morgan wanted to take advantage of it.

"What's wrong with jakkals?" she asked. "If they can't hurt us, why can't we just ignore them?"

"Because Bridge Valley is *our* territory. Your father's people have lived here for generations. We can't permit another pack to come to town, no matter what they are. It's also a practical matter. The more supernatural beings living in one area, the greater the chance that they'll start attracting unwanted attention."

"You mean hunters."

Sylvia nodded. "Do you remember that family of ghouls that moved into the old house on Market Street a few years ago? Remember what happened?"

How could she forget? A hunter had come to town, tracking the ghouls. Dad and her two brothers went out one night, and by the next morning both the hunter and the ghouls were dead. The house had been burnt to the ground along with all the bodies, including the hunter's.

"Jakkals are worse than ghouls," Sylvia said. "As loathsome as ghouls are, they at least serve an important function. They're like the garbage collectors of the monster world. But jakkals are a perversion of the natural—" She paused, smiled a little. "Or should I say *unnatural* order? Ghouls feed on death, but jakkals worship it. They carry it within them, like a disease. They're disgusting, and the world would be a better place if their entire species was rendered extinct."

Morgan had never heard her mother talk this way before. The anger, the sheer venom in her voice... It was clear that Sylvia hated jakkals with all of her being. She hated Greg without even knowing him. But then, Morgan didn't know Greg either, not really. They'd only spoken briefly before their mothers had freaked out. But she'd felt a connection. She didn't believe in love at first sight or anything like that. That sort of thing only happened in movies. But she *did* believe in listening to her instincts, and her instincts told her that Greg was a good person, and he could be trusted. Did her mother's instincts tell her something different? Or was she so blinded by her hatred that she refused to listen to them?

Sylvia continued. "If for some reason we ever run into that boy again—or any of his pack—do not allow them to get close enough to attack you."

Morgan was confused. "I thought you said they were harmless."

"They are… in general. Just do as I say, please?"

"All right."

Morgan thought of Greg's kind face. She couldn't imagine him being dangerous. The idea seemed laughable. But she didn't look dangerous, did she? None of her family did.

"What did Dad say when you told him about the jakkals?"

At first Morgan thought that Sylvia wasn't going to answer her, but then she said, "He's going to see if he can find the jakkals' den and ask them politely to leave our territory."

Morgan thought her dad's idea of *politely* was apt to be a bit more confrontational than hers. She hoped a fight wouldn't break out. She didn't want anyone getting hurt. Especially Greg.

"He told me something else." Sylvia's tone was less angry now. More worried. "A pair of FBI agents showed up asking questions about Clay Fuller's death. And earlier, a writer from out of town tried to interview him about Clay, but your dad turned him down."

Morgan had a cold, sick feeling in the pit of her stomach.

"Hunters?" she asked softly.

"Maybe. We'll have to be on guard for the next few days."

She shook her head in disgust. "Jakkals and now hunters. How much do you want to bet the carrion-eaters led them here?"

Morgan couldn't take any more. "You're being racist, Mom."

Sylvia turned to look at Morgan for a moment, then looked forward again.

"I'm not racist," she said. "I'm a monster."

As they drove on in silence, Morgan wondered if the two conditions were mutually exclusive.

After a bit, Sylvia said, "At least we won't have to worry about Amos Boyd blabbing to the media anymore." Her mouth twisted into a cruel smile, and Morgan could see a hint of fangs.

"What do you mean?" Morgan asked, afraid of the answer.

"Never you mind," Sylvia said. "And don't tell your father I said that."

Sylvia continued smiling as she pried a small shred of meat from between her too-sharp teeth.

Morgan caught the scent of human flesh and shuddered. She didn't want to know what *that* was about. She turned away from her mother, gazed out the window, and thought.

She'd only just met Greg, and they'd spent less than five minutes speaking, but she felt a connection to him. She wanted to see him again, but more than that, she wanted to protect him from her dad—*and* her mom, who in many ways was just as dangerous as he was, if not more so. But Morgan had no idea what she could do. Her family—her *pack*—operated by a strict hierarchy, and she was dead last in the pecking order. Not counting Joshua, of course. She was expected to obey her father, mother, and older brothers in all things. If she continued to insist her family could find a way to live alongside the jakkals, she would be punished. But she had to do something, and soon, if she was to have any hope of saving Greg and his family from hers. She would text him a warning as soon as she was alone, but she didn't know if it would be enough. She didn't know if anything would be enough.

When Alan ended the call with Sylvia he was so furious he wanted to punch a hole in his office wall. He restrained himself, though. No one else in the Sheriff's Department was a werewolf, and he'd have a hard time explaining how he could punch all the way through the wall with a single blow *and* not damage his hand. He ran his tongue over his teeth to check them. They were halfway sharp, and he concentrated until they became human again.

First some writer tried to get an interview with him, then a pair of supposed FBI agents show up asking questions, and to top it all off, there were *jakkals* in his town. This was not shaping up to be one of his better days on the job.

Before he could do anything else, his phone rang. The display identified the caller as Melody Diaz. He *really* didn't want to talk with her right now, but even in a small town, it didn't pay to irritate the press.

"Hey, Melody. How are you doing?"

She didn't bother with pleasantries. "I'm calling to see if you have anything new on Clay Fuller's murder."

He frowned. "Why? You've already covered the story. I don't—" He broke off. "A couple FBI agents came to see me today. They didn't happen to drop by your office, did they?"

Melody didn't respond.

"Look, I understand reporters want to protect their sources and all that, but if you want me to scratch your back, you've got to scratch mine."

Melody sighed. "Fine. Yeah, the agents paid me a visit, along with that true-crime writer you wouldn't talk to. The agents asked some questions about Clay Fuller's death, and then they left. The writer did too, shortly after. I had a feeling the three knew each other, so I stuck my head out the door in time to see them go into The Whistle Stop."

She went on to tell him about sneaking into the bar to spy on them, how they'd left together in an Impala—"An old one, a real classic"—and that she was in her own vehicle right now, tailing them.

"I think they're heading over to Amos Boyd's house to question him, and I want in. If I learn anything, I'll let you know. And don't bother telling me to keep my nose out of it. We both know that's not going to happen."

She ended the call before Alan could say anything more.

He let out a growl of frustration as he slipped his phone back into his pocket. The Crowder family had lived in Bridge Valley for generations, and in all that time, they'd managed to hide more or less in plain sight. At first, they'd lived peacefully, subsisting on animal hearts. But eventually they realized that it was a mistake to deny the more savage aspects of their werewolf heritage. And so the Hunt was instituted. Once a month, the Crowders would abduct someone who wouldn't be missed, turn them loose in the woods, and then the fun would begin. At the end of the Hunt the human would be killed and their heart shared among the family members. No one got more than a taste, but it was enough to satisfy their needs. Barely.

But as technology became an increasing part of people's lives, tracking missing persons became easier. So Alan—a young man at the time—had decided to join the Sheriff's Department where he could not only better conceal his family's... recreational activities, but he had access to people who no one would ever miss. People like Clay Fuller. Alan quickly rose to the position of Sheriff—after all, he *was* his pack's leader, and humans responded to his commanding nature just like werewolves did—and he'd held the job ever since. Things had worked out well enough, and while there'd been a few bumps here and there, the road had been smooth for the most part.

Until the night when the Hunt had gone wrong. Alan had never expected Fuller to make it so far. They played with him too long. They could've brought him down much earlier, but prolonging the Hunt was part of the fun. Unfortunately, Fuller had reached the road, and then Amos had driven up while Sylvia and their twin sons were finishing off Fuller. It was something of a miracle that they'd been able to keep themselves from killing Amos as well. Fuller was a low-life drug dealer, but Amos was well known in town and would be missed if he were to disappear.

Alan wasn't sure what good talking to Amos would do the three men. Amos had already told his story to the media, and while urban-legend enthusiasts had been speculating wildly about his tale online, no serious media outlets believed him.

Alan doubted Amos could tell them anything more, but there was a possibility they might be able to get Amos to remember some new details.

And Melody was tailing the three men too. What if she learned something she shouldn't?

He was tempted to drive out to Amos's place and confront the agents and the writer and, if necessary, take them out. Melody too, if it came to that. He didn't like the odds, though. It would be three on one, and while he was still strong and in his prime, if the men *were* hunters—as he was beginning to suspect—there was a good chance they'd be armed with silver. The man in him knew it would be wiser to wait for a better opportunity to confront the hunters, but the wolf in him demanded he go to Amos's *now*. His pack was threatened, and that threat had to be eliminated.

But then, the hunters weren't the only problem his pack had to deal with at the moment.

When he was growing up, his pack had dealt with jakkals, and he hated the filth as much as his wife did. He would go to the grocery, catch the scent—although the thought of inhaling a jakkal's stench sickened him—and track them from there. And if he lost the trail, he'd search abandoned places that were falling to ruin. Jakkals were creatures of death, and according to the stories, they chose to lair in desolate, lifeless places. A cemetery would have too many visitors, so it would likely be something else. One way or another, he'd find them soon enough.

He didn't want to face the jakkals alone. Not that he was afraid of them. They were smaller and weaker than werewolves—at least in terms of physical strength. But he had no idea how big their pack was, and if the legends were true, they did possess one formidable weapon. He needed backup, and he couldn't ask his human deputies for help. That left him only one choice. Well, two, actually.

He took out his phone once more and called Stuart. His son answered on the second ring.

"Hey, Dad."

Alan didn't bother with pleasantries. "Is your brother with you?"

"Yeah. We're just hanging around the station. What's up?"

Stuart and Spencer Crowder were twins in their early twenties, working as firefighters for Bridge Valley Fire and Rescue. It was useful to have members of the pack working in another area of local government, but they knew the pack came first.

"Tell the chief you and your brother have a family emergency and need to leave. Don't worry: nothing's wrong. But I need your help for a couple hours."

"No problem. Want us to meet you at the station?"

"No," Alan said. He bared teeth once again grown sharp. "At the grocery."

ELEVEN

"You told us this town was clean!" Marta shouted.

The entire jakkal family had gathered in the living room. Nathan and Muriel. Greg's parents Marta and Efren. His older sisters Kayla and Erin, one seventeen, the other nineteen. His sisters looked like younger versions of their mother, although both were slightly taller than Marta. Marta sat between them, while Efren stood in the middle of the room, almost as if he were on trial. Greg sat cross-legged on the floor near Nathan's chair. His wrist still hurt from where Anubis had grabbed it, but the skin was less aged and leathery now, which he took as a good sign.

In some ways, Efren Monsour looked like he didn't belong to the family. He was taller than the rest of them, although most people would consider him average height, and his skin was fairer. He wasn't as thin either, although he was by no means heavy. He was, however, a nervous man, and he often fidgeted and paced when he talked. His voice had a strained, almost whiny quality, as if he were always apologizing for something that deep down he didn't believe was his fault.

"I thought it *was* clean!" Efren said. He held his arms rigid against his body, and his fingers tapped his outer thighs. He looked like he wanted to run and hide and from the way Marta, Nathan, and Muriel glared at him, Greg didn't blame his father.

"It was your responsibility to find us a new town to move to," Nathan said. "A *safe* town. Instead you've brought us—and worse, your *god*—to the territory of a werewolf pack!"

Nathan's voice grew louder as he spoke, and his fangs and claws began to emerge. Muriel reached over to take one of his hands, and his teeth and claws subsided a little.

"Daddy, how *could* you?" Kayla said.

"You're supposed to *protect* us!" Erin added.

"You were gone almost two weeks on your last scouting trip," Marta said. "That should've been more than enough time for you to thoroughly investigate a town this size."

"Two weeks?" Muriel snorted. "He should've picked up the stink of werewolf on his first day here."

Efren tuned to face her. "We've been here almost a month. Have any of *you* caught any trace of werewolf scent in that time?"

No one answered.

Efren relaxed a bit and gave a small, satisfied smile. "You know the longer we remain in human form, the less like jakkals we smell. The same applies for werewolves. If you're right on top of them, you can smell them, but otherwise…" He shrugged as if to say, *what can you do?*

"What you say is true," Nathan admitted. "But two weeks? You should've found *some* sign of the wolves in that time, if only a small one."

Efren looked uncomfortable again, and he began tapping his fingers against his legs once more. "I was gone two weeks, yes. But I didn't spend those two weeks here. Not all of them, anyway."

Marta jumped to her feet, her features instantly transforming into her jakkal self. She grabbed her husband's throat with one clawed hand, and when she spoke, her voice was a low, rumbling growl.

"If you weren't here, where were you?" she demanded. "And don't lie. This close, I'll smell it on you."

Efren showed no sign of transforming. To do so would've meant he was accepting Marta's challenge and intended to fight. He kept his gaze fixed on hers and did his best to speak calmly.

"I scouted two other towns before I came to this one. Both were clean, but they were smaller than Bridge Valley. I believed we might have drawn too much attention if we settled in either place. But when I came to this town, not only did I find it big enough for our needs, the presence of death looms large here. So much so, that I found it… intoxicating."

For a moment, Greg wasn't sure what his father meant, but then he understood. Bridge Valley had a significant problem with drug addiction and overdoses. Jakkals could smell the scent of death and decay the same way a shark could detect a single drop of blood in the water from miles away. So when the jakkals were in the midst of it—in other words, when they went into the town proper—their senses could be overwhelmed if they weren't careful. And it wasn't only the presence of physical death that they could sense. They could sense the dying of the town itself—buildings on the verge of collapse, streets badly in need of repair, a community of people lonely, depressed, and disconnected from one another. In a way, Bridge Valley was like a gigantic animal in the process of dying. A perfect place for scavengers like the Monsours—and for their god.

Efren continued. "Once I was here, I forgot about scouting. All I wanted to do was wallow in the town's darkness and despair. I wandered the streets by day and slept in the open by night. I didn't eat, barely drank. I would've continued like that if I hadn't felt the pull to return to you." He lowered his gaze to the floor, clearly ashamed. "Even then, I almost didn't leave."

As Efren had talked, Marta slowly returned to human form. She slid her hand away from Efren's throat and onto his shoulder.

"This is why you take so long when you're out scavenging in town, isn't it?" she said. "You want to obtain that feeling again."

Greg had the sense that his mother had almost said *high* instead of *feeling*. He supposed there were all kinds of drugs in this world, many of them not obvious.

"I make sure to take the girls along when I scavenge," Efren said. He raised his head and gave his daughters an embarrassed smile. "They aren't as affected by the town's atmosphere as I am—none of you are, it seems—and when they're with me, I know that I can't stay out too long. I have to bring them home."

The family's mood toward Efren had softened, and now Nathan stood and took hold of his shoulder in a gesture of support.

"You have nothing to be ashamed of," Nathan said. "But from now on, you should avoid going into town. The girls are old enough to go on scavenging runs on their own. And it's about time Greg started going as well."

For an instant, Efren looked panicked at the thought of not going into town, but then he nodded.

"Yes, I suppose that would be best."

Marta smiled, kissed her husband, and then embraced him. Nathan also hugged him, and Muriel rose from the couch and joined them. All, it seemed, was forgiven. Greg didn't know if his father would experience withdrawal symptoms, but in any case, he would likely have some hard days ahead of him.

Kayla and Erin exchanged looks, and since everyone else had forgiven Efren, they decided to as well. They rose and joined the other members of the family in what had become a group hug. Not wanting to feel left out and wishing to show support for his father, Greg rose and joined the others.

He knew it was wrong of him, but he felt relieved that his father's problem had drawn the family's attention away from the fact that he'd spoken to Morgan in the grocery. On the drive home, Marta had raved about the werewolf bitch and her tramp of a daughter. Greg had wanted to tell his mother not to call Morgan names, that she didn't deserve his mother's automatic, unthinking hatred. But he wisely kept his mouth shut. As upset as Marta had been, Greg feared Muriel—and especially Nathan—would go ballistic when they found out. But they had been more concerned with the realization that their new town had a werewolf pack living in it than the fact that he'd spoken to one of them.

"So what do we do?" Marta said. "We've always managed to avoid werewolves in the past, but now…" she trailed off.

"We have to move again," Kayla said. "As soon as possible."

Erin nodded, backing her sister up.

"That's not possible," Nathan said. "At least not right away. We can't risk moving Anubis until the Rite of Renewal is carried out successfully. Until then, he'll be too weak."

Marta frowned and looked at Greg. "I thought you performed the rite earlier today."

Greg felt his face burn with embarrassment, and he covered his sore wrist. "I tried, but something went wrong. It didn't work."

Kayla and Erin grinned at him, as if to say, *We knew you couldn't do it.*

Muriel saw the girls' reaction. "Don't be so quick to judge," she said. "I seem to recall that when you were first learning to conduct the rite that one of you dropped the amaranthine before it could be given to Anubis."

The grin vanished from Erin's face.

"And the other sneezed in the middle of speaking the holy words and had to start the entire rite over."

Kayla's grin fell away.

Greg tried not to smile. It seemed his failure to conduct the Rite of Renewal properly had an unintended—but welcome—side effect.

He knew it was crazy for him to feel anything for Morgan. So they'd spoken for a few minutes in the grocery store. So what? It didn't—couldn't—mean anything. But that he felt something for her was undeniable. They might belong to different species, but both jakkals and werewolves possessed strong animal instincts. Was it possible that on some level, one so deep neither of them was fully aware of it, they had recognized each other as... what? A potential match?

But how could he explain this to his family? There was no way they could understand. Tradition dictated that jakkals form close bonds—friendships, marriages—with their own kind and no others. It was important for the continued survival of their people. At least, that's what his parents and grandparents had always told him. He'd accepted this without question, until the moment he'd set eyes on Morgan. Now he wanted to know what was so bad about being close to someone different.

"Why do werewolves hate us?" Greg asked.

Everyone in the family turned to look at him. None of them spoke right away, so he went on.

"They eat the hearts of freshly killed prey, while we eat the hearts of the dead. It's not like we compete for food."

His family members exchanged glances. Muriel was the first to speak. "We honor the lives of those who provide us sustenance by waiting until after they die to take their hearts."

"By then, their souls have passed on to the afterlife," Nathan said. "They do not feel the pain and fear of being killed for their hearts."

"It's more civilized that way," Marta said.

Erin wrinkled her nose. "Plus, fresh meat is *disgusting*."

Kayla nodded. "It must be seasoned by time for it to taste any good."

Greg frowned. "So werewolves hate us because—"

"They're animals," Efren said. "Purebloods may believe they're masters of the wolf that dwells within them, but it's a delusion born of arrogance. They can no more control themselves than a wild beast running loose in the forest."

The others nodded.

"They resent us for being able to live in perfect harmony with our animal aspect," Muriel said. "We have succeeded where they have failed." She spoke these last words more than a little smugly, Greg thought.

He failed to see the logic in his family's explanation. As near as he could tell, werewolves and jakkals hated each other simply because they did. No reason to it at all. He knew better than to point this out to his family, though. They wouldn't listen.

Marta turned the conversation to other matters. "How soon can the Rite of Renewal be attempted again, Father? Either by you or Mother this time?"

She gave Greg an apologetic glance. He knew his mother didn't mean her question as a rebuke to him, but her words stung nevertheless.

Nathan thought for a moment, then he looked at Muriel. "Twenty-four hours after the last attempt?" he asked.

She considered. "At least. And it would be best to wait until the moon shines strong."

Kayla frowned. "I thought the rite could take place day or night, as long as it's within the three days of the full moon's cycle."

"Normally, that is true," Nathan said. "But given that we do not know for certain what went wrong the last time the rite was attempted—" He avoided looking at Greg as he said this "—we should do everything in our power to ensure it succeeds the next time. The magic is stronger during the full moon."

None of the family challenged this, so it was settled. They would have to wait until tomorrow night. All they had to do was hold out until then, and they could—

Greg's phone buzzed in his pocket, and he felt a surge of excitement. Morgan had texted him! It had to be her. The only other people who had his number were his family. He headed toward the bathroom, leaving them still talking over plans. Once the bathroom door was closed, he read the message. When he did, he felt a cold twist in his stomach.

My dad knows about you and your family. PLEASE be careful. M.

His family had been right. The werewolves were coming. He could only hope they could complete the Rite of Renewal before that happened. Because if they couldn't, they'd only have two choices left. Fight—

—or die.

TWELVE

The sun was beginning to set by the time Sam, Dean, and Garth reached Amos Boyd's house. Dean pulled the Impala up the driveway. Autumn leaves still clung to the branches overhanging the driveway, and Sam thought the place must be absolutely gorgeous in spring and summer.

Garth must have been thinking along similar lines. He peered through the windshield and said, "Man, this is a *perfect* place for a lycanthrope to live. A couple miles outside of town, no close neighbors, woods right out your back door. You could run naked and howl at the moon, and no one would bother you."

Sam and Dean looked at him.

"Not that *I'd* run around naked and howl. That would be weird, right?" Garth finished with an embarrassed laugh.

"Hey, we don't judge," Dean said. "Whatever floats your furry boat."

The house soon came into view. Sam half-expected to see that Amos lived in a rustic cabin, but it was a regular ranch-style house—red brick, black shutters, black roof—just like any number of houses you'd find in town. The difference was this one was in a nicer location.

Amos's pickup was parked in the driveway, and Dean pulled the Impala in behind it. The three men got out of the car and paused to take in their surroundings, which in Garth's case meant inhaling the area's scents, and in Sam and Dean's, meant loading their pistols with silver. In their line of work, it paid to be cautious.

"Dudes, I'm picking up some blood scent," Garth said. "We need to be careful. More careful than usual, I mean." Garth had tucked a revolver loaded with silver bullets into his jacket pocket in case they ran into any werewolves of the non-friendly variety. His brow was furrowed, and his lips were pressed into a tight line, almost as if he was fighting a headache. Even though the bullets were housed in the gun and separated from his body by his jacket, they were still close enough to his skin to hurt. Sam was struck by how quietly and unassumingly brave Garth was. He carried a metal that was literally poison to him in his jacket pocket, and he did so without comment or complaint, like a true hunter.

When they reached the front door, Dean knocked. There was no immediate answer, so he knocked again. Still no response.

Dean gave Garth a look. "Maybe he's out running naked in the woods."

Garth frowned. "You think *he's* a lycanthrope?"

"You said this was the perfect place for a fuzz-face to live," Dean said.

"He *was* the first person on the scene of Clay Fuller's murder," Sam said. "Maybe he did it and tried to cover it up."

"By saying that *other* lycanthropes did it?" Garth said. "That doesn't make any sense."

"Maybe he's got some werewolf enemies he wants to frame," Dean said.

"There's an easy way to settle this." Garth moved past Dean and leaned his face close to the doorknob. He inhaled and then straightened once more. "There's no lycanthrope scent on the knob, just one-hundred percent human. One person, too. A male, in his sixties. Has to be Amos, right? The scent's not all that fresh. The last time he touched the knob was several hours ago." Garth hooked a thumb in the direction of the pickup. "And when we walked passed his truck, I could smell that it hasn't been driven for the same amount of time. So he should be home."

Dean raised an eyebrow. "That sniffer of yours comes in handy."

"Yeah, it's pretty awesome," Garth said. "But it has its downsides, too. I can't go within a dozen yards of a gas station restroom, for instance."

"Can you smell anything through the door?" Sam asked.

Garth shrugged. "I can try. Depends on how tight the seal is."

This time he leaned his face close to the door's edge and started sniffing in and out rapidly, sounding like an over-excited dog. After a few seconds, he pulled back so violently that both Sam and Dean reached for their pistols reflexively.

"What is it?" Sam asked.

"There's blood inside," Garth said. "A lot of it." His voice sounded rough, not quite a growl, but close to it.

Dean stepped back to the door and tried the knob. It was

locked, and Sam took hold of Garth's arm and gently pulled him back to give Dean some room. Dean reared back and kicked the door open. It swung inward, and Sam and Dean drew their weapons. Garth, however, did not draw his. His teeth were gritted and his hands were clenched into fists. Sam understood that he was fighting not to change again.

There were two types of Purebloods. Those born that way, and those who become werewolves after being bitten by a Pureblood. Garth had become a werewolf by the latter method, and while Purebloods like him retained their human intelligence when they transformed, the same as any other Pureblood, they had more difficulty controlling their animalistic urges.

"Maybe it would be better if you stayed outside," Sam suggested.

"Yeah," Dean said. "Maybe you can case the property, see what you can smell out here."

Sam thought that Garth might protest, but instead he let out a defeated sigh. "'Sometimes the best way to attack is to retreat,'" he said.

"Another morsel from *The Way of the Fang*?" Dean asked.

Garth nodded.

Sam felt sorry for their friend, but there was no time to commiserate with him. He and Dean had work to do.

Dean entered the house first, and Sam followed close behind. They raised their pistols into firing position and moved through the house, checking the living room, dining room, the kitchen, the hall, bathroom, and the bedrooms. There were spots of blood in the hall, and the linen closet door was open, but it was empty, not even any shelves, which was strange. The window in the master bedroom had been broken, and there was blood on the carpet next to the bed. Dean knelt, touched his fingers to the crimson spot, and then smeared blood between his thumb and forefinger.

"Not quite dry." Dean wiped his fingers on a clean patch of carpet and then stood. "Whatever happened here took place a few hours ago, at most."

"Which is when Garth said Amos got home," Sam said.

Dean nodded.

They left the bedroom and made their way down the hall once more. They checked the garage, but other than some lawn equipment—rakes, a push mower, and the like—and a workbench with numerous tools hanging on the wall above it, the garage was empty. They went back into the house and conferred.

There was a door in the kitchen, which they assumed led to a basement. They hadn't checked it in their initial sweep of the house, but now they returned to it. The door wasn't locked, and Dean opened it easily. The brothers, even with their limited human sense of smell, could detect the coppery odor of blood once the door was open. Neither of them was a stranger to murder scenes, and the blood smell told Sam that they weren't going to find Amos Boyd alive. Still, he called out, "FBI! Mr. Boyd, are you down there?"

Silence.

The basement light was off, so Dean switched it on and the two brothers descended a set of wooden stairs. What they saw when they reached the bottom was enough to shock even them. Blood was everywhere—on the floor, the walls, the ceiling, and splattered onto the various objects Amos had kept stored down here. There was so much blood that it was hard to believe it had all come from a single person. At first Sam didn't see Amos, but then he realized that was because the man had been ripped to pieces and scattered throughout the basement. A head lay on the far side of the basement on the floor, half hidden by the corner of a cardboard box. The face was covered with blood, rendering the features difficult to make out, but Sam had no doubt they were looking upon the savaged remains of Amos Boyd. He also knew that once the parts had been collected and catalogued, the man's heart would be missing.

The brothers lowered their weapons. There was no threat here, not anymore.

"One werewolf did all this?" Dean asked.

"Maybe three. That's how many Amos claimed to have seen."

"Guess they wanted to make sure he couldn't tell his story anymore."

"They succeeded," Sam said.

There were tracks all over the floor, as well as bloody handprints on the walls and on some of the stored objects. Both sets of prints showed their owners had sported claws. There had been no tracks upstairs, and there were none on the basement steps. A moment later, Sam understood why. He'd been so overwhelmed by the scene of carnage before him that he hadn't noticed one of the basement windows had been broken. The killers had left by that route.

"We should call the sheriff," Sam said.

Dean shook his head. "Let's wait and see what we're dealing with first."

Sam agreed. He was about to ask his brother what they should do next when he heard Garth call out from somewhere on the first floor.

"Guys? You need to get up here. *Now*."

Sam and Dean exchanged a look and then ran up the stairs.

Garth stood in the kitchen next to Melody Diaz, holding onto her wrist as if she was his prisoner. An expression of fierce concentration was on his face, and beads of sweat dotted his forehead. The smell of blood and ravaged flesh must have been overwhelming for him, and he was fighting to keep from transforming in front of Melody. So far, he was succeeding, but Sam didn't know how long he could keep this up.

"I found her outside. She was checking out the broken bedroom window."

Garth's voice was low and rough, but still human. Mostly.

"Let me go, damn it!" Melody struggled to pull away from Garth, but his grip was too tight.

"She parked on the road," he continued. "I could see her car through the trees."

"I have just as much right to be here as you do," Melody said. "Maybe more, since I live in this town, and it's my job to keep its residents informed."

Dean gave Sam a look, the expression on his face saying, *Seriously?* Sam shrugged and then turned to Melody.

"You're interfering with a federal investigation," he said. "We could have you arrested if we wanted."

"If you're *really* FBI, then what's *his* deal?" Melody yanked her wrist free of Garth's grip. Sam saw that Garth's fingernails were slightly larger than normal and pointed. He hoped Melody wouldn't notice.

Sam thought fast. "He's a federal agent as well. Undercover. Sometimes we work a case from multiple angles to see what we can turn up."

She looked dubiously at Garth, as if she were having a difficult time imagining him as an agent, but then she said, "I guess that makes sense."

Sam felt relieved. If their cover story hadn't held, they would've been forced to tell Melody the truth about who they were and what they did. And that conversation never went smoothly.

"So what did you find?" Melody asked.

Sam tried to think of a suitable lie, but before he could come up with one, Dean said, "We found Amos. He's down in the basement. All over the basement, actually."

It took a couple seconds for the meaning of Dean's words to sink in, but when they did, Melody's eyes widened in shock and she put a hand to her mouth. "He's dead?" she asked.

"And in about a dozen pieces," Dean said. "Like Humpty Dumpty, only without the shell."

"Oh my God."

Her face paled and her breathing became erratic. Sam feared she might faint, and he hurried forward, intending to catch her, but she waved him away.

"I'll be all right," she said. "I'm not used to covering violent crimes, and to have a pair of murders take place in town so close to each other… Well, let's just say I find it a little overwhelming."

"If you've got a queasy stomach, I'd stay out of the basement," Dean said. He took his phone from his pocket and said, "We need to alert the local authorities. Get some crime scene techs and the coroner out here."

"Agreed," Sam said.

Dean nodded and stepped into the living room, where Sam knew he'd only pretend to make the call. For now, they didn't want the sheriff or his deputies coming to the scene until they'd finished with it.

"Is it really that bad down there?" Melody asked.

Sam nodded.

"How can you ask such a question?" Garth said. "Even *you* should be able to smell the death in this house."

The intensity with which he spoke prompted Melody to take a couple of steps away from him.

"Why don't you go back outside and continue your search of the perimeter, Agent, um, Thrash?" Sam said.

"Yeah. That's probably a good idea."

Garth left the kitchen without looking at Melody again. After a moment, Dean returned.

"The sheriff's on his way." Dean turned to Melody. "Which means you need to scoot on out of here."

Melody started to protest, but Sam interrupted her.

"We're not going to take you in for interfering with an investigation, but that doesn't mean the sheriff won't. Plus, as the editor of the local paper, you need to maintain a good relationship with him, right? Imagine how tight-lipped he'd become if you pissed him off by being here when you shouldn't."

She considered this for a moment. "Okay, but tell me this

much, at least. Was Amos killed the same way as Clay Fuller? Is his heart missing?"

"At this juncture, we can neither confirm nor deny anything," Dean said. "But yeah, that's what we think."

Sam shot Dean a look, but Dean ignored him.

Melody departed then, and Sam and Dean went to the living room and watched through the window to make sure she actually got in her Jeep and drove off. She did, and the brothers stepped outside to look for Garth.

Sam was glad Melody was gone. There was no place for a civilian on a case like this. It was too dangerous, and not only might she get herself killed, they'd be distracted by trying to ensure her safety, which might get *them* killed.

"She's going to be trouble," Dean said.

Sam hoped Melody would stay out of the way until the case was concluded, but he doubted she would. She was inquisitive and persistent. Excellent traits for a reporter, but ones that could become major pains in the ass for the Winchesters.

Sam decided to worry about her later. Right now they had work to do.

They found Garth at the northern side of the house, crouching in front of the broken basement window and sniffing the ground. Even in the dim light of dusk, Sam could see a trail of blood leading from the window across the yard and into the woods.

"This is all Amos's blood," Garth said. "There were three lycanthropes, and while they all entered through the bedroom window, they exited here. Two males, one female. Family by their scent. Mother and sons would be my guess."

Garth stood. He had smears of blood on a couple of fingers, and he raised those fingers to his mouth, almost as if he intended to lick them clean. He seemed to realize what he was about to do, and he stepped several feet away from the blood trail, knelt, and wiped his fingers clean on the grass. Then he stood once more and faced Sam and Dean.

"Sorry about that," he said. "I haven't been around a scene this… extreme since before I became a lycanthrope. It's more of a struggle to control myself than I expected. But don't worry. I'll be okay."

Garth didn't sound as confident as his words suggested, but Sam decided not to make an issue of it. Dean also made no comment, but Sam knew his brother was thinking the same thing he was. If Garth couldn't control himself and wolfed out, would they be forced to put him down? If it became necessary, could they kill their old friend? Sam thrust these thoughts away. When you were a hunter, sometimes it was best to live in the moment and deal with the future when it came.

It was almost full dark now, and the wind had kicked up, rustling dry leaves and causing bare branches to scrape together.

"I'm going to follow the lycanthropes' trail and see where it leads," Garth said.

"We'll come with you," Dean offered, but Garth shook his head.

"Nothing personal, but you guys would only slow me down. Plus, I can move silently, but to someone with enhanced hearing—such as lycanthropes—you'd sound like a couple of extremely large and clumsy elephants crashing through the woods."

"Nothing personal, he says," Dean muttered.

"Be careful," Sam told Garth. "And if you find the werewolves, don't engage them on your own. We know there's at least three, but there might be more if they belong to a pack."

Garth nodded. "'A wise wolf knows when to growl and when to remain silent.' You two head down the road a couple miles and park on the shoulder. I'll meet you there when I'm done."

Before either Sam or Dean could say anything more, Garth assumed his werewolf form, transforming so swiftly that there seemed to be no transition between the two. One moment he was human Garth, and he was werewolf Garth the next. Sam thought that Garth had been holding back the change so long, that once he finally gave in to it, it happened immediately.

Garth gave them a last look with eyes that were now feral yellow, before loping toward the trees, moving with a quiet grace that his gawky form didn't seem capable of. He entered the woods, making no sound despite the dry autumn leaves on the ground. Sam and Dean watched him run until he was lost to the night shadows gathering among the trees.

"I'm getting sick of his *Way of the Fang* crap," Dean said. "It's really annoying."

"I don't think it's that bad," Sam said. "Maybe you could do your own version and call it *The Way of the Hunter*."

Dean opened his mouth, and Sam expected he was going to say it was a stupid idea, but then he paused and grew thoughtful.

"*The Way of the Hunter*," he mused. "That *does* have a nice ring to it."

THIRTEEN

Melody drove away from Amos's property. Night had arrived, or close enough to it, and she had her headlights on. She was leaving with mixed feelings. She now knew that Amos had been killed, but the agents had hustled her out of there before she could learn much more.

She called the sheriff. She'd promised she'd fill him in after her trip to Amos's place, and she knew if she wanted to count on his future cooperation, she needed to make good on that promise.

Alan answered right away. He barked an irritated hello, and Melody said hi in her sweetest voice.

"What is it?" the sheriff said. "I'm kind of in the middle of something right now."

She could hear the sound of a car engine and guessed he was driving. "On your way to Amos Boyd's place, I assume."

"Not at the moment."

She frowned. "Why? You told the agent that you were on your way."

Alan was silent for several seconds before speaking again. "When did this happen?"

Melody had hoped to leverage her knowledge of Amos's death to get Alan to give her an exclusive interview. She'd hint—not threaten—to tell the larger media outlets about Amos's murder if he didn't. But the conversation had taken an unexpected turn, and she was confused.

"One of them called you, not more than ten minutes ago."

"I received no such call."

Was Alan lying to her? Or had the agent lied?

"Like I told you before, I followed those two FBI agents after they left my office. Three agents, if you count their true-crime writer friend. Anyway, they went to Amos's house, and I sneaked inside while they were checking the place out. One of them called you, or at least pretended to. They asked me to leave after that, and I did."

"Why were they there?" Alan asked. "Did something happen to Amos?"

She told him, and when she was finished, he asked, "So you didn't actually see the body yourself?"

"No. They discouraged me from doing so. But I'm sure it was there." But now that she thought of it, was she *really* sure? Maybe they'd lied about Amos's body too. The true-crime writer had insisted he could smell the blood from the basement, but she hadn't been able to smell anything.

"Okay. Don't publish anything about this yet, not until I have a chance to check on it, all right?"

"I won't."

"I'm serious about this. I'm not sure what those agents are up to—or if they're even who they say they are—and I don't want them to know that we're on to them. Not until the time is right."

Melody felt a surge of excitement. It looked like her big story was getting bigger all the time. "I'll hold the story back—on one condition."

Alan sighed. "Yes, you can have an exclusive interview with me when it's all over."

She grinned. "Then it's a deal."

She ended the call and slipped her phone back into her pocket. She had no idea what was going on in her little town, but whatever it was, it would make one hell of a story. When she got home, she planned to start typing up some notes, maybe even take a stab at a first draft. Just because she'd promised not to publish the story didn't mean she couldn't start working on it.

She continued heading toward town, mentally composing her lead paragraph as she drove.

After his conversation with Melody, Alan clenched his hand and shattered the phone into shards of plastic, glass, and broken electronics. He tossed the pieces to the floor of the sheriff's cruiser and held out his hand. The palm and fingers had been cut but he barely noticed the pain. He held his hand out of the open window, and when he brought it back in seconds later, the wounds had healed.

"What's wrong?"

Stuart Crowder sat in the cruiser's front passenger seat, while his brother Spencer sat in the back. The twins were identical. Same tall lean frame, same unruly brown hair, same squarish face that didn't quite match the body. They both cocked their heads slightly to the left when asking a question, both tapped their feet on the floor when bored or impatient. They tended to dress alike too. Flannel shirts, jeans, sneakers, and today a pair of light jackets. He couldn't tell them apart by sight alone, and although she'd never admit it, neither could Sylvia. Morgan said she could, and Alan believed her, although he had no idea how she did it. But unlike a human parent, Alan didn't have to rely on sight to identify his children. Each of them, even the twins, had a unique scent, different from any other werewolf in the world. He could recognize one of his kids blindfolded, in the dark, from a mile away.

"It seems that someone has killed Amos Boyd."

As soon as he spoke those words, the boys' scents changed. They were suddenly afraid.

"I can smell that you've both recently showered, and you used a *lot* of body wash. Maybe an entire bottle apiece. You weren't by any chance trying to scrub away a scent, were you? Like the smell of Amos's blood?"

His voice held a warning tone that said, *Don't you dare lie to me, boys.*

From the back seat, Spencer said, "We did it. Stuart and me."

Alan scented the air. Spencer was telling the truth, but not the *whole* truth. He looked over at Stuart.

"Just the two of you? No one else?"

Stuart and Spencer exchanged glances, then they looked at Alan, and at the same time said, "Mom was there too."

Anger flooded him, and with it came the change. Fangs and claws sprouted, and his eyes blazed yellow.

"Why the hell did you do such a thing?" he demanded in a thick, animalistic voice.

"Mom asked us to," Stuart said.

"She told us it had to be done," Spencer added.

"She said Amos has already drawn too much attention to himself by telling his story to the media."

"She said we should've killed him when he first saw us, and that we had to fix our mistake."

"We had to shut him up permanently."

Together, they finished. "For the good of the pack."

Alan wanted to slam on the cruiser's brakes and teach his sons a painful lesson about giving in to their animal instincts. But he knew it hadn't been their fault. Sylvia was the lead female in their pack, and the boys could not disobey her. Not that they'd wanted to. Stuart and Spencer were closer to the wild side of their werewolf nature than anyone else in the family. They lived for the Hunt, and for the killing that followed. Sylvia said it was a phase, but Alan wasn't so sure. They were twenty-three. If they hadn't learned to live in harmony with their animal selves by now, when would they?

"Don't be mad," Spencer said. "We eliminated a threat, didn't we?" He sounded defensive.

Alan felt a growl beginning deep in his chest, and he knew that if he didn't get control of himself now, he wouldn't be responsible for his actions. With an effort of will, he forced his anger down and concentrated on assuming his human form. It wasn't easy.

"What you did is make a problem a hell of a lot worse than it needed to be."

And if those FBI agents really are hunters, you just confirmed for them that there are werewolves in the area.

He was the ultimate leader of his pack. Sylvia should've consulted him before taking such a drastic step. And once she *had* taken that step, she should never have concealed it from him. He wanted to call her and demand to know what she'd been thinking. But he'd destroyed his phone, and while he could borrow one of the boys', it would be better for him to cool down before confronting her. Arguments between werewolves could rapidly descend into fighting, and he wanted to avoid that. On the other hand, as pack leader, it was important that he maintain discipline. The longer he allowed Sylvia to believe she'd gotten away with this, the weaker his position in the pack became. And that was something he simply could not allow. Sylvia's actions were tantamount to challenging him for leadership of the pack. And werewolves didn't let a challenge go unanswered.

He was about to turn the cruiser around and head home to have it out with his wife, when Stuart said, "I think I smell something."

"Me, too," Spencer said.

Alan eased his foot off the gas and allowed the cruiser to slow. Once they'd gotten the jakkals' scent at the grocery, they'd been driving around town with the windows open, hoping to encounter it again. With any luck, it would lead them to the carrion-eaters' den. They were on the eastern side of Bridge Valley now, near Happyland, an amusement park that had closed in the late eighties and never reopened. Bridge Valley had started going downhill then, and now it was a shell of its former self, plagued with poverty and drug abuse—a perfect hunting ground for their pack. But Alan had to admit that he missed Happyland. He'd been a kid when it closed, and he'd spent many joyous hours there, pretending that he was no different than all the other children around him. A *human* child.

But Happyland had died and he'd grown up. He challenged his father for leadership of the pack and killed him. Alan's mother had in turn challenged him, and he'd been forced to kill her too. His brother and sister had both decided against challenging him, but rather than remain under his leadership, they'd left town to form their own packs. A sad situation, overall, but it was the way of his people. One day Stuart or Spencer—or perhaps both of them—would challenge him. If he was strong enough, he'd be victorious and remain leader. If not, he'd join his parents in death.

Alan inhaled deeply, and recognized the scent from the grocery. It was both like and unlike that of a werewolf, but with an unpleasant taint of rot that turned his stomach. It made sense that jakkals would choose to lair in Happyland. It was old and abandoned, in its own way a graveyard, and it was enclosed within high metal fencing. The park was large enough to provide plenty of room for a pack to remain hidden.

The thought that the filthy carrion-eaters had taken up residence in a place Alan had loved as a child filled him with rage. If he couldn't vent his anger on Sylvia yet, the jakkals would do quite nicely as substitutes.

Happyland was two miles ahead of them. The sun had been slowly setting while they'd been searching for the jakkals. Now nighttime had fallen, and the full moon hung near the horizon. Perfect.

Alan parked by the main gate. It was rusty, but still sturdy enough, and it was locked with an equally rusty chain and padlock. In Happyland's prime, the park's name had been spelled out in an arch of neon letters that lit up the night. The sign had long since fallen down, and the only illumination came from the cruiser's headlights. But Alan's night vision was excellent, and he could make out the shadowy forms of buildings and rides inside the park.

The stench of jakkal was stronger here, so much so that Alan had to breathe through his mouth. Spencer made a gagging sound.

"This is worse than getting squirted in the face by a dozen skunks!" he said.

"Two dozen!" Stuart said.

"Looks like we found the place." Alan turned off the engine. "Let's go."

He got out, and the boys waited for their father to start walking toward the fence, then fell in behind him. *As it should be,* Alan thought. He stopped when he reached the gate. He could easily break the chain and open it, but he wanted to make as little noise as possible to avoid warning the jakkals. Instead, he climbed over the gate and dropped down silently on the other side. A moment later, Stuart and Spencer landed just as silently next to him.

The three stood and assumed their werewolf forms. Stuart and Spencer's breathing became faster then, and Alan could smell the excitement coming off them. The boys had gotten the scent of prey. Alan gave them both a warning growl, the werewolf equivalent of a command to heel. The twins bristled, but they didn't move until Alan started walking, and they matched his pace as they followed.

They picked up the jakkals' trail almost immediately: a single line of scent that led toward the middle of Happyland. It appeared the carrion-eaters were careful not to wander throughout the park. A sensible precaution, but one that meant Alan and his sons had a single clear trail to follow. Alan found himself feeling a bit disappointed. The jakkals were making this too easy.

As the werewolves made their way through Happyland, they passed rides Alan remembered from his youth. The moonlight draped the machines in glowing blue-white, giving them an otherworldly aspect. They looked much smaller than he remembered, shabbier too, as if Happyland had always been a cheap, rickety small-town amusement park, despite his happy memories. Many of the buildings' roofs had collapsed over the years, and most of their paint had faded or flaked away entirely. The asphalt paths were shot through with cracks, and debris—chunks of concrete, broken lengths of wood, fallen signs—littered the place. They could hear animals close by. Rats, raccoons, and birds mostly, but there were a few groundhogs and opossum as well. When Alan and his sons drew near them, the animals grew silent, sensing the presence of predators in their midst.

The werewolves reached a section of the park where game booths lined the path. Most of the words on their signs were illegible now, but a few could still be made out: Big Six

Wheel, Knock 'em Down, Dartmaster… Alan had played most of these games when he was a boy.

He was surprised how many emotions were stirring in him. He might look human most of the time, but that was a disguise. He was a monster twenty-four-seven, and to a creature like him, humans were good for only one thing: food. And yet, he couldn't help remembering what it had been like in Happyland when he was kid, when he walked and ran and played in the midst of other children. *Human* children. They hadn't seemed like food to him then, had they? Even if the smell of them sometimes made his mouth water, especially when their pulses raced and he could hear the beating of their tender little hearts. They'd simply been kids, as he had been, and while he would never admit this to anyone, he missed the days back before he'd come to understand what being a monster was all about.

He was lost in his thoughts, unaware of the thin metal wire stretched across the path until his shin connected with it. There was a tall wooden pole to his right with a fluorescent light atop it that likely hadn't been activated in decades. As the wire pulled taut, there was a *click-clack* sound. The pole wobbled and began falling toward him. He leaped forward to avoid it, and Stuart and Spencer leaped backward. The heavy pole crashed to the asphalt where Alan had been standing a few seconds ago. It bounced a couple of times, rolled a bit, and then stopped.

It seemed the jakkals had set a trap for anyone who might come calling without an invitation—and they'd no doubt laid the scent trail to lead any intruders directly into it. The trip wire had been stretched across the path between two booths. This much he could see now, but he wasn't certain how the rest of the trap worked. The falling pole would've killed a human. A werewolf could've been severely wounded, making them easy prey. But the pole was more than a trap—it was also an alarm. The jakkals now knew that someone had come to Happyland.

Alan ran. His sons followed, all three of them moving inhumanly fast. They needed to reach the carrion-eaters before the jakkals had a chance to escape. The werewolves encountered two more traps along the way, but now that they knew to look for them, they easily avoided them.

As they'd driven through Bridge Valley searching for the jakkals, Alan had told his sons about the carrion-eaters:

They're scavengers. Smaller and weaker than we are, but they have one important advantage. If a jakkal manages to bite a werewolf, the wound won't heal, at least not any faster than a human injury. And if the wound is severe enough, you could bleed to death. My grandfather encountered a jakkal once, a lone one whose pack had cast him out for some reason. He caught a whiff of the man when he was leaving a bar. He found him sitting on the ground in an alley. The man looked like he was asleep, but when my grandfather got close, the jakkal transformed, sprang to his feet, and slashed Grandpa's face. The jakkal fled and Grandpa staggered out of the alley, blood dripping from his wounds. He healed eventually, but his face remained scarred for the rest of his life. So watch yourselves.

The scent trail led Alan and his sons to a round brick building with a black roof in the middle of the park. The sign above the entrance was still legible: PARK ADMINISTRATION. The stink of jakkal was strong here, and Alan knew they'd found the scavengers' den. He stopped twenty feet from the entrance and motioned for Stuart and Spencer to do the same. The twins' breathing was harsh and rapid, and they whined softly. He could feel their eagerness to rush forward, break into the building and begin killing. He was more experienced at controlling the wolf inside him, but even he had to fight it. He had his boys to think about. Controlling their animal impulses was difficult for them, and they'd already given in once when they'd helped their mother kill Amos Boyd. He didn't want them to kill again so soon, not unless they had to. Doing so would only erode what self-control they had.

"We know you're here!" he called out. "Show yourselves and let's talk. I promise that none of you will be hurt."

He meant this, although he wasn't confident that he could deliver on his promise. It all depended on what the jakkals did.

Your move, he thought.

FOURTEEN

Greg, in jakkal form, crouched behind a trashcan next to
what had once been a small burger joint. He had never been
in anything remotely resembling a fight before, and he was
scared. His mother, father, sisters, and grandfather had also
taken up positions in the vicinity, all of them spread out to
make it harder for the werewolves to determine their precise
locations. If they'd been grouped together, their combined
scent would've been easy for the werewolves to detect. But
spaced out as they were—along with the fact that their
scents were already in the immediate area—rendered them
practically invisible. At least, that was the hope.

Muriel had remained behind to guard Anubis and, if
necessary, wake him. She wasn't certain she could do so since
the Rite of Renewal hadn't been completed this month, but
if she was forced to try, she would.

Greg held no weapon. *You are all the weapon you need*,
Marta had told him before they left their quarters and took
their separate positions. He knew she'd meant her words to

be reassuring, but he would've felt better if he had something more solid—a knife or a club of some kind—to hold onto.

There were three werewolves, one older, two younger. Related, most probably. Father and sons, he guessed. Morgan's father? Maybe. He could detect the family connection from their scents. The older werewolf wore a sheriff's uniform, which made him doubly dangerous. The older werewolf promised he only wanted to talk, but Greg knew better than to believe him. They had all assumed their werewolf forms, and there were many ways to hunt prey. Luring them out into the open was an effective tactic—*if* the prey was foolish enough to fall for it.

Greg hid opposite the old restrooms. Nathan lay flat on their roof, concealed in the shadow of a tree next to the building. He rose to his feet in jakkal form, but he made no move to join the werewolves on the ground.

"What do you want, *iwiw*?"

Nathan used the ancient Egyptian word for dog. The word was meant to resemble a dog's bark, and when applied to werewolves, it was considered a grave insult, or so Nathan had told him. The werewolves didn't look particularly upset, though.

The older werewolf—the pack's leader, Greg thought— looked up at Nathan.

"Bridge Valley is *our* territory," he said. "We've been here for generations. You are not welcome."

"You got that right!" one of the man's sons said.

The leader's face darkened as if he were angry at his son, but he didn't take his gaze from Nathan.

"We did not know your kind inhabited this town," Nathan

said. "Otherwise, we would not have come here."

Greg understood that Nathan was projecting strength, one leader to another, but he wished his grandfather sounded less confrontational. The leader of the werewolves seemed to take Nathan's words in stride, but his sons were becoming increasingly agitated. They swayed back and forth, clawed hands clenching and unclenching, heads jutted forward, teeth bared.

"In that case, you won't have any problem packing up and leaving, will you?" The werewolf leader paused, and then added, "Carrion-eater."

Nathan's lips curled back from his fangs. "It will be our pleasure. Give us forty-eight hours, and we will be gone."

"Twenty-four," the werewolf leader said. "And believe me when I say that's being generous."

Nathan growled so softly that Greg wasn't sure he actually heard anything.

"Twenty-four hours," Nathan repeated. "Very well." He paused, and then added, "*Iwiw*."

Regardless of whether the werewolves knew the precise meaning of the word, there was no mistaking the derision in Nathan's tone. One of the sons let out a roar of anger and ran toward the restroom building.

"Stuart! No!" the werewolf leader shouted.

Greg didn't think. All fear fled him when he saw his grandfather in danger. He left his hiding place behind the trashcan and raced toward the werewolf. Greg slammed into him before he could leap onto the roof. They went sprawling, snarling, snapping, and clawing as they rolled on the asphalt. Greg was no longer thinking, was no longer really *Greg*. Not the rational part of him, anyway. For the first time in his life, he had completely given in to his animal side, and it was magnificent.

The werewolf's teeth and claws raked his flesh, but the wounds didn't trouble him. Injuries inflicted on a jakkal by a werewolf healed just as swiftly as normal ones. But the same couldn't be said for the werewolf. Blood poured from the places where Greg had taken a bite out of him. The werewolf might be stronger, but Greg could hurt him. In a few more moments this battle would be over and his foe would lie dead at his feet, a bloody, ragged ruin. The werewolf's blood tasted like sweet honey in his mouth, and he was greedy for more. He was about to sink his fangs into the werewolf's throat when he felt something grab hold of his neck and pull him roughly backward. He smelled Nathan's scent, and he whirled on his grandfather, growling.

"Get control of yourself, boy!" Nathan snapped.

Greg was tempted to take a swipe at his grandfather, but his instincts told him this was his pack leader, and he must obey. He closed his eyes and felt his animal bloodlust ebb. When he opened his eyes once more, he had returned to human form.

Greg looked over his shoulder and saw the werewolf leader stood with his hands on his son's shoulders. He spoke to his boy in soothing tones, almost whispering. The son's breathing remained heavy, and he kept shooting murderous glances at Greg, but in the end, he too calmed and regained his human appearance. His wounds did not heal, though, and his shirt was soaked with blood. Now that he was human again, he seemed to realize how badly hurt he was and grimaced in pain. Nathan and the werewolf leader resumed their human forms too. The other son remained in his werewolf shape for several more seconds, glaring at Greg murderously, but then he returned to human form as well.

The werewolf leader looked at Nathan. His face was dark with anger.

"When I pulled my son away from your grandson, I smelled something on the boy I didn't expect: my daughter's scent."

Greg went cold at the werewolf leader's words.

Nathan frowned, but he didn't take his gaze off the werewolf leader's face.

"Keep your pup away from my daughter, or I'll return and kill the lot of you."

The werewolf leader turned his glare on Greg then, and Greg—although frightened—did not look away. After a moment, the werewolf leader turned his attention back to Nathan.

"Twenty-four hours," the werewolf leader said. "Not a second more." Then he put an arm around his wounded son and began to lead him away. The other son gave Nathan and Greg a last dark look before following after his father and brother.

Greg and Nathan watched the werewolves depart silently. A few moments later, his father, mother, and sisters joined them.

"That went better than I expected," Marta said.

Nathan put a hand on Greg's shoulder. "I'm proud of you, boy. I could not have done better in my prime."

His grandfather's words made Greg's heart swell with pride. His pack had needed him, and he hadn't let them down. He felt tired, and more than a little embarrassed at having been taken over by his animal side like that, but his parents and his sisters looked at him with newfound respect, and he liked that. One thing bothered him, though. What would Morgan think when she learned what he'd done to her brother? Would she hate him? The next time they met—if there was a next time—would she consider him an enemy? Just another carrion-eater that should be killed? He hoped not. He'd done what he'd had to do, and in the same circumstances, he would do it again. But that didn't mean he had to feel good about it.

Greg looked at Nathan. "Do you think they'll keep their promise?"

Nathan shrugged. "It's difficult to say. Even Pureblood werewolves are ultimately slaves to their bestial nature. We did harm one of their own, and they might seek revenge. But the problem isn't if we'll have enough time to leave, but rather if Anubis is ready to be moved before the werewolves return."

"Anubis would be ready now if I hadn't screwed up the Rite of Renewal," Greg said.

Nathan gave him a reassuring smile, but Greg could see the worry in his grandfather's eyes. "Everything will be fine," Nathan said. "You shall see."

Greg wished he could believe that.

FIFTEEN

"Dad, I—"

"Shut up," Alan growled.

Stuart held his brother's shirt pressed tight to his wounds to slow the worst of the bleeding. He fell silent, and Alan thought as he drove.

He couldn't take Stuart to a hospital. Not only wouldn't he be able to explain how his son had gotten his wounds, but even in human form a werewolf's metabolism functioned differently than a human's. Stuart's heart, respiration, and blood pressure readings would arouse doctors' suspicions. There was no other choice than to take Stuart home and tend to his wounds there. He had a first-aid kit in the cruiser, and he hoped its supplies would be enough to do the job. Pureblood werewolves had almost no experience treating injuries or illness since their bodies resisted all disease and healed wounds rapidly—with the exception of those caused by silver, of course.

But even wounded as he was, Stuart was still a werewolf.

As long as his wounds were treated soon, there was an excellent chance he would heal, if far more slowly than normal. Alan had briefly examined Stuart's injuries before they'd driven away from Happyland, and luckily, most of them didn't look too serious. Even transformed, the jakkal boy was younger than Stuart. If he'd been mature, their brief battle might've had a very different outcome.

Alan could still smell Morgan's scent mingled with the stink of the jakkal boy. He gripped the steering wheel so tight it creaked. He was more than her father; he was the leader of her pack, and it was his responsibility to safeguard her until she was ready to mate. When that day came, he and Sylvia would make inquiries of other packs to find potential suitors for her. Meetings would be arranged, nature would take its course, and Morgan would select her mate. This was the way of their people and had been for thousands of years.

But for Morgan to display interest in a *jakkal*, of all things? He'd rather she fell in love with a human. At least they could be transformed into werewolves. When he'd detected Morgan's scent on the boy, he'd wanted to slice him open from throat to groin, but Stuart had been wounded. They couldn't afford any more fighting. Not then.

Sometimes he *hated* being pack leader.

"We should've killed them all," Spencer said in a whiny voice. He sounded like a child that had been denied dessert.

Alan understood how his son felt, but he knew if they'd tried to kill the jakkals, they all would've been badly wounded, if not worse. They'd only seen the old jakkal and the boy, but from the different scents in the area, Alan knew there were enough to outnumber him and his boys. Not good odds when your opponents could deal injuries you couldn't easily heal from.

He didn't respond. Let Spencer sulk for a while. Now that they'd dealt with the jakkals, he needed to turn his attention to their other problem: the hunters. They'd gone to Amos's house, and they'd let Melody follow them. His promise of an exclusive interview would hopefully keep her from writing a story for a day or two, but not much longer. Fuller's death had already brought too much attention to Bridge Valley, but if news of Amos's death got out, it could very well attract national news interest—*It appears a serial killer is at work in the small Indiana town of Bridge Valley!* He couldn't have that. Something had to be done about Melody, and soon.

Stuart moaned and his head slumped forward. Alan feared his son had passed out, but then the boy drew in a hitching breath and raised his head once more. His eyes were half-lidded, but at least he was conscious. How long he'd remain that way, Alan didn't know. If only there was some way to boost his boy's natural strength and help him heal more swiftly. But how?

Then it came to him.

A heart. A fresh one. A *human* one. One that Stuart had to himself. It might not heal his injuries completely, but it could give his body the extra strength needed to speed his healing.

A slow smile spread across Alan's face. He knew just where to get a heart, and he'd be killing the proverbial two birds with one stone. After he got Stuart settled in at home, he was going to pay Melody Diaz a brief but very satisfying visit.

* * *

Dean and Sam had parked the Impala on the side of the road several miles from Amos Boyd's house. While they waited for Garth to return, they changed into civilian clothes. Dean felt a thousand times better, and he wondered if they could take a tip from Garth and pretend to be writers as their cover story. That way, they could wear whatever they wanted.

It seemed to Dean as if they'd been waiting for hours when Garth—features human once again—finally emerged from the woods and hopped in the Impala.

"It's about damn time," Dean said. "You find the pack's den?"

"I think so," he said. "I followed the lycanthropes' trail to a house several miles east of here. Big place, lots of land, no close neighbors. It's a perfect place for a pack to live. They can change outside day or night without anyone seeing them, and they have easy access to the woods for hunting."

"Sounds like you found Werewolf Central. Let's get rolling." Dean started the Impala, pulled onto the road, and headed east.

"'The sooner the hunt's begun, the sooner the prey's between your teeth,'" Garth recited.

"That one's kind of creepy," Sam said.

"It's just a metaphor," Garth said, sounding a little defensive.

"Did you pick up any scent trails besides the werewolves that killed Amos?" Sam asked. "We know there are at least three, but it would help if we had some idea of how many total we might be up against."

"There was lycanthrope scent all over the woods," Garth said. "Trails that overlapped one another, some new, some old. This is a pack that's been around for a very long time." He thought for a moment. "If I had to guess, I'd say that currently, it's a small pack. Probably a single family. Two parents, maybe three grown children."

"That makes it easier," Dean said.

Werewolf packs tended to be on the smaller side so they could better avoid being noticed, but a family would fight all the harder to protect each other. That made this pack even more dangerous. He was glad to hear that the children were adults. He didn't want to have to hurt little kids, even if they were monsters. Killing kids was one thing Dean couldn't stomach, no matter what species they were.

"How do you boys want to play this?" Garth asked.

"Simple is best," Dean said. "They don't know we're coming, so I say we arm ourselves with silver bullets and silver blades, go in the front and back, and start taking out the furballs one by one."

"I thought you'd say something like that," Garth said. "And it's a decent plan, don't get me wrong. But I can't sign on for that."

Dean had no idea what Garth was talking about, but then Sam said, "You want to talk with them first."

Garth nodded. "I want to give them a chance to turn away from a life of violence and join my pack. 'The more voices, the stronger the howl.'"

"Would you cut it out with the werewolf philosophy crap?" Dean said. "This pack has killed at least two people and probably a hell of a lot more. And you want to *talk* with them? They're monsters, pure and simple, and you don't talk to monsters. You put them down so they can't hurt anyone ever again."

Garth was silent for a moment, then he said, "Monsters like me?"

Dean felt sudden shame. "That's not what I meant. You're a hunter—or you were. You know how the job works. It's kill or be killed."

"It doesn't have to be like that," Garth said. "Not always. Since the last time I saw you guys, I've managed to convince seven lycanthropes to join my pack."

"And how many have you had to kill because they wouldn't join?" Dean asked.

"Sixteen," Garth said.

Dean continued. "And of the ones you brought home, how many stayed savage and had to be killed?"

Garth hesitated before answering.

"Three."

"So out of twenty-three werewolves you've encountered, only four are still alive."

"Dean…" Sam said, but Dean ignored his brother and went on.

"That's not a lot. And you think there are at least five werewolves where we're going. Even if a couple are willing to listen to you, the rest are going to rip your throat out as soon as you open your mouth." Dean almost added, *And I can relate to that*, but he managed to restrain himself. "I say we go in guns blazing, and if any of the werewolves are still alive when we're done, *then* you can talk to them."

"Because the only good monster is a dead one, right?" Garth said bitterly.

Garth began to softly growl, and Dean felt a sudden chill.

He was ready to reach for his Colt, which was currently in the glove box along with Sam's gun. Emotionally, he believed that Garth would never hurt him or Sam, but intellectually, he feared he couldn't take that chance. But before he could move, Garth jumped out. The Impala was doing forty-five, but Garth hit the ground, rolled once, and came up gracefully onto his feet.

Dean slammed the brakes, and the Impala skidded to a halt in the middle of the road.

In the crimson glow of the car's brake lights, Dean could see anger and hurt on Garth's face. Then Garth transformed and loped into the woods where he was quickly swallowed by the night.

Dean turned to Sam, who was scowling at him. He sighed. "Yeah, I know. I'm a dumbass."

Melody sat on the floor of her living room, leaning against the couch and typing on her laptop. When she'd sat down to work, she'd told herself she'd only do so for an hour or two, then maybe have a glass of wine and watch some TV to unwind. She lived alone, and so when she worked at home she usually lost track of time and stayed up way too late. She needed to be better about getting a full night's sleep, both for her mental and physical health.

Who am I kidding? she thought. Relaxing wasn't her thing. She was an admitted workaholic, and it was a rare moment that didn't find her writing a story for the paper, whether literally typing one up or trying to brainstorm ideas and composing articles in her head.

So I love what I do. Sue me.

While she liked her little office downtown, she much preferred working at home. She owned a small two-bedroom house in one of Bridge Valley's nicer neighborhoods—no rehab clinics on her block—and while the second bedroom was nominally her home office, when she was at home she did most of her work in the living room. It felt cozier, especially when she had a fire going in the fireplace. She wore a pair of fuzzy pajamas and slippers, and she *did* have a glass of wine on the coffee table next to her computer, so at least she was relaxing a little, right?

She'd promised the FBI agents and the sheriff that she wouldn't publish anything about Amos Boyd's murder before she got the go-ahead from them, but she liked to be prepared. This way, when she got permission to publish, she'd be ready to go.

She was well aware that this story—coming so soon after Clay Fuller's death—would garner a lot of media attention. How could it not? The witness to a murder allegedly committed by three "animal people" was killed in a horrific fashion only a few days later. The situation was absolutely bizarre, and such stories appealed to people's morbid curiosity. Plus, there was an element of conspiracy to it. It was reasonable to assume that Amos was killed to silence him. Add to that three men claiming to be federal agents who'd come to town to investigate Fuller's death, and now Amos's. The whole thing was a bona fide mystery.

Melody enjoyed working at *The Bridge Valley Independent*, but that didn't mean she wanted to spend her entire career there. She wanted to live and work somewhere exciting, and this story would help her achieve that goal. Part of her felt guilty for exploiting the deaths of two people solely to advance her career, but someone was going to write about these murders, so why shouldn't it be her? She'd already written a story about Fuller's death, and she knew she could pull bits and pieces from it to recycle for this new article. What she was struggling with was how to write about the agents and following them to Amos's house. She wasn't used to putting herself into a story.

It was five minutes after nine when she heard the back door burst open. Startled, she tried to jump to her feet and banged her knees against the underside of the coffee table. She managed to stand without knocking anything else over and ran to the fireplace. She grabbed a metal poker, and turned to face the entryway to the kitchen. There was a full moon out tonight, and enough light filtered in through the windows to reveal the silhouette of a person. Whoever it was stood still, features hidden, save for a pair of eyes that glowed with yellow light. Those eyes terrified her to the core of her being. She could feel them sizing her up, deciding how much effort it would take to bring her down. She felt frozen to the spot, unable to move, afraid to even breathe.

This must be what an antelope feels like when it realizes it's being stalked by a lion, she thought. *The antelope must believe that if it stands still long enough, maybe the lion won't see it. Then the lion will move on, and the antelope will avoid death for one more day.*

She didn't think she was going to be that lucky.

She heard the figure's breathing, a heavy animal sound, and then it began to growl. She knew then that whatever this thing was, it wasn't human. Still holding onto the poker, she ran for the front door.

She only managed to take three steps before whoever—*whatever*—had broken into her house raced into the living room, grabbed hold of her wrist, and spun her around. Her first thought was the thing was damn fast. Her second thought was it was a monster—yellow eyes, sharp fangs, long curving claws. Her third thought was the intruder was Alan Crowder. Which wasn't possible. Alan was human. He couldn't be a monster.

Could he?

It came to her in a flash then. Alan was connected to the animal people that had killed Clay Fuller and likely Amos Boyd too. More than connected; he was one of them. And she'd called him after leaving Amos's home, letting him know what she'd learned. And evidently Alan had decided she'd learned too much.

She tried to pull free of his grasp so she could swing her makeshift weapon at him, but his fingers clamped around her flesh and bone like iron, and she couldn't move her arm. It was at that moment when she knew she was going to die. No more late-night work sessions at home. No chance for a better job in a bigger city. No more glasses of wine.

Alan's lips drew back from his fangs in what might have been a snarl or a smile. Perhaps, she thought, it was a little of both.

He rammed his free hand into her chest with astonishing strength. She felt his claws cut flesh, break ribs, and take hold of her heart. Then he pulled it from her chest in a spray of blood. She had just enough life left to hear his howl of triumph, then she collapsed to the floor.

Garth had described the werewolf pack's house well enough that the brothers knew what to look for: a two-story house on a large expanse of land, no close neighbors, about two miles from Amos's place. Sam was confident they'd locate it. The question was whether they'd find it in time to help Garth. Then again, maybe he didn't need their help. Without meaning to, they'd been treating Garth as a kind of goofy sidekick rather than a hunter in his own right. He'd been making contact with other werewolves for a while now. Maybe they should give him the benefit of the doubt.

"When we get there, I think we should give Garth some time to talk with the werewolves before we bust in and start shooting," Sam said.

"I'm not sure that's a good idea," Dean said. "Garth's only one guy, and he's going up against a pack."

"A small pack," Sam said.

"He'll still be outnumbered."

Sam couldn't argue that point. "Even so, we need to trust him on this."

"Why?"

Sam didn't have to think about his reply. "Because he's family."

Dean grimaced, an expression Sam knew well. Dean made the same face every time he was going to do something that went against his better judgment.

"Fine. We'll give him ten minutes."

"Fifteen?"

"Ten," Dean said firmly.

Sam knew this was as good as he was going to get from his brother, so he nodded.

"And we'll just have to hope Garth doesn't get torn to shreds while we sit around twiddling our thumbs," Dean said.

Sam knew how Dean felt. He didn't like hanging back any more than his brother did. But you had to take chances when you were a hunter. Sometimes you had to give them too.

The Impala glided down the road, headlights slicing through the darkness. Sam gazed out of the passenger-side window and thought about another time when he and Dean had taken a chance. It had turned out far differently from what either of them had expected.

Sixteen

Near Seattle, Washington. 1992

Sam didn't remember falling asleep, but he must have, because when he opened his eyes the TV was off and the motel room was dark.

Someone's at the door, he thought.

Then he heard knocking. The sound was soft, as if whoever it was didn't want to wake any people staying in nearby rooms. Sam recognized the rhythm of the knocking. Three slow, three fast. It was Bobby.

Dean was up and moving before Sam could get out of bed. He quickly unlocked the door and Bobby staggered inside. He slumped against the wall to steady himself, and he might've fallen if Dean hadn't reached out. Bobby's face was ashen, and the right arm of his army jacket was covered with blood.

"Get me… onto bed," Bobby gasped. "And… watch the arm."

Sam hurried forward to help Dean, and together the two of

them steered Bobby to Sam's bed. Bobby collapsed and rolled onto his back, wincing in pain. Dean tried to get him to sit up enough so he could get his jacket off, and Sam closed and locked the door. Dean managed to get Bobby's left arm out of its sleeve, and when Sam saw how badly wounded Bobby was, his breath caught in his throat. Bobby's arm had a trio of long gashes running from his bicep to the inside of his forearm. Sam couldn't tell how deep the wounds were because they were bleeding too badly.

"Get a towel!" Dean shouted, and Sam ran into the bathroom, grabbed a rough white towel, and rushed back to the bed. Dean snatched the towel from Sam and pressed it against Bobby's injuries. Bobby took in a hissing breath, but he didn't cry out. Sam was impressed by how brave Bobby was being. Later, Bobby would tell him the only reason he hadn't shouted from the pain was because he'd been wounded so many damn times in his life, he was used to it by now.

"Get the first-aid kit," Dean said. Blood was soaking through the white towel, turning it red, and the sight made Sam's stomach do a flip. He tore his gaze from the widening crimson stains and ran to get the kit.

For the next half hour, Sam and Dean tended to Bobby's injuries, following his instructions. At times it seemed he might pass out, but he managed to remain conscious. While they worked, he told them what had happened, pausing now and then to catch his breath.

"By the time I got to the hospital the rain had let up, which I appreciated. I hate sitting a stakeout in the rain. I parked in the visitor lot and starting walking around, keeping an eye out for hospital security. Last thing I needed was to have rent-a-cops haul me in for taking a nighttime stroll on hospital grounds. And I didn't want to answer any questions about why I was carrying a gun loaded with silver bullets in my jacket pocket.

"I must've walked for several hours, but I only had to duck security once. It was getting cold, and I was starting to think the werewolf had moved on to other hunting grounds, when I heard growling. The lot was almost full, and there were plenty of places for a werewolf to hide. Too many. I was heading toward one of the lot's fluorescent lights so I could better see the damn thing when it came at me."

Bobby paused in his story to take a sip from his flask. Once fortified, he continued.

"Little good *that* did me. The werewolf came at me so fast all I saw was a blur out of the corner of my eye. I managed to step to the side in time to avoid being gutted like a fish, but I still got tagged."

He nodded to his injured arm. By this point, Sam and Dean had cleaned the wounds—which turned out not to be as deep as Sam had feared—and Dean was now in the process of stitching up the gashes.

Normal kids don't do stuff like this, Sam thought. He didn't know how he felt about that. Part of him liked being able to do things most kids couldn't, but another part of him resented having to take on so much adult responsibility so soon.

Bobby continued his story.

"The werewolf hit me so hard, I spun around and nearly fell. I managed to draw my gun, and just as the werewolf was coming at me again—straight on this time—I got a shot off. The thing let out a loud yelp, and instead of attacking me, it veered off and ran away. I don't know how badly I wounded it, but it was able to keep running at full speed, so I knew I missed the thing's heart. The wound won't heal right away since it was caused by silver, but it won't be fatal. Since the werewolf got hurt in the parking lot, it'll probably go looking for a new hunting ground. Tonight's the last night of the full moon's cycle, which means someone else will have to die next month before we learn where the thing has set up shop."

Bobby couldn't tell them much about the werewolf's appearance. It had moved too swiftly for him to make out any distinct features. It was an adult and it was wearing a shirt and pants, but that was all Bobby knew. He wasn't even sure what gender it was. After the werewolf fled, Bobby had managed to return to his truck and drive back to the motel—"Bleeding all over my damn seat"—and stagger to the door of their room.

When Dean finished playing doctor, Sam handed Bobby several prescription pain pills from the supply in the first-aid kit. Sam had no idea how hunters like Dad and Bobby managed to get their hands on prescription meds, but they did. He'd asked Dad once, and John Winchester had smiled and said, "You need all kinds of friends when you're a hunter."

Bobby swallowed the pills and chased them down with another pull from his flask. He then sighed, handed the flask to Sam and lay his head back on the pillow and closed his eyes.

"I did the best I could, Bobby," Dean said, "but we should get you to a hospital and have a real doctor fix you up."

Dean sounded unsure, even worried, and that surprised

Sam. He was used to Dean being the always-confident older brother, but if *he* was worried, then the situation had to be even worse than Sam feared.

Bobby spoke without opening his eyes. "You did good. And I've been stitched up on the fly more than a few times. I'll be all right as long as I get a chance… to rest."

A few moments later, Bobby's breathing deepened, and Sam knew he'd fallen asleep.

The boys cleaned up as best they could. They threw the blood-soaked towel in a dumpster outside, and they did their best to scrub out the bloodstains on the carpet. They couldn't do anything about the bedclothes Bobby lay on, which were also bloodstained. Later, when he was up and moving around, they'd strip the bed and throw the blankets and sheet into the dumpster as well.

When they were finished, it was past midnight. Both of them sat on the other bed and watched Bobby as he slept.

"His breathing's regular," Dean said. He got up and placed his fingers against Bobby's neck. After a minute he said, "His pulse is strong too."

"You're not a doctor," Sam said.

"No, but I've watched a lot of episodes of *Heartbreak Hospital*," Dean said, as if this somehow qualified him to look after the sick and injured. Sam didn't challenge him. Dean's medical knowledge, however scant, was better than his.

Dean sat on the bed once more and they continued watching Bobby sleep, almost as if they were sitting vigil. After a while, Dean said, "You sleepy?"

"No. You?"

"Nope."

A few moments passed, and then Dean said, "Still a long time until the sun rises."

Sam turned to look at his brother. He already had an idea of where Dean was going with this, and he didn't like it. But he listened as Dean went on. And when his brother had finished explaining his plan, Sam surprised himself by saying, "Let's do it."

SEVENTEEN

Present Day

Garth moved through the woods as swift and silent as a shadow. There were many difficult things about being a lycanthrope—chief among them the hunger that only heart meat could satisfy, and for which animal hearts were a poor substitute. But *this*—moving through the forest, his mind and body so attuned to his environment that he was practically one with it—this was his favorite thing about being a Lupine American. The full moon sang in his blood, making him feel even stronger, faster, and *wilder* than usual. The sensation was more intoxicating than any drug, and he had to fight to keep from being swept away by it. He knew if he gave in, his animal side would take over completely, and then he would be all instinct and hunger. He would be in danger of doing the one thing he'd vowed never to do: kill a human for nourishment.

The moon strengthened a Pureblood's animal side, and Garth's pack preferred to avoid changing during the cycle of the full moon if possible. Easier to avoid temptation that way. But when you hunted rogue lycanthropes, you didn't always have a choice about when you transformed. He thought there might be a good "fangism" in there somewhere—*Hear the song of the moon, but don't let it lead you astray.* Could use a little work, maybe, but not bad.

He knew he was doing his best to distract himself. But it was no use. Dean's words had hurt, and no matter how hard he tried to shove them to the back of his mind, he could still hear them.

I say we go in guns blazing, and if any of the werewolves are still alive when we're done, then *you can talk to them.*

Garth hated the W word.

The hell of it was that he understood how Dean thought. It hadn't been that long ago that he'd been a human hunter, and his attitude toward supernatural entities had been simple: they were dangerous, if not downright evil, and they had to be destroyed, banished or whatever it took to prevent them from harming anyone. Shoot first and don't bother asking questions later.

But then he'd become a monster himself, and his outlook changed. It wasn't out of simple self-preservation, either. When he realized he'd become infected from the lycanthrope's bite, he'd considered putting a silver bullet in his head before he changed and killed someone. But during his time as a hunter he'd heard rumors about a cure, and while he'd always considered the stories to be bullcrap, it was the only hope he had. So he began making inquiries among the hunters he knew. He didn't go to Sam and Dean, although he knew he should have. It wasn't that he'd been afraid of them killing him. In fact, if he had to be put down, he'd rather they do the job than some random hunter who'd tracked him down. He didn't go to them because he was embarrassed, pure and simple. He'd screwed up and let a lycanthrope bite him, and while he'd killed the one who'd done it, that didn't change the fact that he'd once again pulled a Garth, allowing his reckless—not to mention unearned—self-confidence get the better of him. He looked up to Sam and Dean. He knew they weren't perfect—who the hell was?—but they were two of the greatest hunters of all time. They were his role models, and he didn't think he could bear seeing the disappointment on their faces when he told them what had happened. So he didn't reach out to them, and he didn't plan on seeing them again until he was cured.

But his search for a cure ran into one dead end after another, and by the time the next cycle of the full moon rolled around, he found himself in Wisconsin, holed up in a ratty motel after another failed attempt to find a lead on a cure. He hadn't changed since being bitten, although there had been times when he felt the wolf growing inside him, becoming stronger as it waited patiently for its time to be freed from its human prison.

He decided to end his life before the sun fell. His revolver was still loaded with silver bullets—minus the one that had killed the lycanthrope who'd bitten him. He'd tried to unload the gun so he could clean it, but the silver bullets burned his flesh so severely that he'd given up on the idea. Now he was glad. The gun was already loaded and ready to go. He considered leaving a note, but he wasn't sure what to say. He almost went with *I'm sorry I screwed up and became a monster. Goodbye.* He decided that wasn't good enough, but since he couldn't think of anything better, he gave up on writing a note. He hoped Sam and Dean would never find out what happened, but if they did, he hoped they'd understand.

But the moment he was sitting clothed in the bathtub— easier to clean up the mess in there—and beginning to raise the revolver to his head, the lycanthrope in him, as if sensing the danger it was in, emerged. The transformation was so swift and startling that he dropped the revolver, which hit the tub with a loud *clang*. He'd expected the change to hurt, and it did this first time, but it also felt *good*. His senses expanded in ways he never could've imagined, and his body surged with so much energy, so much raw *power*, he feared his physical form couldn't contain it and he'd explode. And then—

He just sat there.

He was a lycanthrope. One look at the claws on his hands confirmed this. But he was also still Garth. The wolf aspect of him was separate, but he could feel this new part of his mind intertwining with the old, merging with it, becoming one. His body wanted him to get out of the tub, leave this disgusting room—which now reeked of a hundred different foul smells that he preferred not to think about—go outside into the fresh air and open space and *run*, fast and free. He was hungry, yes, and for one thing in particular, which was gross, but he felt no overriding impulse to go out hunting humans.

It was then that he began to understand that there might be more to being a lycanthrope than he'd thought.

He climbed out of the tub and checked himself in the mirror. His sharp teeth felt weird, and he cut his tongue when he ran it over one elongated incisor. The small wound healed instantly, which was even weirder. The yellow eyes were cool, though.

He had changed while the sun was still up, and he could still think. He'd thought the lycanthrope who'd bitten him had been the kind that turned into a savage killing machine only three nights a month, and he'd believed that would be his fate as well. Now he understood that he'd been bitten by a Pureblood, which made him one, too.

He focused on his reflection in the mirror and imagined the yellow-eyed fanged Garth returning to his all-too-human self. At first, nothing happened, and Garth feared he might be stuck like this, but then he felt a sensation of release, of letting go, and his lycanthrope features receded and he was once again plain old Garth Fitzgerald IV.

That night he decided to find some woods, change, and explore his newfound capabilities. He was astounded when, after running among the trees and sniffing every delicious scent he could find for over an hour, he ran into another lycanthrope. A female. At first, they both fell into defensive positions, claws up, teeth bared, throats growling. But after a moment, the woman lowered her arms and became human.

"Hi. I'm Bess."

And the smile she gave him was the most beautiful he'd ever seen.

That was how he'd met the woman who would become his wife, and how he came to join her pack. And aside from some trouble that Sam and Dean had helped them clear up, life with the pack had been good. It was that life—one where you could be safe and accepted, where you could just be a person instead of a monster—that he wanted to help other lycanthropes find. Or at least give them a shot at.

He thought Sam understood. He wished Dean could too.

But he couldn't afford to worry about that now. He didn't know how much time Sam and Dean would give him to talk to the Bridge Valley pack, but he knew it wouldn't be long. Not after the lycanthropes—or at least some of them—had committed two murders.

Two that you know of, he thought.

He had to make every moment count. Otherwise there was an excellent chance the entire pack would be dead within the hour.

He gritted his sharp teeth and poured on the speed.

Garth slowed to a walk when he broke out of the woods. He'd reached the pack's property, and you approached another pack's den with extreme caution. Purebloods were never more dangerous than when protecting their home.

There was a wooden deck at the rear of the house, along with a patio door. The vertical blinds were closed, but light filtered between them, so he knew someone was home. Maybe the entire family. Transforming during the full moon was extra exciting for some Pureblood packs, and they liked to have a meal on those evenings—a *light* meal—after which the pack would transform and go out to hunt.

He smelled no food. Maybe this pack preferred to hunt on empty stomachs.

The emptier the belly, the sweeter the meat.

That fangism was a keeper.

He knew better than to go up to the patio door and knock. That would be creepy even if he hadn't been a lycanthrope. He intended to go around to the front, take a quick look to make sure Sam and Dean weren't there ready to break down the door and start shooting, and then he'd return to human form and ring the doorbell, nice and civilized. He'd done this sort of thing before, and he'd found—

He was halfway across the backyard when the patio door exploded in a shower of glass shards. A female lycanthrope came racing toward him, moving faster than any lycanthrope he'd ever known. She leaped off the deck, soared twenty feet through the air, and landed in front of him in a crouch, snarling, saliva running from her mouth.

Garth came to a sudden halt and stuck out his hand.

"Hi! I'm Garth, and I'd like to—"

That was all he got out before the woman let out an ear-splitting cry of rage and attacked.

When they located the house, Dean drove past and parked the Impala on the side of the road about a mile away. Neither of the brothers spoke while they sat, and after fifteen minutes Dean said, "Let's go."

They got out of the Impala as quietly as they could. Both brothers were armed: Dean with his Colt M1911A1 and Sam with his Taurus PT92AFS, each pistol loaded with silver rounds. They also carried silver blades for up-close combat. They had their weapons out and ready. As fast as werewolves were, you didn't want to waste time drawing your gun. You'd most likely be wolf chow before you had a chance to get off a single shot.

Their plan was simple: they would enter the house from the rear and kill any werewolves that came at them. If Garth had managed to convince the werewolves to talk with him, the brothers would hold their fire, although Dean would do so grudgingly. He still felt bad about upsetting Garth, and he wanted to give him the benefit of the doubt. Garth might have saved only a few werewolves, but that was a hell of a lot better than none. But Dean doubted Garth's message of peace and love would be well received by this pack. They'd murdered two people over the last couple of days and had probably killed a lot more. From what Dean understood, once a werewolf tasted a human heart, it was almost impossible for them to stick to a diet of only animal hearts. When the Bridge Valley pack learned that Garth's pack abstained from eating human hearts, they'd stop listening to his sales pitch. And once that happened, Garth would be in big-time trouble. Dean hoped to hell he was wrong, for Garth's sake, but he couldn't help feeling their friend had made a serious—and potentially fatal—mistake.

Dean was itching to get moving. He saw a pair of headlights off in the distance, coming toward them, and they hid behind a sturdy pair of oaks. They'd remain hidden until the vehicle passed, and then they'd resume their approach to the house. But the vehicle slowed as it drew closer, and when it reached the werewolf pack's house, it turned into the long driveway. It was a sheriff's cruiser. Dean had no doubt that

Alan Crowder was behind the wheel. The sheriff was one of the pack, probably their leader.

Great, Dean thought. *The exact moment Sammy and me are ready to bust in on Werewolf HQ, Papa Wolf comes home.*

Dean looked at Sam. "This isn't good," he said.

"No, it's not."

They started running toward the house.

Eighteen

Alan was on high alert when he pulled the cruiser up to the garage, parked, and got out. He carried a plastic cooler containing Melody's heart, and as he walked to the front door he scanned his surroundings and scented the air, but he didn't detect any sign of intruders. Still, something wasn't right. He could *feel* it.

He went inside and closed, locked, and bolted the front door behind him. The instant he entered the house, he smelled the presence of another werewolf. The change swept over him in an instant and he ran, following the foreign scent into the dining room. He stopped when he saw Sylvia—in human form—holding a revolver to the temple of a scrawny man. She wore a yellow rubber glove over the hand holding the weapon. The man was bound to one of the dining table chairs by heavy chains covered in duct tape. Alan normally used the chains to bind one of the family when they disobeyed him and were in need of a "time out."

Speaking of Sylvia, Alan was glad to see the wounds he'd

inflicted on her as punishment for killing Amos Boyd had mostly healed. The skin at the left corner of her mouth was still a little raw, but it would repair itself soon enough. Stuart, Spencer, and Morgan stood close by, watching. Joshua was in his high chair, happily munching on bits of toasted oat cereal, oblivious to what was happening. Stuart was shirtless, face pale, his chest wrapped in blood-soaked bandages. Given the extent of the boy's wounds, Alan was surprised Stuart wasn't lying in bed, but he was glad the boy was here. He was proud of his son's determination not to give in to weakness.

Alan looked at the scrawny man and thought, *Were you ever in the wrong place at the wrong time. You're lucky she didn't tear you to pieces.* After her punishment, Sylvia would've wanted to make sure Alan had the opportunity to question their prisoner, even though she must've been eager to vent her fury on someone. *Good girl,* he thought. The twins' eyes gleamed as they stared at their captive, and Alan knew they were imagining all the things they'd do to him. Morgan just looked confused and worried.

Alan placed the cooler on the table and looked at Sylvia. "I see we have a guest."

"An uninvited one." Sylvia didn't take her eyes off the intruder. The man might not look like much of a threat, but he was a werewolf, and werewolves were always dangerous.

Alan didn't recognize the gun she was holding to the scrawny man's head, nor did he understand why she wore a rubber glove. And then he smelled it: *silver.* The scent of the metal caused his nasal passages to burn, as if he'd inhaled the odor of some caustic chemical.

As if reading his mind, Sylvia said, "It's his gun. I took it from him when I captured him."

The man was a werewolf, so why had he been packing silver? Merely having the gun on him had to have been uncomfortable, if not painful. It didn't make any sense. Werewolves fought each other with tooth and claw, the way nature intended. They didn't lower themselves to use human weapons—especially not silver.

"He says his name's Garth," Stuart said. "And that he's come to help us." Both Stuart and Spencer snickered.

"It's true," Garth said.

The man sounded calm despite being chained up and having a gun pressed against his head. *He's not a coward. I'll give him that,* Alan thought.

Sylvia looked at Alan and smiled. "You've got fresh blood on your uniform." She inhaled deeply, savoring the smell. "I take it your shopping trip was successful."

"It was."

Alan opened the cooler, withdrew Melody's heart, and held it up for everyone to see. Stuart and Spencer began drooling, and Sylvia took her eyes off their captive long enough to give the heart a hungry glance. Even Joshua forgot his cereal and turned toward the heart, his small nostrils flaring as he drank in the scent of the meat, although he was much too young to eat it. Only Morgan didn't seem excited. If anything, her lips pursed in an expression of distaste, if not outright disgust. So far, she'd resisted eating human heart meat, and it wasn't the way of the pack to force children to do so until they were ready. But Morgan wasn't a child anymore, and it was high time she acted like it.

And as for Garth, Alan found his reaction to the heart most interesting. His entire body trembled and he breathed through his mouth instead of his nose, as if he couldn't bear the smell. His head was turned halfway to the side, as if he were trying to look away from the heart but couldn't quite make himself do it. Alan could hear the rapid beat of the man's pulse, and he could smell warring emotions in his scent: shame, anger at himself, but most of all, *desire*.

"That's Melody's heart, isn't it?" Garth said. His voice was low and deep, more animal than human. "I can smell it."

Alan ignored his question. "You've never tasted human heart meat before, have you?"

Garth shook his head. "It's the way of my pack," he said, his voice shaky. "We don't believe in violence and we don't kill humans. We eat only animal hearts."

Alan's stomach turned at the very idea. Sylvia sneered in disgust, and both boys made comical retching sounds. Morgan didn't react at all. If anything, she looked thoughtful. Alan found that more than a little disturbing, and he resolved to have a father-daughter talk with her as soon as possible. About this, and about her talking to that jakkal boy.

"I came here because of Clay Fuller's murder," Garth said. "I suspected there were lycanthropes in this area, and I wanted to offer you a chance to join my pack and live peacefully. No more killing humans, no more being a slave to your animal nature, and no more hunters coming after you. You can be free."

Alan looked at Garth for a long moment, and then he burst out laughing.

"That's the most ridiculous thing I've ever heard. We already *are* free. We accept what we are and live true to our nature. Can you say the same?"

Garth didn't answer.

"And just how peaceful *are* your intentions," Alan said, "when you come to us carrying a gun loaded with silver bullets?"

Again, Garth had no response.

Alan raised Melody's heart to his mouth. His teeth became fangs, and he bit off a sliver of meat. It was beyond delicious. It was as if something vital was missing at the core of his being, and the meat was the only thing that could make him whole again. He wanted to chew it, savor it until he could no longer resist and had to swallow it. Instead, he opened his mouth and removed the sliver with his free hand. Then he tossed the rest of the heart to Stuart.

The boy caught the organ on the fly and jammed it greedily against his mouth. He transformed and began devouring the heart like a starving animal. He left his son to his grisly meal and stepped toward Garth.

Now that he stood within inches of the man, he got a deeper read on his scent. He was Pureblood, but he hadn't been born that way. And unless Alan missed his guess, he hadn't been transformed very long ago. A few years back at most. He was what Alan had always heard referred to as a turnblood. Technically Pureblood, but a step down from the real thing. Turnbloods tended to be slightly slower and weaker than actual Purebloods, and they had a more difficult time balancing their human and wolf sides. The poor sonofabitch had never stood a chance against a werewolf as magnificently fierce as Sylvia.

Alan could smell something else on Garth: the scents of the two FBI agents that he suspected were really hunters. He was working with them. A werewolf working with hunters, against other werewolves? What was the world coming to?

Smiling, Alan lifted the piece of heart meat to Garth's mouth. Garth pressed his lips together tight and turned away.

"Come on," Alan said. "One little taste won't hurt you. Don't you want to know what you're missing?"

Garth didn't turn his head back toward the meat, but his nostrils flared, and Alan knew he was drinking in the sweet scent of Melody's heart. He couldn't help himself.

"Melody told me you were at Amos's place," Alan said. "You're the writer who wanted to interview me this morning, aren't you? Except you're not really a writer. That was just your cover story. Like your friends being FBI agents was their cover story."

Moving swiftly, Alan grabbed the back of Garth's head and tried to force the meat into his mouth, but he kept his lips shut tight.

Sylvia—who still held the gun to Garth's head—grinned in malicious delight.

"Open your mouth," she said. "Or I'll spray your brains all over the room."

Alan kept his eyes on Garth, but he heard Spencer laughing. Not Stuart, though. He was still busy eating. Morgan made a soft, almost canine whine, as if she was distressed by what her father and mother were doing. The sound filled Alan with anger and disappointment.

First she talks to a carrion-eater, and now she displays weakness in front of an enemy.

Obviously, he and Sylvia had been too easy on her. They should never have allowed her to attend school with humans. She'd spent too much time around them, and it had softened her. That was all right, though. It was nothing that couldn't be beaten out of her in time. And as for the jakkal boy… Alan thought it would be best if he were no longer around. That way, Morgan wouldn't be tempted to see him again. And if Alan was going to kill the boy, he might as well kill the rest of his family while he was at it. But that was a matter for later. Right now, he had his plate full right here.

Garth still hadn't opened his mouth, and now tears began to trickle from his eyes. They weren't tears of anger or sadness. It was simply his body's reaction to the great war he was fighting inside himself—the battle of man versus beast—and Alan knew the beast always won in the end.

That's when Alan heard the sound of footfalls in the backyard. Someone—two someones—were heading their way, running all out. The wind was blowing in the wrong direction for Alan to pick up their scents, but he didn't need to smell them to know Garth's friends were attacking.

"I hear them too," Sylvia said. "What should we do?"

Alan thought fast. He released his grip on Garth's head and removed his hand from the man's mouth. Garth immediately sighed in relief. Never one to waste heart meat, Alan popped it into his mouth and swallowed it.

"Keep the gun on him," Alan told his wife. Then he looked at Stuart. The boy's mouth was red with gore, but he'd finished the heart. He looked stronger than he had a few moments ago.

"Stay with your mother," Alan told him. "Protect her and Joshua if necessary. Spencer, Morgan, follow me."

Alan transformed as he ran for the front door. At first he heard only Spencer following him, and an instant later he heard Morgan hurrying to catch up. He allowed himself a satisfied smile. Maybe she wasn't as far gone as he'd feared.

When he reached the front door, he threw it open, and he plunged into the night, his son and daughter close behind.

Nineteen

God, that was close!

Garth felt a strange mix of reactions. He wanted to throw up at the thought of what he'd almost done. He had never smelled anything so wonderful in his entire life. He hadn't just wanted to eat the heart meat. His body had screamed that he *had* to have it, and if he didn't get it, his empty, aching stomach would devour him from the inside out.

I'm in control, he told himself. *Not the wolf. Me!*

And then he realized: Sam and Dean were coming.

"Look out!" he shouted. "It's a trap!"

Sylvia snarled and clouted him on the head with the gun—hard. His vision blurred and he fought to hold onto consciousness, but he felt himself sliding into darkness. His last thought was *I hope they heard me*, and then he was out.

Dean and Sam were within twenty feet of the Crowders' deck when the werewolves attacked.

One good thing about hunting monsters by the light of the full moon, Dean thought. *As long as you're in the open, you can see them coming.*

The sheriff led the charge, and following close behind were a man in his twenties and a teenage girl. Crowder's kids, Dean figured. All three had wolfed out, and the front of Crowder's uniform was stained dark. Dean knew it was blood. Garth's? He hoped not.

We should never have let him go alone, he thought. But just then he heard Garth shout from inside the house.

"Look out! It's a trap!"

No kidding, Dean thought.

Dean turned toward Crowder and fired his Colt. Crowder leaped to the side, avoiding the silver bullet that hurtled toward him. Dean fired a second round, but Crowder ducked. Dean would never get used to how fast these damn things were.

Sam fired a round at the son. Like his father, the boy veered to the side. The girl hung back, however, watching her father and brother attack with an expression that Dean couldn't read. She almost looked… sad? Whatever emotion she was feeling, it was keeping her out of the fight, which was fine by Dean. One less furball to worry about.

Crowder quickly closed the distance between them. Dean swiped his silver blade in a wide arc. Crowder retreated several feet to avoid getting sliced, and Dean fired another shot. He aimed for the bastard's heart, but Crowder ducked to the side. He wasn't quite fast enough this time, and the silver bullet grazed his left shoulder. Crowder howled with pain, and Dean smiled grimly.

First blood to me, he thought.

He and Sam were fighting back to back. Like him, Sam had gotten off a couple of shots and was slicing his silver blade through the air. Dean had no idea if Sam had managed to wound Crowder's son. He hoped so. The girl still held back, watching. What in the hell was going on with her?

Dean had taken his attention off Crowder for only a split second, but that was all the man needed. He drew his service weapon and aimed it at Dean.

"That's cheating!" Dean said.

Crowder grinned, displaying a mouthful of sharp teeth.

Crowder fired, and it was Dean's turn to avoid getting shot. "Down!" he warned his brother. Sam threw himself to the ground the same time Dean did. Dean rolled, came up on his feet, and hurled his blade at Crowder. The silver weapon spun end over end as it flew toward the werewolf. He caught the blade in his left hand before it could strike him. Unfortunately for Crowder, he caught the wrong end of the blade, and he cried out as sharp edges of silver cut into his hand. He dropped the blade as if it were red-hot and blood began to stream from the wound. Sam was on his feet as well, and he had drawn his gun. This was their chance. Dean drew a bead on Crowder's chest and began to squeeze the Colt's trigger.

But before he could fire, a gunshot split the night. At first he thought Sam had fired, but he quickly realized that the sound came from the house. He looked to the deck and saw a female werewolf—Crowder's wife?—holding an unconscious and chained Garth by the back of his shirt. In her other hand—her *gloved* hand—she held a revolver, the barrel pointed at Garth's temple.

"Surrender or he gets a head full of silver!" she shouted.

It's Garth's gun, he thought. *They took it when they captured him.*

"Let him go," Dean shouted. "Or I'll put a silver bullet through your husband's heart!"

"And I'll do the same to your son!" Sam shouted.

"If you do, I'll mourn their loss," Sylvia said. "But I'll still kill your friend."

Instead of looking betrayed by his wife's words, Crowder grinned savagely, as if he were proud of her.

Goddamned monsters, Dean thought. He tossed his gun and blade to the ground. A second later, he heard Sam discard his weapons too.

Dean curled his hands into fists. Maybe the werewolves were going to kill them, but he wasn't going to go down without a fight, and he was sure Sammy felt the same. But to his surprise, the werewolves didn't attack.

"Put your hands up," Crowder said. He still held his own gun pointed at Dean. His left hand continued to bleed, but he didn't seem to care.

The Winchester brothers did as the sheriff ordered.

"Spencer, get their weapons," Crowder told his son. "Take off your shirt and use the cloth to protect your hands. The silver will still hurt, but not as much."

Spencer did as his father commanded.

"Morgan, get in the house."

"Dad, I'm sorry, I—"

"*Do what I say!*" Crowder roared in a guttural animal voice. Morgan—who appeared entirely human now—looked as if she might cry. She turned and ran toward the house. Crowder's wife kept the revolver against Garth's head. Her eyes gleamed in the moonlight, hungry and eager.

Crowder handed Spencer his gun. "If either of them moves, shoot him," he said.

Spencer nodded. Crowder walked over to Dean and Sam.

"Keep your hands up if you don't want to get shot," Crowder said. "Or maybe I'll just gut you myself. Might be more fun that way."

"Yeah?" Dean said. "Make sure to use your right hand, then. Your left one's a mess."

Crowder growled. When the sheriff reached the brothers, he ordered Sam to put his hands behind his back, and he closed a pair of handcuffs around his wrists. He did the same to Dean.

"I always carry spare cuffs," Crowder said. "Some of the things I do aren't exactly legal, so I have to make do on my own. For example, I can't very well call one of my deputies to come over and help me take a couple nosy hunters into custody, can I?"

Once the brothers were cuffed, Crowder took his gun back and motioned for the Winchesters to begin walking toward the house.

"Get moving," he said. "There's still plenty of night left." He gave them another fang-filled grin. "More than enough for us to do a little hunting of our own."

"I don't think this is a good idea."

Greg stood at the head of the table and watched Anubis, the god still and quiet as death itself. Next to Greg, the fire in the brazier burned bright and strong. Nathan and Muriel stood on one side of the table, while Marta and Efren stood on the other. Kayla and Erin stood at Anubis's feet, and from their expressions, his sisters were as doubtful about this as he was.

"If you are thrown from a horse, you must get back on and ride as soon as possible," Nathan said. "It is the only way to regain your confidence."

"This isn't another lesson," Greg protested. "This is for our *survival*—and our god's!"

While Anubis slept, the god was vulnerable, which was why he needed the jakkals' protection. When he woke, he was power itself. Even when he'd been only partially awake, his mere touch had caused the skin of Greg's wrist to age. If the Rite of Renewal went wrong again, what might Anubis do this time?

But unless the ritual was completed, Anubis would fall into a much deeper sleep and he might never awaken. If the rite failed this time, it would be another day before they could attempt it again, but that would be past the sheriff's deadline for leaving town. They could not afford to make any more mistakes. *He* couldn't.

"You will not fail," Muriel said. "You are jakkal. The blood of our ancient ancestors flows through your veins. Their spirits will guide you."

Erin rolled her eyes, but she didn't say anything.

Greg looked to Marta for help, but his mother only shook her head. The family had made its decision, and this was the way it was going to be. No protest, no appeal, no reprieve.

Greg loved his family, but right then he hated them too.

There was nothing else for it. He had to conduct the rite and pray that he succeeded this time. Because if he didn't, it could mean the end not only of his family, but of Anubis himself.

He began.

At first his hands shook as he prepared the amaranthine, and he had trouble concentrating. But as he went on, he found himself thinking of Morgan. He concentrated on the memory of her smiling face and he grew calm, his movements sure and confident. He cut his palm with the Blade of Life Everlasting and added his blood to the amaranthine, and when it came time to speak the holy words, his voice was strong. When he poured the amaranthine into Anubis's mouth, he didn't spill a single drop.

When finished, he stepped back and held his breath. He feared Anubis would possess Nathan or another of his family and attack him. But Anubis's chest expanded as he took in a single deep breath and let it out slowly, filling the chamber with the sweet scent of rotting flowers. Anubis then fell still once more. One deep breath was all he took during the Rite of Renewal, but that was enough to sustain him for another month. That, and the amaranthine in his system.

Greg grinned in disbelief. He'd done it! All by himself, for the first time. No, he realized, not by himself. Morgan—or at least his memory of her—had helped.

The family smiled and congratulated him, clapped him on the back, and hugged him. Even Kayla and Erin seemed pleased and impressed. Nathan and Muriel led the family out of Anubis's chamber, which had once been a meeting room back when this building served as the park's administration offices. They left their god sleeping peacefully and gathered in the living room, which had once been the building's main lobby.

"Do we start packing now?" Kayla asked. Not that any of them had much in the way of possessions. Jakkals believed in traveling light.

"There is the question of where we will go," Muriel said.

"We have never moved Anubis without having a new home prepared for him first," Nathan said.

Efren spoke. "We could live on the road for a time, staying where we can until we find a more permanent place."

Marta pursed her lips in distaste. "That sounds so…" She trailed off, unable to think of the proper word.

"Disrespectful?" Erin offered.

"Sacrilegious?" Kayla added.

"Yes," Nathan said. "Our god is not mere freight to be carted from one location to another."

Greg couldn't believe what he was hearing. "But the sheriff said if we weren't gone in twenty-four hours—" he began.

"To hell with the *iwiw*!" Marta said, practically spitting the word. "I'm tired of cowering before their kind. We are Anubis's chosen people, and I say it's time we start acting like it! Do we really believe the sheriff will keep his word? He's a werewolf. They lie as easily as they breathe."

Nathan nodded. "He could return at any moment and attack us."

"And next time he'll bring his entire pack," Muriel said.

All the more reason to leave, Greg thought. But he didn't speak this aloud. He knew they should go, but part of him was excited at the idea of remaining in Bridge Valley and being near Morgan. Plus, he remembered what it had felt like to wound the sheriff's son. He'd felt strong, powerful. But even so, he wasn't sure fighting was the answer.

"We need to prepare," Marta said.

"We need *neteru*," Muriel added.

Everyone fell silent at this. Greg could not remember a time when that word had been spoken by any member of his family. He knew what *neteru* were, of course: it meant guardians. But he'd never seen one before, and as far as he was aware, no one in his family had ever made any. He'd come to regard them as a myth that had been passed down by jakkals from one generation to the next, and no one— not even Nathan and Muriel—had ever told him otherwise. But now here they were, discussing *neteru* as if they were not only real, but something that could be obtained as easily as dropping by a convenience store for a gallon of milk.

"And we will need some silver," Nathan said. "To set traps with."

Greg thought his family was acting insane. He had successfully performed the Rite of Renewal, and even though he was the youngest, he was now considered a full adult. Still, it was not his place to contradict his elders, as much as he might like to.

"The girls and I will go out to procure some silver," Efren said. "There are several pawn shops in town that are open late."

"Marta and I will inspect the traps we already have in place," Muriel said, "and ensure they are in working order."

Jakkals were quite skilled at building traps. They had been ever since helping to create elaborate—and usually deadly— precautions to deter tomb robbers in ancient Egypt, back when their kind was known and respected by humans as servants of the great Anubis.

"Good," Nathan said. "Then Greg and I shall see to the *neteru*. We shall not run. We shall stay and fight!"

The rest of the family cheered, but Greg knew that by choosing to make a stand, they were committing to a battle that they might not win. Or survive.

TWENTY

"Chains? Seriously?"

Sam and Dean sat on the basement's concrete floor. Aside from a furnace and a water heater, the room was completely bare. Their backs were to the wall, wrists still cuffed, ankles encircled by heavy chains secured with padlocks. Duct tape had been wrapped around the chains as an additional measure—as if they weren't enough. Garth lay unconscious on the floor nearby, also in chains. Sylvia Crowder hadn't put a silver bullet in his head, but whatever they'd done to him, it looked to be having a lasting effect.

"I guess they don't want to leave anything to chance," Sam said. Like Dean, he'd been struggling to get free of his bonds, but the brothers' efforts had proved useless. "They probably keep chains around in case they need to use them on other werewolves." Sam nodded toward Garth. "Or if one of the pack members disobeys Crowder's orders and needs to be punished."

"I doubt the basement's empty because they haven't finished moving all the way in," Dean said.

"Yeah. It's their own personal jail, and they don't want to put anything down here that prisoners might be able to use to escape."

"Or fight back," Dean said. He jerked his arms and legs. "Not that anyone this side of Houdini could get out of these damn things."

Garth moaned then, and without moving or opening his eyes, he said, "Man, this place *stinks*!"

Garth rolled slowly onto his back, sat up and opened his eyes. The basement was lit by a single weak bulb on the ceiling, but Garth winced as if he were staring full on into the sun.

"What happened?" he asked. His voice started out soft, his words slurred, but his speech became stronger and clearer as he went. "Last thing I remember I was in the dining room, trying to convince the family—" His eyes widened then, and he winced once more. "She hit me on the head with my own damn gun!" He looked at Sam and Dean.

"How bad is it?" he asked.

"Your head's got so much blood on it, you look like you ran full speed into a brick wall, then backed up and hit it a few more times," Dean said.

"Your skull had a dent in it when we were brought down here," Sam said. "But that healed. I take it you're better now?"

"I don't know about *better*," Garth said, "but I'm functional. Still got a bit of a headache, though. I don't know why Sylvia hit me. It would've been easier to kill me." Before Sam or Dean could respond, he said, "Wait. I get it. They wanted to use me as leverage against you two—which is why you're down here with me, inside of up there—" he raised his head toward the ceiling "—kicking ass." He sighed. "I'm really sorry. Dean, you were right. Talking to them *was* a dumb idea."

"Hey, you did what you thought was right," Dean said. "If Sammy and I had a dollar for every time we did something that ended up turning around and biting us in the ass—"

"We'd be extremely wealthy men," Sam finished.

"What's done is done," Dean said. "We're just glad you're alive. Now we have to find a way to make sure all three of us stay that way."

Garth's mouth and chin were wet with blood, and it didn't look to Sam as if it was the result of any injury. Had Garth managed to take a bite out of one of the Crowders before being captured?

"You said it stinks in here," Sam said.

"Yeah. Can't you guys smell it? The whole basement stinks of body odor, desperation, and fear. They've kept other people down here. A *lot* of them."

"Three guesses what they did with them," Dean said. "And the first two don't count."

"They keep their victims prisoner until they're ready to harvest their hearts," Sam said.

"Clay Fuller was probably down here," Dean said. "You think he escaped and they had to hunt him down?"

"Maybe," Sam said. He turned to Garth. "Can you transform and break out of the chains?"

"I don't know." Garth gave his bound wrists a shake. "Crowder would've made sure these chains can hold me. It takes a lycanthrope to know how to catch a lycanthrope." Garth's face brightened. "Hey, that's another fangism!"

"Forget that and see if you can break free," Dean said.

Garth changed and tried to pull his arms and legs apart. His brow furrowed, his lips drew back from his fangs in a snarl, and his whole body shook from the effort. But the chains did not break.

Garth slumped forward and dropped his chin to his chest. When he raised his head once more, he was human again.

"No good. Maybe if I had some time to work on weakening them…"

The basement door opened and Crowder came down, boots thumping on the wooden steps. His sons followed, and Sam realized they were twins. One of them had been hurt, and his chest was wrapped in bandages. Sam was immediately curious. What could injure a werewolf in such a way that the wound wouldn't heal almost immediately? Even an injury caused by silver would heal given enough time, unless the injury was to the heart, of course. Something else had to have hurt him, but what?

Crowder and the twins stood several feet away from Sam, Dean, and Garth. Crowder, it seemed, wasn't a man who liked to take chances.

"It's been an eventful couple days for my pack, fellas," Crowder said. "First these two and their mother let Amos Boyd witness them killing Clay Fuller—"

"But, Dad, we told you it wasn't our—" the uninjured twin began. But before he could finish, Crowder snarled, whirled around, and struck his son's face with a clawed hand. The son yelped and clapped a hand to his bleeding cheek. His eyes filled with fear. He took a step back and lowered his head, still keeping his hand pressed to his wound.

"Sorry," he murmured. Drops of blood pattered to the concrete floor, but they were already slowing as the wound began to heal. Crowder gave his other son a look, as if daring him to say something. The boy lowered his gaze, and Crowder turned back to face the hunters.

"And then, after bringing the media's attention to our little town, they decided it would be a good idea to kill Amos so he couldn't talk any further." He shook his head. "*And* without asking my permission. As I'm sure Garth knows, among my people, that's about as close to a cardinal sin as we get." He put his hands on his hips and regarded them for a moment. "And you three show up while all this is going on. I figured you were all hunters who'd come to investigate reports of the 'animal people' that killed Fuller. But it occurs to me that you might be here for another reason. Are you working with *them*?"

Sam exchanged glances with Dean and Garth. What the hell was Crowder talking about?

He went on. "They said they didn't know there was a pack living in Bridge Valley when they moved here, but what if they were lying? Maybe they decided to get rid of us and hired you three to do the job. Considering the mess you've made of it, though, I hope they didn't pay you very much. Whatever it was, you guys aren't worth it."

"You must've been hitting the wolfsbane too hard," Dean said, "because we have no idea what you're jabbering about."

The twins started growling and took a step toward Dean, but Crowder held up a hand.

Garth frowned and inhaled deeply. "You three smell funny.

I mean, you smell like lycanthropes, but you've got some other scent clinging to you. A weird one. It's kind of like wolf scent, but not. And it also smells kind of like... garbage?"

Crowder looked at Garth for a long moment, his gaze intense. "You really don't know them, do you?" he said.

"Enough with the cryptic references!" Dean said. "Who are you talking about? Are there even more of you furry bastards in town that we need to kill?"

Crowder bared his teeth, which—while not quite fangs— had grown sharper.

"Werewolves are nothing like jakkals," he said. "We're predators. They're carrion-eaters."

"Jackals?" Sam didn't think Crowder was referring to the animals.

Despite the situation, Garth grinned like a little kid. "You've got jakkals in town? I didn't think they were real!"

"They're real, all right," Crowder said, "and there's a pack of them holed up at the old amusement park. So you've got nothing at all to do with them? No, of course you don't. The creatures are cowards at heart. It's not in their nature to fight back."

Crowder's gaze flicked toward the wounded twin for an instant before fixing once more on Sam, Dean, and Garth.

"Did you guys tangle with these jakkals?" Dean asked. "Did one of them take a bite out of Lon Chaney Junior over there?"

The son with the bandage on his chest growled and lunged forward, but Crowder grabbed the waistband of his jeans and pulled him back. Crowder snarled at him and he fell silent.

"Sounds as if jakkals aren't quite as timid as you make them out to be," Sam said. He'd never heard of jakkals before. Whatever they were, they either had to be rare, really good at keeping a low profile, or both.

Crowder sniffed. "Even a rabbit will fight if it has no choice. But it's a moot point. Come sunrise, the jakkals will be dead. But before that, we're going to have a little fun." He grinned. "And we're going to have a midnight snack."

"Nice bloodstain on the uniform," Dean said. "I take it cleanliness isn't a top priority for the Sheriff's Department."

"That's Melody's blood," Garth said. "The sonofabitch killed her."

"And fed her heart to my boy," Crowder said. He gestured to the bandaged twin. "Heart meat is the best medicine for my people."

"And it was delicious," the boy said. "Just what the doctor ordered."

Crowder turned to Garth. "What did you think of the piece I tried to feed you? You might not have tasted it, but it sure looked like you wanted to."

Sam was shocked to hear this, and from the expression on his brother's face, he knew Dean felt the same.

Garth didn't answer. He lowered his gaze, ashamed.

The three werewolves laughed, but Garth kept his head down, as if he couldn't bring himself to meet Sam and Dean's eyes.

Sam was relieved to hear their friend hadn't tasted Melody's heart, but he couldn't imagine how Garth must be feeling right then. Not only had he been talking to Melody a short time ago, he'd never been tempted by human heart meat before tonight. Would it be harder for him to resist his more savage instincts now? Sam didn't know.

Crowder turned to his sons. "Bring the tall one. We'll save the other for another night."

"What about Garth?" the unbandaged twin asked.

Crowder considered a moment. "We'll keep him too. I've never hunted one of our kind before. It'll be a nice change of pace." Crowder looked at Sam. "I hope you're faster than you look. It's no fun if we catch you too quickly."

He nodded to his sons to get to work and walked toward the stairs. The twins each took one of Sam's arms and lifted him into the air as if he weighed nothing. They carried him up the stairs, following Crowder.

Sam realized what had happened to Clay Fuller. He hadn't been food, or at least not *only* food. They'd hunted him before killing him. He'd been entertainment as well as sustenance. Dinner and a show.

And it looked like it was his turn next.

TWENTY-ONE

Morgan remained in the dining room while her mother went upstairs to change. On a hunt, Sylvia liked to wear clothes she could move freely in but which weren't too expensive, since they always got ruined by the time she was finished. Joshua sat in his high chair, nibbling on bits of oat cereal. She stood at the sink, working on the dishes. Or rather, she pretended to wash dishes while she listened to what was being said in the basement. Her werewolf hearing was more than sharp enough to make out what her father and the other men said.

She knew her parents and brothers would want to hunt one of the humans tonight, but to hear that her dad planned to attack the jakkals afterward… She'd wanted to believe that he would give Greg and his family twenty-four hours to leave town, but she'd been foolish to do so. Alan and Sylvia Crowder were werewolves. They believed in solving problems with strength and action, not with conversation and compromise. She figured the only reason her father hadn't tried to kill the jakkals earlier was because Stuart had been wounded. After eating the heart, he was likely strong enough to participate in a second attack on the jakkals, and naturally her other brother would want to take part as well. Morgan thought they might even make *her* go. Who was she kidding? *Of course* they would. Her father would want her to prove her loyalty to the pack by helping to kill the jakkals. Alan would likely command her to kill Greg as a way of punishing her for talking to him in the first place.

She didn't want to do that. She *couldn't*.

She had one thing going for her. Werewolves—or at least the ones in her family—couldn't resist hunting. As much as her parents and brothers might want to fight the jakkals, they'd hunt one or both of the humans first. It was their nature. That meant she had time to warn Greg. With any luck, he and his family would be able to leave Happyland before the hunt—and the feast that followed—was finished.

Not for the first time, Morgan wondered what made her different from the rest of her family. She had the same instincts and drives they did—she loved hunting and she needed to eat heart meat to sustain herself. But she only ate animal hearts. She didn't want to hunt humans. More than that, she believed killing humans was wrong. Alan and Sylvia had sneered at Garth's offer to join his peaceful pack, but it sounded like the perfect life to her. She loved her family, but she couldn't overlook or accept their cruelty. She'd leave tonight and take Joshua with her so he wouldn't have to become a monster like the rest of their family—*if* she thought she could get away with it. But her parents would hunt her down before she could get very far, and punish her so severely she'd regret ever being born. Or worse, they'd kill her outright and bring Joshua back home, to raise him as one of them.

She turned to look at Joshua, tears in her eyes. He was happily chewing on cereal while playing with a couple of bits, maneuvering the crunchy little O's through the air as if they were planes. Seeing him like this, she had a difficult time believing he was destined to be a monster. If humans had free will—if they could *choose* who they wanted to be—why couldn't her kind?

Her thoughts broke off as the basement door opened and her father entered the kitchen. Stuart and Spencer followed, carrying one of the humans. So they'd decided to hunt just one tonight. *Why not?* she thought bitterly. That way they could make their blood sport last longer.

Sylvia came into the kitchen a moment later, wearing a pair of black leggings and an old T-shirt. Her feet were bare. She looked at Alan.

"You going to change, hon?"

"No, I'll never get these bloodstains out of this uniform." He patted his chest. "Might as well keep it on."

Sylvia turned to Morgan. "Sweetie, would you mind watching your little brother while we're out?" she asked.

Morgan smiled. "I'd be happy to."

The twins carried Sam outside, Crowder and his wife close behind. The boys tossed Sam onto the deck, and he landed hard on his left side. Crowder unlocked the handcuffs, the twins cut through the duct tape around Sam's legs and

Sylvia unlocked the padlock on Sam's chains. They stepped back, giving Sam room to remove his chains and get to his feet. Both his wrists and his legs throbbed, but that was the least of his worries. All four of the werewolves gazed upon him with dark anticipation, and their nostrils flared as they inhaled deeply.

They're taking my scent, Sam thought. *Getting ready to hunt.*

"I can't tell you how much we're going to enjoy this," Sylvia said. "You're so much healthier than the ones Alan usually brings home."

Alan bristled. "I do the best I can."

She reached out and touched his cheek. "Of course you do, love, and we all appreciate it. All I'm saying is it'll be nice to hunt someone who isn't already half dead when they start running." She lowered her head and turned to Sam. She smiled, showing teeth grown sharp. "And he's a hunter too. He should prove quite entertaining."

Sam understood what was going on here. The Crowders' prey needed to be people who wouldn't be missed, or whose disappearance wouldn't come as a surprise. People like Clay Fuller: a drug dealer who might've vanished because of an unsatisfied customer or aggressive competitor. As sheriff, Crowder had access to a never-ending supply of small-time criminals, and he could have his pick of the litter.

"So how does this work?" Sam asked. "You guys give me a head start, I haul ass into the woods, and after—what?—five, maybe ten minutes you come after me?"

Sam was calm as he spoke, and the werewolves exchanged uneasy glances. Sam supposed they were used to their prey pleading for their lives, terrified at the thought of what the werewolves would do. Sam was glad to disappoint them.

"That's about it," Crowder said.

"What if I decide not to run?" Sam asked. "After all, you're just going to kill me eventually. Might as well get it over with now and save myself a lot of effort and false hope."

"But it's not false," Sylvia said. "If you manage to find your way out of the woods, you're free to go. You win, we lose. People need a strong motivation if they're to run their best."

"And there's no stronger motivation than survival," Crowder said.

"Clay Fuller got out of the woods," Sam pointed out. "But that didn't seem to stop you from killing him and taking his heart."

"You have my word that, in the unlikely event you make it out of the woods alive, you'll remain that way," Crowder said.

Sam knew he was lying. Crowder would never allow any of their prey to live long enough to go to the authorities. But there was no point in saying so.

"So what now?" Sam asked. "Does one of you fire a starter's pistol or do you just shout, 'Ready, set, go!'"

Crowder gestured to the yard beyond the deck.

"Just start running," he said, "or we'll tear you to pieces right now."

Sam could tell by the man's tone—and by the way Sylvia and the twins were looking at him—that Crowder wasn't kidding. So he hopped off the deck and ran toward the woods, the full moon shining overhead, howls of excitement rising into the air behind him.

* * *

Near Seattle, Washington. 1992

"Look out!" Sam shouted. He had his seatbelt on, but he put his hands on the dashboard of Bobby's pickup to brace himself anyway. Dean sat in the driver's seat, gripping the steering wheel so hard his knuckles were white.

"I see it!" Dean said.

They were heading straight toward a light pole. Dean yanked the steering wheel hard to the left, and the pickup swerved away. Sam shouted for Dean to slow down. Dean shot him an angry glare, but he eased his foot off the gas, and Sam began to relax as the pickup slowed.

"I thought you said Dad gave you driving lessons," Sam said.

"He did." Dean paused, then added more softly, "Once."

Now that they were on their way to the hospital, Sam was having second thoughts.

"I'm not sure we should be doing this," he said.

"You heard Bobby. If we don't stop the werewolf tonight, it will be a whole month before it comes back. We have to kill it before it attacks someone else! He can't do it, and Dad's not here. That leaves you and me."

"But we're just kids," Sam said.

Dean shrugged. "So what? Dad's taught me how to shoot… a little. And we got Bobby's gun, which is loaded with silver bullets. Besides, werewolves don't eat kids' hearts. They're too small, and they're not ripe yet. They taste awful, like green bananas."

Sam frowned, fairly certain Dean was making this last part up.

Sam would rather have stayed in the motel room with Bobby. The idea of hunting a werewolf terrified him, and it didn't help that they'd watched part of that stupid movie, *Night of the Blood Moon*. But in the end, Sam had agreed to accompany Dean for one simple reason. He loved his brother and couldn't let him go into danger alone.

Dean nearly got them into several accidents on the way to the hospital, but he avoided them all—if only just. They continued driving around lost for a while until they found signs directing drivers to the hospital. They pulled into the visitors' lot and looked for a place to park.

A thought occurred to Sam then. "Have you ever parked before?"

"Sure I have," Dean said. "Nothing to it."

But he looked nervous, and Sam figured he was lying.

They found a space between an SUV and a van, and Dean painstakingly attempted to park between the two vehicles. There wasn't a lot of room between them, and Dean had to back up several times and make another attempt to fit the pickup in. During his final try, he scraped the side of the van, but the pickup was parked, more or less, and he turned off the engine.

"See? Nothing to it," Dean said.

Sam rolled his eyes. The pickup was squeezed in so tightly between the SUV and the van that they couldn't open the pickup's doors wide enough to get out. They had to roll down the windows and crawl out that way.

It had started to rain again, although it wasn't much more than a sprinkle. They'd put motel towels on the driver's seat because of how much Bobby had bled on the drive back from the hospital. But some blood had soaked through anyway, and Dean's pants had a few splotches on the bottom. Ordinarily, Sam might have teased his big brother about this, but not now, not here.

Dean carried Bobby's gun in his right jacket pocket. The pocket wasn't deep enough to conceal the whole weapon, and its handle stuck out. It didn't look secure in the pocket, and Sam was afraid the gun would fall out if Dean wasn't careful. Sam carried Bobby's silver knife. He didn't have the sheath for it—he had no idea where Bobby kept it—and no way was he going to stick this sharp thing in one of *his* pockets. Sam knew that, like Bobby, they'd have to keep an eye out for hospital security making the rounds. Two adults hanging out in the visitors' parking lot in the middle of the night would've been suspicious enough, but two *kids*? If security spotted them, the guards would come running to make sure they weren't lost or in some kind of danger.

We are in danger, Sam thought. *But not the kind any security guard can help us with.*

The moon was hidden by the cloud cover overhead, and Sam was grateful. He knew werewolves didn't need to see the moon to be affected by it, but as scary as being here was, it would've been worse if a full moon hung in the sky above them. It would've been too much like *Night of the Blood Moon*. He was also glad they were in a well-lit parking lot instead of an eerie forest, like in the movie. But then he realized that the lot was kind of like a maze. They couldn't see between the vehicles, not until they stood close to them, and anything could be hiding in the spaces between.

Suddenly, a spooky old forest didn't sound so bad.

"What do we do now?" Sam asked Dean, whispering.

Sam was surprised when his big brother didn't answer right away. He was used to Dean always knowing what to do, or at least *pretending* to know. But Dean had to think a minute.

"I guess we go slow through the lot and see if we find the werewolf."

"Or it finds us," Sam said.

"Or that," Dean agreed.

So they began walking, keeping close to the vehicles, crouched low. Dean took the lead, but Sam was right behind his brother, so close that he bumped into him several times. But Dean didn't complain. He just kept moving forward, attention focused and sharp. Sam periodically glanced behind them to make sure they weren't being stalked from the rear. Each time he turned to look, he expected to see a wild-eyed creature with fangs and claws racing toward them, but he saw nothing. He listened for any sounds of movement but the rain had picked up, making it difficult to hear any other sounds.

Sam told himself that the werewolf probably wasn't in the area anymore, that Bobby had scared it away when he'd wounded it. Like Bobby had told them, the werewolf would move to a new hunting ground, and it wouldn't be heard from until next month. They were wasting their time. On the one hand this was reassuring, as Sam didn't particularly want to tangle with a werewolf. But on the other hand, he couldn't stop thinking about what Dean had said back at the motel. If they didn't stop the werewolf here and now, more people would die next month. Maybe a lot more. He'd never considered the responsibility that rested on a hunter's shoulders. Every action they took had the potential to save lives or lose them, depending on how things went down. No wonder his father and Bobby worked so hard and rarely took time off. Every moment they weren't hunting was another moment when someone was potentially dying at the hands of a supernatural creature.

The rain grew worse, coming down faster and harder now, accompanied by lightning flashes and booms of thunder. Sam figured they'd been at it for at least an hour, maybe longer. He was cold, wet, and tired, but one thing was good: he was too irritated and uncomfortable to be scared anymore.

"Let's go back to the truck and sit inside until the rain lets up," Sam said. He would've preferred they ended their stakeout and returned to the motel room. The warm, and above all, *dry* room. But he didn't trust Dean to drive in the rain. Better to sit in the truck and wait for the storm to blow over than end up wrapping Bobby's truck around a telephone pole on the way back to the motel.

Dean scowled, clearly unhappy with the idea of giving up. But he said, "Okay."

They were currently on the west side of the lot, just about as far as they could be from the pickup. They turned and began heading back the way they'd come. But they stopped after only a few steps. There, standing in the middle of the lane between two rows of vehicles, stood a woman. Her long white hair was wet and plastered to the front of her brown sweater, which was soaked and hung limply on her slight frame. She wore blue slacks and a pair of open-toed brown shoes, which revealed her toenails were sharp werewolf claws. Her hands were clawed as well, and her mouth was filled with wicked-looking fangs. Her eyes were those of an animal, bestial and shining with bloodlust.

It's an old lady, Sam thought, surprised, although he couldn't have said why. Monsters had to get old too, didn't they?

The sweater's right arm had a ragged tear through the sleeve, just beneath the shoulder. Sam figured that was where Bobby had wounded the werewolf, but she didn't appear any the worse for wear. Maybe the silver wound had healed, or maybe she was too excited by the prospect of two fresh, young hearts to care about her injury.

She bared her teeth in a half-snarl, half-grin, and then she ran toward them, claws out, ready to rend their flesh.

Present Day

"I'm really sorry I got you into this mess," Garth said. He sat next to Dean, his back to the wall.

Dean wanted to tell Garth not to feel guilty, that it wasn't his fault. But he was too worried about Sam—out there in the night, running for his life—to think about anything but escape right now. Sammy was as smart and resourceful as any hunter ever born, but he was being hunted by a family of werewolves. And he was unarmed. Those weren't good odds, no matter how you sliced it. Sam needed backup, and Dean was determined to get out of this damn hole in the ground and give it to him. But how? Garth had started working on loosening his bonds as soon as the Crowders had closed the basement door, but he'd made little progress. At the rate he was going, Sam would be dead and his heart divided among Crowder's pack before Garth managed to break out of his chains. Dean felt helpless, and he hated it.

The basement door opened, and someone started coming down. Dean felt his stomach drop. Had they already finished with Sam?

It was Crowder's daughter, and she was alone. She hurried over and knelt next to them, an expression of guilt and concern on her face.

"You come down to take a nibble or two while the rest of your family is out chasing my brother?" Dean said.

The girl—Morgan, if he remembered right—didn't answer. Instead, she raised her right hand and sharp claws emerged from her fingers. She swung her hand toward Garth, and at first Dean thought she meant to attack him. But instead she cut the duct tape away from his chains with a few quick swipes. Then she transformed completely and pulled on the chain around Garth's wrists while he struggled to break them from the inside. Together, they were successful. The chain broke, and Garth's hands were free. The first thing he did was rub the dried blood—Melody's blood—from his mouth and chin. Then they broke the chain wrapped around his legs. Working swiftly, the pair moved onto Dean, broke the handcuffs around his wrists, and then freed his legs.

When they were all standing—and Garth and Morgan were human again—Dean looked at the girl and said, "Not that I'm complaining, but why did you free us?"

"I'm not like the rest of my family," Morgan said, her words coming out in a rush. "I don't like hurting people, and

I won't eat their hearts. I want to go with Garth and join his pack. I want to live like them. And I want to take my baby brother with me. I want him to grow up in a good place, surrounded by good people."

Dean looked at her a moment before turning to Garth.

"I'll be damned. It looks like you made a convert after all."

Garth smiled.

TWENTY-TWO

Nathan drove the ancient station wagon and Greg rode in the passenger seat. It was the middle of the night, and the streets were mostly deserted. Not only was Bridge Valley a sleepy little Midwestern town, it was a weeknight, and it felt to Greg like he and Nathan were the last people on Earth.

"It's late," Greg said. "What if he won't let us in?"

"Don't worry. We pay him well enough that he'll do whatever we ask—within reason. He will allow us entrance."

Jakkals might have been scavengers by nature, but that didn't mean they were poor. They simply didn't believe in wasting things. But the extended family of jakkals—which Nathan had once told Greg numbered in the hundreds—had acquired a significant amount of wealth over the centuries, primarily by selling gold (which they handled *very* carefully) and jeweled artifacts they'd carried out of ancient Egypt. They kept their funds stored in various banks throughout the world, and all the packs could access this money when needed. The jakkals mostly did odd jobs to earn whatever money they needed and saved their bank funds for their most vital expense: bribing funeral home owners and morgue attendants. Dead human hearts weren't easy to come by—unless you were willing to kill the humans yourself, remove their hearts, and allow them to age until they were ready to be eaten. Nathan had once admitted to Greg that in times of great need, and only when there was no other choice, jakkals had been known to procure their sustenance through violent means. But jakkals weren't predators, and they preferred to acquire their food peacefully. This had the added benefit of drawing less attention to themselves, which was why they were practically unknown to those who studied supernatural lore—a fact the jakkals took great pride in.

So they paid humans who worked with the dead to harvest the hearts of their "clients" before burial or cremation. The arrangement was mutually beneficial and caused no harm to anyone. Although Greg supposed the families of the "donors" wouldn't be pleased to discover one of their loved one's major organs had been purchased like meat at a deli counter.

"Mr. Everton may be less than pleased to be awakened at this hour," Nathan said, "but he will open his door to us, no questions asked." He paused, and then added, "Although after tonight, it's doubtful he will do business with us ever again."

They drove until they came to a two-story house framed by a pair of large elms. A wooden sign in the front yard read *Everton Funeral Home: The Best in Eternal Rest.*

Greg looked at his grandfather, and Nathan shrugged. "So the man has a poor sense of humor. At least he's open to bribery."

* * *

True to Nathan's word, the owner of the funeral home—middle-aged, grumpy, and wearing a robe over pajamas—wasn't pleased to have visitors at this hour. He was, however, quite happy to see the envelope containing three thousand dollars in cash, which Nathan handed to him. With a smile on his face, Everton ushered them inside and led them to the door of his basement workroom.

"You'll have your pick tonight," he said. "There was a two-car accident on the highway yesterday. Two passengers in one car, three in the other. All fatalities. A terrible thing." He shook his head. "But good for business, I suppose. As you might imagine, the bodies were not in the best condition, and my assistants and I had to do quite a bit of restoration work on them. Please do be careful while you're, ah, shopping."

Nathan smiled and patted the black leather satchel he carried. "I always am."

The satchel contained tools for cutting into dead bodies, but they wouldn't be needed any more than the plastic cooler Greg carried. They were merely props, meant to reassure Everton that nothing was out of the ordinary. Well, no more so than usual.

An apologetic expression came over Everton's face. "I've already embalmed them. I hope that won't be a problem."

Jakkals might prefer their meat to be rotting, but they would never eat food that had been spoiled by chemicals. But Nathan smiled and said, "No problem. Not tonight."

Everton frowned, but he said nothing. Greg figured that for

three thousand dollars, Everton didn't care what they did or why. He asked them to lock up after they were finished, bade them good night, and headed back upstairs to bed. Greg didn't see how the man could sleep given what he thought his midnight visitors were about to do, but he supposed it took all kinds.

Once they were in the workroom, Nathan put his satchel on the floor and Greg set the cooler beside it. This was the first time Greg had ever gone on a harvesting run. Nathan or Muriel usually took care of the task, as they were the pack's Elders, but sometimes his mother, father or sisters went along. Now that he was here, he was somewhat underwhelmed. He'd pictured the workroom as something out of an old-time horror film—stone walls and floor, bodies on tables concealed beneath white sheets, an assortment of sinister-looking medical instruments spread out on a gleaming steel table… Instead, it was depressingly mundane.

The bodies—five of them, as Everton had said—were laid out on wheeled mortuary cots. The bodies themselves were uncovered, evidently because they were still being worked on. Greg didn't like this. It felt disrespectful to him. Past the cots was an embalming station: a porcelain table next to a sink with a spray nozzle attached to the end of a hose. Set against the wall near the porcelain table was a waist-high cabinet atop which rested an embalming machine—a clear plastic canister with a thin black hose emerging from it. Burial rites were the province of Anubis, and as his children, they were important to jakkals. Greg felt a curious mixture of awe at being in the presence of modern embalming equipment and repulsion at how sterile and impersonal it seemed. There was no magic or mystery here, and he found that sad.

Nathan walked to the closest body, and Greg followed. Of the five, there were three men and two women, ages ranging from mid-twenties to late forties. Greg wondered what their relationships to each other had been. Family? Friends? He supposed it didn't matter now. Their souls had gone into the afterlife, leaving behind the meat they'd once inhabited. But now that he was standing in the presence of the bodies, he was having second thoughts about what he and his grandfather were about to do.

"Grandfather, these people... They have relatives and friends. If we take them as *neteru*..."

"Their loved ones will have nothing to bury and no graves to visit in the years to come. This is unfortunately true, but our need is great. Anubis gave us the ability to create guardians. It is our god's wish that we do this—as long as we do not abuse the power. And remember, we are doing this to protect our god as much as we are to protect ourselves."

His grandfather's explanation rang hollow to Greg. He couldn't escape the feeling that what they were doing was wrong. But he nodded and said no more on the matter.

Although Everton and his staff had done a good job preparing the bodies for burial, it was obvious to Greg that they had been in poor shape when they'd been brought here. Cuts and abrasions had been sewn or sealed with glue and covered by makeup, and a couple of the heads were slightly tilted, indicating broken necks or even decapitation. Everton might be less than ethical when it came to making extra profit, but his skills at body preparation appeared to be quite good. Still, the repairs that had been done to these bodies were merely cosmetic, and there was no telling how intact they were internally.

Nathan noticed Greg looking closely at the bodies and said, "Do not worry. Once they become *neteru* they will be whole and strong—at least for the time they last."

On the drive to the funeral home, Nathan had explained to Greg how what the jakkals called *kheper*—the rebirth—worked. Unlike werewolves, the jakkals' bite did not transfer their condition to others. It did something else, something miraculous.

"Always use the right wrist," Nathan said. "One bite, no more. Swift and sure."

Nathan took the right wrist of the corpse closest to them—a stout man with a great deal of body hair—in his hands, bent down, and opened his mouth. His teeth grew sharp, and with a single fast motion, he bit into the wrist's soft flesh. He remained like that for several seconds before pulling his teeth from the wrist and allowing the arm to drop back to the table. He wrinkled his face in disgust.

"I *hate* the taste of embalming fluid," Nathan said.

They watched the corpse closely, and after a few moments, the fingers on its right hand twitched. Then, without any more warning, it opened eyes that glowed with crimson light and abruptly sat up. The man turned to look at them, but there was no sign of awareness in those glowing eyes. He had become *neteru*, a soulless guardian who would obey the commands of the jakkal who'd revived him.

Nathan smiled at Greg.

"That's one. Only four more to go."

Greg didn't feel right about forcibly resurrecting these people when they had no choice in the matter. But Nathan was his Elder, and his pack was in danger.

Greg selected a corpse from the four remaining and walked toward it.

TWENTY-THREE

Morgan sat in the front passenger seat of the Impala, Joshua on her lap. The cold didn't bother werewolves much, but she wore a jacket and she'd put Joshua's coat on him. She wanted to make sure he was comfortable. She was his big sister, after all. But now that she had fled her family and taken Joshua with her, she was starting to have second thoughts.

The hunter named Dean had told her where the car was parked. The plan was for her to wait there with Joshua while Dean and Garth tried to help Sam escape her family. Then, if all went well, Garth would take her to live with his pack. She didn't like the idea of never seeing Greg again, but she had to think about Joshua's future as much as her own. She didn't want her little brother to grow up hunting humans. His best chance was for him to be raised among Garth's people.

She was well aware that she had put the rest of her family in danger. She'd shown Dean and Garth where her mother had hidden their weapons, and now they were armed with silver once again. The hunters would shoot her family if necessary, maybe even kill them. She understood they'd do so out of self-defense, but that didn't make her feel any better about it. Her family were murderers—*monsters*—but despite this, she still loved them. They were her pack. By freeing Dean and Garth, she'd signed their death warrants.

Maybe I'm not so different from them after all, she thought.

As if picking up on her conflicted emotions, Joshua began to fuss. She hushed him and began rocking him gently back and forth. He soon quieted and nodded off. As she held him, she listened. She'd heard the howls of her family as the Hunt began, but since then she'd heard nothing. No more howls, and more importantly, no gunshots.

She began to worry that her family would win, and why not? They were strong, swift, and utterly without mercy. How could two human hunters and one not-so-savage werewolf possibly hope to defeat them? If her family survived—a prospect that seemed more and more likely—they would attack Greg and his family next. After the Hunt, her parents and brothers would be riding high on bloodlust, and they would be eager for the killing to continue.

She shifted Joshua to one arm, and with her free hand she slipped her phone out of her pocket and began to text. She was grateful that she'd been impulsive enough to ask Greg to exchange numbers. It just might save his life.

This is Morgan.

I think my dad plans to break his promise and attack you and your family tonight.

Protect yourselves!!!

She sent the text. But as soon as she did, she began to have doubts. What if Greg didn't see the message in time? What if he *did* see it, but he had trouble convincing his family they were in danger? She needed to go to Greg and explain the situation to his family in person. That was her best chance to convince them. She quickly sent Greg another text. *On my way.*

She changed and then, holding Joshua close, began running toward town. In her werewolf form, she was swift and tireless, and she wasn't restricted to the roads and could run cross-country.

But no matter how fast she ran, she feared it might not be fast enough.

The stink of formaldehyde filled the station wagon, and even with all the windows rolled down, Greg had to breathe through his mouth to keep from gagging. Once all five *neteru* had been reanimated, Nathan and Greg had led them out of Everton's funeral home and packed them into the car. Three of the living corpses fit in the vehicle's back seat, while the remaining two curled up in the station wagon's cargo area. They must've made quite a sight as they drove through town, Greg thought. Two jakkals and five resurrected and very naked dead people in a station wagon. Any police officer who pulled them over would be in for a surprise.

Despite the undeniably grotesque nature of the *neteru*, Greg was amazed that a simple bite could restore life—if only temporarily—to the dead. Truly, Anubis had given his children great gifts. But Greg didn't know if he'd ever get the taste of embalming fluid out of his mouth.

Nathan had explained that the magic which animated the

neteru would last for approximately twelve hours. Less, if the corpses were forced to exert themselves. After that, they would begin to rapidly decay and would soon collapse into sand. Until that moment they would fight fiercely and with superhuman strength at the jakkals' command. The only way they could be stopped before their time was up was if their bodies were destroyed. The *neteru* sounded formidable, and Greg hoped they would be a match for the werewolves, but he really didn't know.

Nathan had the radio on and tuned to a classical music station, which seemed perfectly appropriate given jakkals' affinity for the ancient past. He had the volume up and hummed along to the music as he drove.

The cold November wind blowing in through the open windows was pleasant, almost calming. Greg found himself wondering what Morgan was doing now. Did she know that her father and brothers had threatened his family? Did she know that he had wounded one of her brothers, and did she hate him because of it? He hoped not. He could text her and find out, of course, but he wasn't sure that was a good idea. His family planned to fight the werewolves the next time they came to Happyland, which he supposed made him and Morgan enemies, technically. It was better for them to avoid any further contact.

A terrible thought occurred to him then: what if Morgan came to Happyland with the rest of her family? What if during the resultant battle the two of them ended up facing one another? He didn't want to hurt her. Whatever happened, he hoped it wouldn't come down to that.

He felt his phone vibrate in his pocket, and when he took it out he wasn't surprised to find he'd received a pair of texts from Morgan. Just as his family had anticipated, the werewolves were planning on attacking them before the twenty-four-hour grace period was up. But it was the second text—*On my way*—that both thrilled and concerned him. He was excited at the prospect of seeing Morgan again, but he was afraid of how his family might react to her presence. Could he convince them that she wasn't their enemy? And if he couldn't, what would they do to her?

"Anything important?" Nathan asked.

Greg debated whether to tell his grandfather about Morgan, how she wasn't like the rest of her family, that she was on their side. But in the end, he couldn't risk it. Jakkals hated werewolves, and he feared he couldn't convince his grandfather that Morgan could be trusted.

"No," he lied. "Everyone is just about finished setting the new traps."

He didn't know if this was true, but he figured it was a likely guess, which made it kind of like the truth. Sort of.

"Good," Nathan said.

They drove on for a few more moments in silence before Greg spoke again.

"Grandfather, are you worried about fighting the werewolves again? Our people weren't meant to be warriors."

"We are meant to be whatever Anubis wants us to be," Nathan said. "No, I am not afraid, for I know my god is with me. We jakkals have been running from one place to another since our species was born. It is a relief to finally take a stand, however events play out. But we will not be without weapons. We have our bite from which the *iwiw* cannot easily heal, we have our traps, and we have them." Nathan jerked his chin toward the *neteru*. "And if it becomes necessary, we shall revive Anubis and he will fight for us as well." Nathan gave Greg a smile. "Have faith, my grandson."

Greg returned the smile but didn't otherwise reply. Faith was all well and good, but a dozen automatic weapons loaded with silver rounds would be of a lot more use when the werewolves came. He turned back to the window, let the wind blow over his face, and tried not to think of what the next few hours might bring.

Sam ran through the dark. He wasn't scared, exactly. He'd been close to death too many times to be frightened. But just because he wasn't scared of dying didn't mean he looked forward to doing it—especially when it meant being ripped apart by a pack of bloodthirsty werewolves. So while he wasn't scared, he was determined to avoid his pursuers and fight back once they caught up to him. And they *would* catch him eventually, sooner rather than later.

He had a couple of things going for him, though. He'd already been through a portion of these woods when he and Dean had first approached the Crowders' house. And the Impala was close by. The Crowders had taken their keys along with their weapons, but there were more in the Impala's trunk, including silver ones. Sam would have to break a window to get into the car, and he'd just have to listen to Dean complain until they got it replaced.

He had one other thing going for him. The Crowders would do everything they could to draw out the Hunt, to build the anticipation that would make the final kill all the sweeter. From the news reports he'd read, Clay Fuller had been killed several miles from the Crowders' home. Even if they'd given the man a huge head start, they could've easily caught him before he'd gone as far as he had. They'd let him run as long as they could to prolong their fun, so Sam knew he had some time. The question was whether it would be enough.

Sam headed toward the Impala. Over the years, he and Dean had been forced to find their way in all kinds of conditions and they had both learned to memorize the routes they took, in case they had to retrace their steps. He might not come out of the woods at the exact spot where the Impala was parked, but it would be close enough. The trick would be getting into the trunk and arming himself before any of the werewolves figured out what he was doing.

He judged he was within a quarter mile of the Impala when he heard soft growling somewhere off to his left—between him and the car. Sam caught a glimpse of movement out of the corner of his eye. He instinctively ducked and avoided a sweeping strike from a werewolf. One of the twins, he thought. The werewolf's claws struck the trunk of a tree and a large chunk of bark was torn off.

Sam reached toward the ground, fingers scrabbling to find anything he might be able to use as a weapon. His hand closed around a rock the size of his fist. Sam straightened up and slammed the rock into the left side of the werewolf's head. There was a sickening *crunch*. The werewolf let out a roar of pain, staggered, then collapsed to one knee. Sam hit him again. This time the werewolf slumped to the ground, moaning.

Still holding onto the rock, Sam started running again. He heard rustling to his left and knew another werewolf was there, blocking his way to the Impala. He veered right and headed deeper into the woods. He knew the twin he'd struck would recover far sooner than he'd like, but for the moment, he now faced three werewolves instead of four. As if that was much better.

He continued running, mind racing. He tried to think of some kind of plan, but he came up blank. The problem with werewolves was while the animal part of them was predictable, the human part was anything but. That made it difficult—if not impossible—to plan when fighting them. Something he and Dean had first learned the hard way when they'd been kids.

Near Seattle, Washington. 1992

The werewolf's long white hair trailed behind her as she ran toward them, rippling in the wind like the tail of a kite. Sam gripped the silver blade so tight his hand hurt, but he didn't raise the weapon. He'd never seen a creature this terrifying before—all teeth and claws and mad hunger—and he froze. All he could do was stare at the old woman werewolf as she came at him. He couldn't even close his eyes or turn his head, couldn't even blink as death rushed toward him.

Dean stood, raised Bobby's revolver, and fired. Once, twice, three times. The first two shots missed as near as Sam could tell, but the third struck the werewolf in the chest. Her eyes rolled white and she collapsed to the ground. She lay on the asphalt as rain pattered on her body.

The instant the werewolf went down, Sam's paralysis broke. He tried to look at Dean and saw his brother still holding the revolver in a two-handed grip, eyes wide and body trembling.

"Dean? You okay?"

Dean continued staring at the werewolf's lifeless form for several moments before finally answering Sam's question.

"Yeah, I'm good."

He didn't *sound* good, but Sam knew they didn't have any more time to talk. Someone would've heard the gunshots and called security—which meant they had to get out of here. *Now.* Sam stood and put a hand on Dean's shoulder. "Can you drive?"

The question snapped Dean back to reality. "I got us here, didn't I?"

Without another word, the brothers ran to Bobby's pickup and climbed inside. Dean had replaced Bobby's gun in his jacket pocket, but once they were inside the truck, he didn't return it to the glovebox. They put on safety belts, Dean fished the keys out of his pocket, and with a hand that still shook slightly, started the vehicle.

Sam was looking at Dean when he saw a blur of shadowy movement. It seemed to come from behind the pickup, but when he turned to look, he saw nothing. He figured he was just jumpy from what had happened, and he thought no more of it.

Dean backed out of the parking space and then headed for the exit. Sam saw red-and-blue lights in the distance approaching rapidly. Dean saw them, too, and he tromped on the gas pedal. The pickup swerved from side to side on the wet asphalt before Dean got control of it once more, and they roared out of the visitors' lot and onto the road. Sam turned around to watch, afraid he'd see a dozen police cars on their tail, lights flashing and sirens wailing. But no one was behind them. A hospital security vehicle had stopped in the lot they'd just vacated. They'd probably found the werewolf, Sam thought. Werewolves reverted to human form in death, and the security officers who arrived on the scene would discover a normal-looking—albeit dead—human woman, with a wound on one arm and a large bullet hole in her chest. No one would know that she'd been a monster. They would think she was a harmless old woman who'd been killed by an unknown assailant for an unknown reason. No one would ever know the truth. Bobby had once told Sam that protecting people from the knowledge that the supernatural was real was, in its own way, equally as important as saving lives.

If folks knew the truth about what really goes bump in the night, they'd never feel safe again. We help give them peace of mind, and even if it's a damn lie, it's a necessary one.

So people would think that he and Dean were murderers. Not that the brothers would ever be caught—hopefully—but that's what everyone would assume, and it made Sam sad. He didn't want credit for killing the werewolf, especially since Dean had been the one to shoot it. But the idea made him finally realize, perhaps for the first time in his life, that hunters were killers. Yes, they only killed to protect others, but that didn't change the fact that they still took lives, even if they were unnatural ones. If he grew up to become a hunter, he'd have to kill. A lot. What effect would that kind of life have on a person? Would they become as cold-hearted a predator as the things they hunted? Is that what had happened to Dad? Had he become something he wasn't proud of, something he didn't want to expose his boys to? Maybe that was part of the reason he was gone so much of the time. Maybe, in his own way, he was trying to protect his sons.

Sam faced forward once more. "Do you remember the way back to the motel?"

"Of course I do," Dean snapped. Then after a moment, he added, "But let's see if *you* do."

Sam smiled.

TWENTY-FOUR

Present Day

These were the times when Alan felt most alive. Running through the night in his true form, strong and free, the moon singing in his blood. The world was alive with scents and sounds, a symphony of sensory input that was as intoxicating as it was overwhelming. For him, the Hunt was secondary. He enjoyed it well enough, and he *definitely* enjoyed the heart meat that came at the end of a kill. But Sylvia, Stuart, and Spencer *lived* for the Hunt. They could stalk and kill a different person every night and they'd never tire of it. They'd bathe in victims' blood and gnaw on their hearts even if their bellies were full to bursting. In a way, he admired them. The pack Sylvia grew up in had been closer to the old ways of their people, to the primal essence of the wolf. Alan's pack had become too much like their prey, and they had been weaker for it. It was Sylvia's wildness that had first attracted him to her, and she'd passed it along to her two eldest sons. It was too early to tell which way Joshua would go, but it seemed clear that Morgan took after his side of the family. Perhaps when it was time for her to select a mate, she'd choose someone who would balance her, someone wild like her mother. Otherwise, she'd remain weak. Werewolves did not tolerate weakness in their ranks. If Morgan didn't toughen up, she wouldn't last long. As her father, the thought saddened him, but as pack leader, he wouldn't allow emotion to get in the way of his responsibilities. And if the time came when Morgan had to be put down, he'd do it himself. It was the least he owed her as her sire and her leader.

He was grateful that the two hunters and their werewolf companion had come to town. Sylvia and the boys wanted to hunt more often than was prudent. There were only so many people who could disappear in Bridge Valley without raising suspicion. He'd done what he could to select prey that wouldn't be missed, but it was becoming difficult to keep up with his family's demands. The three captives—for they would hunt the weak werewolf, too, the one that stank from eating animal hearts—would supply them with fun for a little while, maybe all the way to Christmas if they spaced the hunts out far enough.

He heard Spencer's guttural growl off to his left, then the heavy sound of rock striking bone and a cry of pain. Their prey changed course and ran deeper into the woods. Alan knew that Spencer had been trying to direct him to run into the thickest part of the woods and prolong the Hunt. But the hunter had turned the tables.

Alan could smell his son's blood, but he did not run toward him. Spencer would recover quickly enough on his own.

Until then, he'd pay the price for his carelessness by missing out on the Hunt. If he didn't recover in time, he'd miss out on his share of heart meat.

Rather than being angered that the hunter had hurt his son, Alan was pleasantly surprised. It seemed as if tonight's Hunt was going to be something special. The hunter wasn't going to make it easy on them. He wouldn't have had it any other way.

Feeling more excitement for a Hunt than he had in a long time, Alan howled and doubled his speed as he plunged through the woods.

Garth ran ahead of Dean. Sam was facing four lycanthropes, and he had no silver to fight with. As resourceful as Sam was, those were lousy odds, and Garth was determined to even them. He not only had his gun loaded with silver bullets tucked into the waistband of his pants, but he also carried Sam's pistol and silver rounds, and Sam's silver knife. The silver bullets so close to his flesh were uncomfortable, but the knife—even though its handle was leather—hurt like hell. It felt as if his hand was on fire, but since the silver wasn't actually in contact with his skin, he suffered no damage. But even if he had, he wouldn't have cared. All that mattered was reaching Sam before the Crowders killed him.

Garth had no trouble tracking Sam. His scent was like a blazing beacon shining through the darkness. He could smell the Crowders' separate scents in a crisscrossing pattern as they moved through the woods, never far from Sam, always driving him onward. Thank Fenris they wanted to play with him for a while, or he'd already be dead.

One of the Crowders had been wounded. The twin named Spencer, Garth thought, although his scent was much like his brother's. Garth could smell the boy's blood—from a head wound, he judged—and he smiled, baring his fangs. Even unarmed, Sam was still dangerous as hell.

As he ran, Garth became aware of a sound like whispering. It was the voice of the wolf inside him. It came softly at first but grew louder with each inch of ground he covered.

You are wolf, it said. *Hunter, killer, feaster. Strong, swift, savage, merciless...*

And accompanying the voice was a nearly overwhelming explosion of scent, more intense than anything he'd ever experienced before. That wasn't true, he realized. He *had* experienced this, back in the Crowders' dining room. It was the smell of Melody's heart. He could join the other lycanthropes, take part in their Hunt, perhaps even share in the reward at the end. The thought of sinking his fangs into a sliver of the man's heart meat made his mouth water. Then Garth realized what he'd been thinking.

Sam's not just a man—he's my friend!

He felt the animal part of him rising to the forefront of his consciousness, threatening to take over. The scent of human heart had aroused in the wolf a deep, all-encompassing hunger. The beast wanted meat, and it wasn't about to let this weak little man whose body it was forced to share stop it. Garth could feel himself slipping away. It was as if he were drowning in darkness, sinking into depths from which he would never emerge. With his last conscious thought, he relaxed his grip on Sam's knife and let the blade slide down. He then tightened his grip around the metal before it could slide through his hand. The metal seared his skin and the knife's edges cut into his flesh. Blood flowed from the wounds, but the pain cleared his mind and drove the wolf away. He was grateful, even as the agony doubled him over. He readjusted his grip on the knife and managed to keep stumbling forward until the pain passed—mostly—and he was able to straighten and run normally once more.

The wolf's voice receded into the background of his mind. But it was still there, still whispering, urging him to deny his humanity and allow his true self to run free and unrestrained. To hunt as it would, kill when it pleased, and devour the succulent heart meat of humans, as it had been created to do.

Garth still smelled Melody's heart, although it was nowhere near as strong as it had been. He could ignore it for now, but he feared they would grow stronger. And when that happened, would he be able to resist it, or would the part of him that was Garth Fitzgerald IV be destroyed by the wolf? If that happened, his worst nightmare would've come to pass: the man would die, leaving behind only the monster.

He decided he'd fight that battle when he had to. Right now, Sam needed him.

Dean ran through the woods, Colt in one hand, silver blade in the other. Somewhere up ahead of him was Garth. Dean didn't give a damn which of them reached Sam first, so long as they reached him in time to help him fight the Crowders.

The werewolves might've had a head start on them, but the hunters had a couple of advantages of their own. Dean figured the Crowders wouldn't kill Sam right away. Not only would they want to play with their food before they ate it, Sam was far more skilled at fighting and surviving than the werewolves' usual prey. And the Crowders thought he and Garth were still chained up in their basement. They wouldn't be expecting their other two prisoners to be hunting *them*. With any luck, their attention would be so focused on Sam they wouldn't realize he and Garth were coming for them until it was too late.

Of all the monsters he and his brother had ever faced, werewolves were among the most challenging. They were a perfect fusion of human and beast, fiercely savage killing machines with a singled-minded focus on their goal: to feed. You knew where you stood with a werewolf. There were no lies, betrayals, or trickery like you had to deal with when hunting a demon or a witch, and while werewolves *did* kill, often in a horrific fashion, they did so swiftly. The Crowders were different. They planned their hunts, abducting people to serve as playthings, until they were finally brought down and allowed to die. He'd seen Amos Boyd's ravaged corpse. There had been nothing quick about his death. The Crowders had wanted to make him suffer, had luxuriated in his blood and pain. The Crowders might think they lived in harmony with their animal selves, but as far as Dean was concerned, they were more aligned with the worst aspects of their human side. To put it simply, the Crowders gave werewolves a bad name.

At that moment, he heard several shots come from deeper in the woods. The fight was officially on.

"Save some for me," Dean said, and ran in the direction of the gunfire.

Twenty-Five

Sam had been running full out since the Hunt began, and his lungs were on fire and his legs felt like rubber. He wasn't running now so much as stumbling forward, gasping for breath while his pulse pounded like a trip hammer. He couldn't keep this up much longer, and if he knew that, it was certain the Crowders did too. They wouldn't tire—their supernatural stamina let them run as long and far as they wished. They could've easily run him to ground a dozen different times by now. But they wanted to make the fun last as long as possible.

That gave him an idea.

He stopped at a large elm tree, pressed his back to it, and waited. He didn't have to wait long.

Shadowy figures emerged from the darkness and came slinking toward him. Four of them. It seemed the twin he'd struck in the head had recovered. Sam still held the rock, but now he let it fall. A single rock wouldn't do him any good now.

Crowder approached, Sylvia to his right, Stuart and

Spencer flanking their parents. "What's wrong? Need to catch your breath?" he mocked.

"Maybe he's decided to stand and fight," Sylvia said. "He *is* a big, brave hunter after all."

The twins laughed at this. The werewolves continued moving forward, fangs bared and claws raised.

Crowder's upper lip curled away from his teeth in a sneer. "He's no hunter. *We're* the hunters. It's what we were born to be. He's just another meal, nothing more."

The werewolves stopped within ten feet of Sam. They made no move to attack, and Sam allowed himself a small smile.

"Sorry," he said, "but I *am* tired. And I think I might've twisted my ankle." This was a lie, but he knew that even the werewolves' hyper-strong senses wouldn't be able to determine if he was telling the truth, not from where they stood. He put his weight on his left foot to help sell the lie.

"If you can stand on both feet, you can run on them," Sylvia said.

Sam shook his head. "I don't think so. I guess you'll just have to kill me right here."

"You can't just quit!" Spencer said. "You owe me after hitting me in the head like you did."

Sam had guessed right. The Crowders wanted to hunt as much as kill. By stopping here, he'd interrupted their fun. They wanted him to continue running before they finally feasted. But he could only stall them for so long before they decided to say to hell with it and tore him to bits. Time for step two of his plan.

"Owe you what?" Sam said.

Stuart answered for his brother. "A chase! The meat tastes so much sweeter after a good run."

"I don't see what that has to do with you," Sam said. "It's not as if *you're* going to get any of my heart."

Stuart growled and took a step forward, but his father raised a hand and Stuart stepped back.

"I'm pack leader," Crowder said. "*I* decide who gets meat and how much."

"That doesn't seem fair," Sam said. "Not in this case, anyway. Spencer was the one I hit with the rock. He's the one I humiliated in the eyes of his pack. He deserves the biggest piece. Like he said, I owe him."

Spencer turned to face his parents. "He's right! But I should get more than a piece. I should get the whole thing. I deserve it!"

Stuart snarled and took several steps toward his brother. "You deserve nothing! You were brought down by a human armed with nothing more than a rock. Your weakness brings shame to the pack. You should return to the house now before we remind you how we deal with weakness."

Sam figured the twins' blood would be up after chasing him, and they wouldn't be thinking and reacting rationally. Sam and Dean might not be twins, but they were brothers, and Sam knew how angry brothers could become with each other.

"Stop it!" Crowder roared.

But neither twin paid him any attention. They were too focused on each other.

"*I'm* weak?" Spencer said. "I didn't let myself get wounded by a carrion-eater. Besides, you got to eat all of the reporter's heart. You've had enough meat for one night."

"*Boys...*" Sylvia said in a low warning tone.

Sam could feel the tension between the four werewolves thrumming in the air. It wouldn't take much more for their anger to overwhelm them, and then they'd begin fighting each other. And when that happened, Sam would hightail it out of there.

Crowder looked at Sylvia. "Spencer *does* have a point," he said.

Sylvia snapped her teeth at her husband. "Are you *crazy*? Stuart's right! Spencer was weak tonight, and he deserves to be punished."

"I'm pack leader," Crowder said.

Sylvia growled back. "And I'm your mate. Do you *really* want to go up against me?"

She took a step forward, raising her claws. Crowder raised his own claws and rushed toward her. The twins ran at each other, and Sam felt grim satisfaction. The moment the four were at each other's throats, he'd start running again.

But instead of clawing at each other, Crowder and Sylvia went into each other's arms and kissed. And instead of coming to blows, the twins high-fived each other. Alan and Sylvia broke apart, and all four werewolves burst into laughter.

"Nice try, hunter," Crowder said. "But just because we're monsters doesn't mean we're stupid."

"It was amusing," Sylvia said, "and turning the tables on you like we did... You should've seen your face!"

They all laughed once more.

"A memorable end to an unusual—but satisfying—Hunt," Crowder said. "But it *is* the end."

The werewolves growled in unison and started advancing slowly toward Sam. He desperately wracked his brain, hoping to come up with a last-minute idea that would save his life. But he couldn't think of anything. After all the years he'd spent on the road with his brother, all the things they'd done and seen, his time to die—and stay dead this time—had finally arrived.

He heard leaves rustling, and then caught sight of a shape pulling away from the darkness—a shape that looked remarkably like Garth. And he was holding Sam's gun in one hand and a silver blade in the other. He shouted, "Catch!" and hurled the pistol toward Sam. It flew through the air in a perfect arc, passing over the Crowders' heads. Sam snatched it out of the air and started firing.

The Crowders' inhuman reflexes saved them. Before Sam caught the gun they were already scattering. One of Sam's rounds struck Alan in the left shoulder, staggering him but not bringing him down. Another round missed Sylvia entirely, and then she and her husband melted into the night and were gone.

The twins were still there. Garth thrust the silver blade at Spencer's chest. Spencer turned to the side, avoiding a fatal blow, but the tip of the blade slashed across his right ribs. Spencer raced away, howling in pain and frustration. Instead of fleeing with his brother, Stuart knocked Garth to the ground, and Garth lost his grip on the silver blade. Stuart snatched up the blade. Grinning, he raised the knife high over his head and began to bring it down in a vicious swipe, aiming directly for Garth's heart.

Sam took aim, but before he could fire, three shots came in rapid succession. Stuart's arms flew out—the blade tumbling from his grasp—and he looked at Sam as if he couldn't believe what had happened. Then he stiffened and collapsed to the ground in silence.

Dean walked up to Stuart, Colt still trained on the werewolf. Garth—in human form once more—rose to his feet and joined him, and Sam walked over to gaze down at Stuart's corpse with them.

"He's dead," Garth said. He tapped his ear. "I can't hear a pulse."

Sam smiled at Dean and Garth. "Took you guys long enough," he said. He bent down to retrieve his silver blade. "Thanks, by the way."

Garth continued to gaze upon Stuart's body, an expression of sorrow on his face.

"Look," Dean said, "I had to—"

Garth held up a hand to stop him. "I know. I'd have done the same thing in your position. It's just a waste, you know? It didn't have to end this way for him."

Given what Stuart had been and how he was raised, Sam wasn't sure it could've ended any other way.

"Do you think the others will circle back and attack?" Sam said.

"I doubt it," Garth said. "They'll go somewhere and lick their wounds before deciding on their next move."

"So we go back to their house and take them down before they can regroup," Dean said.

"Their house is their den," Garth said, "and normally that's exactly where they'd go at a time like this. But not now. They know that's the first place you'd look for them. They'll go someplace else."

Sam nodded toward Stuart's body. "They'll come back for him, though, won't they?"

"Eventually," Garth said, "but not right away. Werewolves like the Crowders—Purebloods who tend more to the wild side of their nature—aren't as sentimental as humans. They'll put Stuart out of their minds for now and concentrate on getting revenge against us. They might consider Stuart a weak link, but he was still a member of their pack, and his death must be avenged. But we don't have time to worry about that right now. We need to take care of Morgan and Joshua. If their family finds them in the Impala—a car with Winchester scent all over it…" He trailed off, but the implication was clear. Morgan and her brother would be killed.

"And *why* are they in our car?" Sam asked.

"I'll tell you on the way," Dean said. "Garth, you want to go on ahead?"

Garth nodded, took on his werewolf form, and dashed off into the woods. Within seconds, he'd merged with the darkness and was lost to sight.

"You up for some more cardio?" Dean asked.

Sam nodded, and the brothers started running after Garth.

Near Seattle, Washington. 1992

The farther they drove from the hospital, the lighter Dean's mood became, until he'd gone from stunned silence to exhilarated chatter.

"Man, that was scary! But awesome too! Did you see those *teeth*? And the way she growled! I thought for sure we were dead meat, but I kept cool and fired anyway, and I got her. Did you see that, Sammy? I *got* her!"

Sam didn't understand his brother's excitement. Even though it was all over, he was still scared. In a way, he was relieved too. The werewolf was far more terrifying than any movie monster could ever be. She'd been *real*. But they'd stopped her, and Sam now knew that monsters, no matter how frightening or powerful, could be defeated. You just needed to know their weakness.

The brothers managed to get back to the motel without getting pulled over, which Sam considered to be something of a miracle. The same space where the pickup had been parked before was still empty, and Dean slid the truck into it. When he finished, the vehicle's left tires were well over the line, but he hadn't hit anything, so Sam considered that a win.

It was close to two a.m., and both of them were tired to the bone. Dean's earlier excitement at their victory over the werewolf had ebbed, and now he was quiet and subdued. As they walked toward their room, legs heavy as lead, Sam said, "I hope Bobby's still asleep."

"Me too."

Bobby would be angry at them for going off on their own. And now that they were back safe and sound, Sam knew that Bobby would be right. What he and Dean had done was incredibly stupid, and they were lucky the werewolf hadn't torn them to bloody ribbons and feasted on their hearts. But if they could get inside the room without waking Bobby, he wouldn't find out as long as he and Dean kept their mouths shut. Sam knew he'd feel guilty not telling Bobby about tonight, but he'd rather live with that guilt than get yelled at. And if Dad found out what they'd done—

No, better to keep it to themselves for the rest of their lives.

When they reached the door to their room, Dean quietly took the key from his pocket and started to put it in the keyhole. But before he could turn it, the door flew open and Bobby—beads of sweat on his too-gray face—said, "Where in the *hell* have you two idjits been?"

Dean stepped forward, putting himself between Sam and Bobby. "Don't be mad at Sammy. It was all my idea. I made him come with me."

Sam appreciated his big brother standing up for him. But he didn't think it was fair for him to accept all the blame. "I *wanted* to go," Sam said. "I—"

His words were cut off by an ear-piercing shriek that sounded half-human and half something else. Sam and Dean turned to see the werewolf they'd killed leap up out of the truck bed and onto the top of the cab. Her sweater was still dark with blood, but her wounds didn't seem to have slowed her down. She snarled and fixed her feral-eyed gaze on them.

Bobby didn't hesitate. He pulled Sam and Dean into the room, slammed the door shut, and threw the deadbolt. He pulled them to the other side of the room. An instant later, they heard a heavy *thud* as the werewolf threw herself at the door. It shuddered, but the deadbolt held.

"Let me guess," Bobby said. "You two geniuses went to the hospital to kill the werewolf, and you shot her with a silver bullet. You thought you'd hit her in the heart, but you missed, and when you left, she hopped in the back of the pickup and caught a ride back with you."

The werewolf slammed against the door once more, growling and snapping. The deadbolt still held, but there was a small shower of plaster dust as the deadbolt started to come loose from the wall. Sam knew the door wouldn't withstand another impact.

"You mean we had to shoot her in the *heart*?" Dean said.

Bobby sighed. "Remind me to teach you boys what a double-tap is."

Dean still carried Bobby's gun in his jacket pocket. Bobby calmly pulled it out, raised it with shaky hands, and aimed at the door.

The werewolf threw herself against it for a third time, and it burst open. She raced into the room, mouth open wide in a scream, claws extended, ready to tear into them.

Bobby fired one round. It struck the werewolf in the heart, and this time when she went down, she stayed down. He slumped, and Sam and Dean grabbed hold of him before he could fall to the floor.

"I swear," Bobby said, "you boys are going to be the death of me yet."

Sam and Dean packed up their stuff quickly after that, and the three of them departed the room, leaving the werewolf— who now looked like an old human woman—where she lay. Dean offered to drive, but Bobby told him to shut up and get in the truck. When they were all squeezed into the front seat, Bobby started the pickup and, driving with his uninjured arm, maneuvered them out of the parking lot.

They spent the remainder of the night in the pickup, parked at a twenty-four-hour burger joint. Dean wanted to go in and get some burgers, but Bobby told him to be quiet and get some sleep. In the morning, they drove to another town and got a room at a different motel. Bobby lay on one bed while Sam and Dean sat on the other, eating snacks and watching TV. The local news station carried a report about a woman—Juanita Schultz—who'd been found dead at a motel in a neighboring town with multiple wounds. The police had no idea why Ms. Schultz had been there, but she'd made the news earlier in the year when her husband Brent had gone in for bypass surgery and died on the operating table. She blamed the entire surgical team and threatened a lawsuit against the hospital. She stood outside the hospital's main building every day, rain or shine, holding signs with slogans like *Don't Come Here if You Want to Live!* And *Hospital of Death!*

"That's why she was prowling around the hospital as a werewolf," Bobby said. "She was hunting the surgical team she blamed for her husband's death."

Sam asked Bobby how Ms. Schultz had become a werewolf in the first place, but Bobby said they'd probably never know.

He closed his eyes. Sam thought he had fallen asleep, but then he said, "You boys might be idjits, but you did good." Several seconds later, he was snoring softly.

Sam and Dean exchanged grins. Dean started flipping through the channels, looking for something good. He stopped when he landed on a movie: a vampire in a dark suit and cape was moving quickly up the stone steps of a castle, a hungry look in his eyes.

"Sorry," Dean said. "I'll keep looking."

"Don't," Sam said. "This is okay."

Dean looked at him a moment. "You sure?"

Sam nodded and settled back to watch. "Yeah. Real life is way more scary than this stuff."

TWENTY-SIX

Present Day

Greg was relieved when he and Nathan reached Happyland. He didn't think he could stand the smell of formaldehyde much longer. Nathan entered the park through a side gate and pulled the station wagon up to the Monsours' temporary home. Greg got out as fast as he could and opened all the vehicle's doors. Then he and Nathan ordered the *neteru* to exit the station wagon and lined them up downwind from the building. The next step would be to determine the best locations in the park for the *neteru* to stand guard. For that, they would have to consult with the rest of the family.

Greg was impatient. He wanted to sneak off and meet Morgan before his family found out she was here. Maybe he could find a different place in the park for her to hide, somewhere far enough from his family that they wouldn't pick up her scent.

Greg expected the others to come out and greet him and Nathan once they returned, but no one emerged from the building. Greg had a sudden bad feeling. What if the werewolves had attacked while he and Nathan had been gone? The rest of their family might be dead, and the werewolves could be lurking close by, ready to attack him and Nathan any instant.

He told himself not to be foolish. If his family had been wounded he'd smell their blood. He'd also detect the werewolves' scents, and while the scents of the father and sons who'd confronted them earlier that day still lingered in the area, there was nothing fresh. So—

Wait. There *was* a fresh werewolf scent. Two of them, in fact, and he recognized them.

The door to the office building opened and Marta, Efren, Muriel, Kayla, and Erin emerged. They were all in jakkal form, and Morgan—in human form—walked between them, carrying her baby brother.

"We had *visitors* while you were gone," Marta said. The way she said *visitors*, like it was something you'd find floating in a sewer, told Greg what she thought of Morgan and her brother showing up here.

Morgan looked at the crimson-eyed *neteru* with a combination of wonder and disgust. She gave Greg an uncertain smile. He wanted to go to her, to reassure her that everything would be all right, but he knew he couldn't. He didn't want to give his family any excuse to show hostility toward Morgan and her brother. And if his family knew how strongly he felt about Morgan, they might hurt her just to teach him a lesson about getting too friendly with an *iwiw*.

Nathan scowled and changed into jakkal form.

"What is *she* doing here?" he demanded. He turned to

Greg. "She's the one whose stink you had all over you earlier."

"I don't know why she's here," Greg said truthfully. Yes, she'd texted him that she was 'on her way,' but he didn't know the reason she'd come here. Then he surprised himself by adding, "Don't talk about her like that. She hasn't done anything to hurt us."

Nathan's eyes widened in shock. Greg figured he couldn't have surprised his grandfather more if he'd suddenly sprouted a second head.

His sisters snickered.

"Greggy has a girlfriend," Erin said in a sing-song voice.

Kayla sneered. "I can't say much for his taste in women."

Muriel glared at Greg. "He is your Elder! You must show respect!"

"I do respect Grandfather," Greg said, amazed at how calm he felt. He'd never gone against his family before, but now that he was, he found he wasn't afraid. "As I respect you, Grandmother, and the rest of the family." He gave Kayla and Erin a quick glance. "Even my sisters. But just because Morgan is a werewolf is no reason to treat her poorly."

"Her father—" Efren began.

"She isn't her father," Greg said. "Just as I am not you."

Efren drew back, almost as if Greg had struck him. Marta began growling.

"We don't have to fight, Mother," Greg said. "But if it comes to that, I now have two *neteru* under my command."

Now it was Marta's turn to look as if he'd hit her.

Greg smiled at Morgan. "I got your texts. Sorry I didn't get here before you."

"That's okay," she said. "Your family's not happy Joshua and I came, but they haven't mistreated us." There was something in her voice that seemed to imply she might've added *Not yet*.

"It's good to see you again," he said. "Despite the circumstances."

She smiled. "Yes," she agreed.

The rest of Greg's family started talking amongst themselves. They sounded worried, but also excited. They were looking forward to fighting.

Greg continued speaking to Morgan. "You must have known that my family would not welcome you. And if *your* family finds out you are here…"

"Like I said, my family is coming soon. They mean to kill you all."

"This news comes as no surprise to us," Nathan said. "We expect you—"

Greg thought Nathan was going to say *you iwiw*, but he glanced sideways at Greg before continuing.

"—you *werewolves* not to honor your promises."

"There's too much animal in you," Muriel said. "Your lust to kill overrides everything else."

Morgan lowered her gaze, as if she were ashamed. "That may be true for the rest of my family, but it's not true for me. Or for Joshua."

Her little brother had been asleep all this time, but now he opened his eyes at the sound of his name, yawned, and stretched. He looked at the jakkals surrounding him, but he didn't seem afraid, just puzzled. The jakkals' bestial features didn't bother him. *Since he belongs to a family of werewolves, why would they?* Greg thought.

"She's lying," Kayla said. "It's some kind of trick. She's come here to spy on us."

"Or maybe when the attack begins, she'll turn on us," Erin added.

"You give my family too much credit," Morgan said. "Werewolves are simple creatures. The kind of scheming you're talking about isn't something they do. Their entire battle strategy consists of two maneuvers: attack and retreat."

"We're supposed to believe you've come to warn us out of the goodness of your heart?" Marta asked.

"I came in hope of preventing more senseless killing," Morgan said. She glanced at Greg, and smiled, then turned her attention back to Marta.

"I didn't have to come here. There's a werewolf pack in Wisconsin that lives peacefully and only feeds on animal hearts. I could've gone there and taken Joshua with me. But I couldn't just leave and let my family attack without trying to warn you."

Efren snorted. "Werewolves living peacefully? It sounds like a fairy tale."

"It's true!" Morgan insisted. "I met a werewolf named Garth who belongs to that pack. He tried to convince my family to join, but they wouldn't listen. They took him and his two friends prisoner. When my family is done with them, they'll come here next."

"Which is why we should stop arguing and get ready," Greg said.

His family looked to one another, uncertain. Then his grandfather's features became human once more, and a moment later the rest of his family shed their jakkal forms as well.

Nathan put a hand on Greg's shoulder. "You speak sense, boy." Nathan raised his voice to address everyone. "One last vote. Do we still wish to stand and fight, or do we flee, as our people have always done when confronted with danger?"

The family answered with one word.

"Fight!"

Nathan nodded. He then looked at Morgan. "Will you fight alongside us, girl—against your own people?"

She looked shocked, as if the idea of helping the jakkals battle her family had never occurred to her. Then her expression became determined.

"If I'd wanted to run, I would've gone with Garth and his friends. I will fight."

Part of Greg wished that she'd said no. He wanted her to stay out of the battle and hole up somewhere safe until it was all over, one way or another. But a larger part of him admired her for her choice. If their roles had been reversed, he didn't know if he could be as brave.

Muriel spoke then. "If you're truly here to help us, Morgan, there's only one way you can convince us."

"I'll do anything," Morgan said.

"Give us your brother," Muriel said.

Morgan looked shocked, and Greg knew how she felt. He couldn't believe what he'd just heard. But before either Morgan or Greg could say anything, Muriel went on.

"He shall not be harmed—I pledge my life on it. We shall care for him as if he were one of our own. But if you betray us…"

Greg stepped toward his grandmother, ready to protest,

but Morgan put a hand on his shoulder to stop him.

"Will Joshua be safe?" she asked him.

Greg didn't like this situation, but he didn't hesitate. "Yes."

She looked at him a moment and then nodded. She turned to Muriel. "I agree."

"Thank you, child," Muriel said. "Kayla, would you take the baby?"

Kayla didn't look happy about it, but she went to Morgan and held out her hands. Morgan gave her brother a kiss on the forehead. "Try to be good," she said, and then handed him over to Kayla. Joshua looked up at Kayla with wide eyes, but he didn't fuss, and Kayla—despite her initial reluctance—held him gently.

"Let us finish our preparations," Nathan said. "And pray to Anubis that the dawn will see us triumphant."

As pep talks went, it was short and sweet. But Greg feared his grandfather was being far too optimistic. There would be blood, pain, and death before the morning came. That was guaranteed. The only question was who would live and who would die. And Greg knew that question would be answered all too soon.

Garth was waiting for the Winchesters when they reached the Impala. He leaned back against the car, arms folded, scowling. There was no sign of Morgan or her baby brother.

"Where's the girl and the rugrat?" Dean asked. "Didn't they make it?"

"Their scents are here," Garth said. "They didn't stay long, though."

"Did her family get them?" Sam asked.

"Negatory. Morgan and Joshua were the only ones here."

"She ran that way." Garth hooked a thumb northward. "Toward town."

"Do you think she had second thoughts about joining your pack?" Dean asked.

"Maybe," Garth said, "but like I said, she's running toward town. Away from her family."

"Do you know where she might be going?" Sam asked.

"I'm not sure," Garth said. "But I have an idea."

Several moments later, they were all in the Impala, heading toward town.

"You really think she'll go to that jakkal boy?" Dean said. "I mean, they just met today."

"Weren't you ever young and in love?" Garth asked. "'The heart understands before the mind starts thinking.'"

"Spare us the greeting card wisdom, oh great werewolf guru," Dean said.

"Garth might have a point," Sam said. "Crowder said he wanted to attack the jakkals tonight. Maybe she's trying to warn them."

"Maybe," Dean said grudgingly.

"Why are you having a hard time accepting the idea that Morgan is on the side of the good guys?" Garth asked. "Is it because you don't believe in love at first sight? Or don't you believe that monsters can love at all?"

Dean opened his mouth to reply, but when he realized he didn't have a good answer, he closed it again.

"Bess and I are in love," Garth reminded him.

"That's different," Dean said.

"How so?" Garth asked.

"Because… Because you were both adults when you got together," Dean said.

"We weren't any different than Morgan and the jakkal boy. Bess and I knew we belonged together from the first moment we met. It was… instinct, I guess you could say. She told me it's like that for Purebloods sometimes. Love at first smell, she called it."

"That sounds disgusting," Dean said. "But even if it works that way for Purebloods, why would it apply to a werewolf and a jakkal? Seems to me that their people aren't too fond of one another."

Garth shrugged. "The heart wants what it wants. You know what your problem is, Dean? You don't have an ounce of romance in you."

"I've got plenty of romance in me," Dean said. "I've got romance coming out the wazoo."

Sam grinned. "Better get that checked by a doctor."

Garth laughed.

Dean scowled but didn't say anything. He remembered driving past Happyland when he and Sam first came to Bridge Valley, and he headed for the abandoned amusement park now.

Sam grew thoughtful. "It's possible werewolves and jakkals are related somehow. They both transform into canine-type creatures, and they both eat hearts. They're more alike than not."

"Okay," Dean said. "Let's say Morgan is going to her boyfriend. What are we supposed to do when we get there?"

"See if she still wants to come with me back to Wisconsin," Garth said.

"And if she doesn't want to anymore?" Dean asked.

"It's her choice," Garth said. "I won't force her."

"What then?" Dean asked. "Do we kill the jakkals, wait for Crowder and his family to show, and kill them, too?"

"We shouldn't need to fight the jakkals," Garth said. "Not as long as they don't think we're a threat to them. They're scavengers rather than hunters, so they're not as aggressive as werewolves. They aren't normally dangerous. Remember, they feed on human hearts, but only ones taken from people who are already dead."

"What's to keep them from killing people and *then* taking their hearts?" Dean asked.

"They don't do that," Garth said. "Not based on the stories I've heard from my pack, anyway. Apparently, it's some kind of religious thing with them. They won't eat the heart of a person they've killed themselves. Something about it not being respectful to death. To be honest, I don't really understand it."

"If they don't kill humans, that explains why there's no lore on them," Sam said. "If they're not a threat, there's no reason for hunters to go after them."

"All right," Dean said, "so jakkals aren't exactly at the top of the scariest monsters list. But let's say for some reason that you had to gank one. How would you do it?"

"The same way you kill werewolves," Garth said. "Except you have to use gold instead of silver. I'm not sure why. Some kind of connection to ancient Egypt, I guess. The pharaohs were entombed with all kinds of gold goodies, right?"

Dean was glad to hear the jakkals had a weakness. He hated it when he and Sam came up against some monster that could only be killed with some kind of super-rare object, like a spear made from a meteorite that landed in China six centuries ago on the eighth of August at exactly three o'clock in the afternoon. They kept blades made from various metals in their trunk armory, and they had a couple of gold ones. If the jakkals turned out to be not quite as harmless as Garth made them out to be, he and Sam would be ready.

"So we're driving to an abandoned amusement park to save monster versions of Romeo and Juliet from their warring families."

"Pretty much," Sam said.

"Sounds about right," Garth said.

"Okay," Dean said. "Just wanted to get things straight."

Deep in the woods—so deep that few humans had ever set foot there—the Crowders regrouped in a small cave set into a hillside. Years ago, a black bear had lived in the cave, but Alan's father had driven it out, and ever since the Crowders used the cave as an alternate den. No animal would come near it, since the werewolves' unnatural scent lingered there. The cave wasn't big enough for the Crowders to stand upright, so they sat on the ground in human form. Alan had taken a silver bullet to the shoulder, and Spencer had been sliced across the ribs with a silver blade. Alan's hand was also bleeding from when he'd caught the wrong end of the silver blade. Sylvia was the only one who hadn't been wounded.

"Where's Stuart?"

Spencer's voice was small and afraid. Normally Alan might've struck him for displaying such weakness, but after what they'd just been through, he decided to let it pass.

"If he's not here, he's dead," Alan said. "You know that as well as I."

Spencer drew in a sobbing breath, and for a moment Alan thought his son would start crying. If he did, Alan would have no choice but to strike him. But the boy managed to maintain control of himself, and while his eyes were full of grief, no tears fell.

Alan's face remained expressionless, but inside he struggled with his emotions. Chief among them was rage. Rage at the hunters for besting them and killing his son, yes, but mostly rage at himself for allowing it to happen. He was pack leader. It was his job to safeguard and provide for his pack. Tonight he'd failed to do either. His family would've been justified to challenge his leadership. But it seemed that neither Sylvia nor Spencer had the heart for it right now. As angry as he was at himself, he wished one of them *would* challenge him. It was no more than he deserved.

Sylvia spoke for the first time since they'd fled from the hunters. "What of Morgan and Joshua? Do you think…"

"It's possible the hunter and Garth killed them both when they escaped from the basement," Alan said, "but I doubt it. I detected her scent on the two we left chained at the house, but I didn't smell her blood or Joshua's. Garth and the hunter couldn't have gotten free without help." He didn't want to say this next part, didn't want to believe it, but it was the only explanation. "Morgan had to have set them loose."

For a moment, he thought Sylvia intended to defend their daughter, but she said nothing. What could she say? It wasn't the way of their people to deny the truth, no matter how much it might hurt. To do otherwise would be to show weakness.

"So where is she then?" Sylvia asked. "Where's Joshua?"

"Maybe she went with Garth," Spencer said, "and took Joshua with her."

"I think that's most likely," Alan said. "We have to go after the hunters and get them back. And if Morgan refuses to come with us, we'll take Joshua from her and teach her what it means to betray her pack." He would take no pleasure in killing his daughter, but it was his duty as pack leader, especially after tonight's failure. He could not afford to spare her.

"No," Sylvia said.

Alan thought she'd decided to challenge his authority after all. He would have to attack her now to put down her challenge. He didn't want to harm his wife, but he had no choice. He began to change, but before he could finish, she said, "Morgan isn't with Garth or the hunter brothers. She's with *him*."

At first Alan didn't know what Sylvia was talking about, but then he realized what she meant. Morgan was with the jakkal boy, the one who had wounded Stuart at Happyland. And with this realization came the certainty that Sylvia was right.

"You weren't there when the two met," Sylvia said. "Do you remember what it was like when you and I first caught scent of each other? As much as it disgusts me to say this, that's exactly what it was like for them."

Alan remembered. When he had first met Sylvia, the

sensation had been electric. It turned his stomach to imagine his daughter feeling that way for a carrion-eater.

"If she's bonded with him," Sylvia said, "she would want to warn him that you planned to attack his family tonight."

Alan knew Sylvia was right. Garth and the hunters could wait, at least for now. They would try to get Morgan and Joshua back, and if she wouldn't come with them, she could die with the filthy jakkals.

Alan smiled grimly. They'd been cheated out of the kill at the end of tonight's Hunt, but there would be other bloodshed. And when the jakkals were dead, Joshua was recovered, and Morgan had been dealt with—one way or another—then they could track down Garth and the hunters and deal with them as well. When they were dead along with the cursed jakkals, the pack's honor—*Alan's* honor—would be restored.

"Let's go," he said.

Without waiting for Sylvia or Spencer to respond, he transformed and began running toward the house. A moment later, he heard Sylvia and Spencer running to catch up with him. They would check the house and if it was empty, they'd head for Happyland.

And once they arrived… well that's when the fun would *really* begin.

TWENTY-SEVEN

Dean pulled the Impala up to Happyland's front gate and opened the trunk, lifting the false bottom to reveal their mobile armory. Right now, what they were most interested in was the selection of edged weapons. There were silver blades, of course, but also steel, iron, copper, titanium, and gold. There were only two of the latter—the brothers didn't have much call for them—and after handing one to Sam, Dean admired the remaining blade. To be honest, it didn't look much different than a regular knife in the dark. Shame they didn't have any gold bullets. The knives would have to do.

Dean turned to Garth. "Sorry we only have two," he said.

"No biggie. I got my gun, and I got these." He held up his right hand and the fingers lengthened into claws for a moment.

"Don't do that," Dean said. "It gives me the creeps."

Garth grinned.

Dean and Sam tucked silver blades into their belts and made sure their guns were loaded with silver bullets. Dean liked this part of a hunt. Choosing weapons and preparing yourself mentally for the battle to come. It was when he felt most at peace. He sometimes wondered if these kinds of moments would form the basis for his personal Heaven—assuming he ended up there after he died, of course. Naw. His version of Heaven would be sitting behind the wheel of his Baby, cruising down an endless stretch of deserted highway, window down, classic rock blasting on the radio. That, or sitting at a table in a stripper bar, a never empty and always cold bottle of beer in his hand. Either or.

He closed the trunk as quietly as he could, and then the three of them walked up to the gate. It was chained and padlocked shut. Dean got their lockpick tools from the car, and a moment later, the lock was open. He slid the chain free—carefully and quietly—and then opened the gate just wide enough for them to slip into the park.

High overhead, the moon gave enough light to see by, but did little to illuminate the dark shadows around the abandoned attractions. As monster lairs went, Dean thought this was one of the coolest. A closed-down, long-forgotten amusement park? This place couldn't have been more sinister if it tried. The only thing missing was a psychotic clown or two. *Wouldn't Sam just love that?* he thought.

Garth led the way in werewolf form, his superior senses functioning as perfect scouts. He'd smell, see, or hear danger long before either Dean or Sam could. Who knew having a werewolf for a buddy would come in so handy? Even though Dean knew Garth's senses were far stronger than his or Sam's, he still kept his weapons ready and his eyes and ears open. He liked hunts that were clear-cut, with easy-to-identify good guys and bad guys. That way, you knew who to kill and who to protect. But this case was anything but simple. There was Morgan and her baby brother, both werewolves, sure, but both of whom they wanted to save so they could go live happily ever after with Garth's pack. Then there were the jakkals—which he'd never heard of before coming to Bridge Valley. Hell, he hadn't even *seen* one yet. Supposedly, they were non-threatening monsters, a kind of cross between werewolves and well-behaved ghouls. The Crowders intended to kill the jakkals for no other reason than the werewolves were douches. So he, Sam, and Garth had three main objectives: rescue Morgan and her little brother, help the jakkals—who might think the human hunters were coming to kill them— and kill the rest of the Crowders. That was too many moving parts as far as Dean was concerned, which meant there was a lot that could go wrong.

Then we'll just have to make sure it doesn't, he thought.

He gripped his weapons tighter as they continued moving deeper into Happyland.

When she'd first climbed the park fence with Joshua, Morgan had been surprised that so much of the park remained intact, especially the rides. Later, as she and Greg were leading the *neteru* to this spot, he told her Happyland's owner had specified that everything in the park remain exactly as it was on the day it closed. The man had a crazy dream that someday the park would return to life, which of course it never had.

"The place is perfect for my family," Greg had told her. *"It's*

kind of like a pyramid in a way—an ancient monument to a long-dead man."

Now Morgan crouched alongside Greg off to the side of a rust-eaten ride called Verti-Go-Go! (exclamation mark included), behind an old ice-cream cart. It was large enough to provide cover for both of them, but only if they remained close together. Their arms, hips, and legs were touching, and the contact was at once exhilarating and terrifying. Here she was, helping a group of people she'd just met fight against her own family, and all she could think about was how natural it felt—how *right*—to be near Greg.

Well, that wasn't quite all she was thinking about. There was the terrible guilt at betraying her family, even though she knew she didn't have any other choice, and the fear they'd get Joshua back and raise him to be just like them. And she felt guilty for allowing her brother to become a hostage. Kayla was watching Joshua back at the offices the jakkals used as their home. She didn't know if she could trust Kayla to take good care of Joshua—although Greg insisted Kayla would. She hoped Joshua wasn't frightened. Greg's family hadn't let her go inside the office building to say goodbye and reassure Joshua one last time that everything was all right. She had the sense that they had something stored there—something important—that they didn't want her anywhere near. This was fine with her, but she wished they'd let her say goodbye to Joshua. She wouldn't have remained behind even if they'd insisted. It was her family coming, and this fight was just as much hers as it was the jakkals'. Maybe more.

Greg had ordered the two *neteru* he commanded to stand on

opposite sides of the path. She was still getting used to the idea that jakkals could make their own zombies. One, a woman in her thirties with long blond hair, stood concealed in the shadow of the ride. The other, a pot-bellied man in his forties with a shaved head and a salt-and-pepper beard, hid among a group of nearby bumper cars. In the dark, the dead man was so still that he looked as if he might be another piece of equipment. Greg had commanded both of them to shut their eyes so the crimson light emanating from them wouldn't give the undead servants away. Morgan couldn't get over how eerily silent and motionless the *neteru* were. They didn't breathe, and she couldn't detect the sound of their hearts beating since, of course, they weren't. But there was no hiding their scent. They reeked of embalming chemicals. When she'd asked Greg if he was worried her family would be able to smell the *neteru* before the undead creatures could attack, he'd said, *"Sure they'll smell them. But they'll have no idea what they're smelling. Who'd ever guess it was a bunch of animated corpses? Plus, the* neteru*'s scent will mask our own."*

She hoped he was right. If her family was overwhelmed with rage and bloodlust, they would disregard the smell as not-prey. But if their human sides weren't completely dominated by the wolf in them, they might recognize the *neteru*'s scent as something to be wary of.

They were waiting for an attack, and she was nervous, yes, but her mind wasn't on the battle to come. She had planned to leave town with Garth, taking Joshua with her to join Garth's peaceful pack. But doing so would mean leaving Greg, and now that she was here, she wasn't sure she wanted to do that.

The air was split by the sound of an explosion then, not

far from their position. She jumped—the animal part of her *hated* loud noises—but she remained by Greg's side.

It had begun.

Alan landed soundlessly on his feet. As he straightened, he scanned the immediate area and detected no one in the vicinity. He'd chosen to climb Happyland's fence nearly three quarters of the way from the main entrance, on the southeast side of the park where there had been no jakkal scent in the small stretch of woods. He wasn't surprised the jakkals stayed out of the trees. They didn't feel the same connection to the natural world that Alan's people did. As far as he knew, they didn't feel the pull of the moon, either. If they hadn't been so disgusting, he might've felt sorry for them.

Certain that no one was near, Alan motioned for Sylvia and Spencer to join him. They scaled the fence and dropped down beside him. It rankled to be sneaking into the jakkals' territory instead of making a frontal assault, but the wounds to his left shoulder and right hand hadn't fully healed. The cut Spencer had received across his ribs from the silver blade still bled. The pack wasn't at full strength. The jakkals outnumbered them, and while the carrion-eaters weren't as strong and fast as werewolves, they did have that deadly bite of theirs. And thanks to Morgan, they likely knew they were coming. They would be prepared.

So as much as it galled him, he knew a head-on attack would most likely result in the pack's defeat. They had no choice but to use guile and stealth as well as fang and claw. And while it wasn't what the wolf half of him wanted, the human part knew it was the best chance they had of victory.

Alan began jogging northeast toward the center of the park, where the jakkals' den was located, and Sylvia and Spencer automatically fell in behind him. The wolf in him chafed at this slow pace. It wanted to run, but he restrained the urge. He and his boys had activated a trap the last time they'd been here, and he expected there would be more scattered throughout the park. The wolf part of him might hate being cautious, but Alan knew it was necessary. He'd warned Sylvia and Spencer to be on the lookout for traps, and with any luck, between the three of them they would—

Alan had no idea how they activated the trap or which of them had done it. One moment they were jogging through the park, and the next a plastic trashcan exploded in a burst of light and noise. He caught the harsh tang of chemicals in the air an instant before he felt multiple impacts on his right side. It felt like small fires blazing in his arm, side, and leg. He cried out in pain and collapsed. He heard both Sylvia and Spencer fall as well, and he wanted to make sure they were all right, but he hurt too much to move.

At first, he wasn't certain what had happened. They must have set off a bomb—maybe one connected to a motion detector. What he didn't understand was the pain. Werewolves hurt when they were injured, of course, but the sensation faded almost at once as their healing ability kicked into gear. But *this* pain wasn't ebbing. If anything, it was increasing. And then he saw why. Scattered across the ground all around them were pieces of silver. Most of the metal had been deformed by the blast, but a few items were still more or less intact. The jakkals had packed silver jewelry and utensils into a sealed plastic container hidden inside the trashcan. Terrorists might have used nails or ball bearings to make a crude but effective bomb. It seemed the jakkals had put their own spin on the idea. *Smart,* he thought.

"Sylvia? Spencer?" he called. "Are either of you badly hurt?"

It took an effort for him to grit out the words through the pain, but he managed. For a moment, neither of them answered. The sound of the explosion had affected his hearing, and he couldn't detect their heartbeats or breathing. He feared they were mortally wounded, but then Sylvia said, "Minor wounds here. Irritating, but not fatal."

"Same," Spencer said. "My right leg got chewed up pretty good, though. I'm not going to be running marathons any time soon."

Now that they were easy targets, he expected the jakkals to come racing out of the shadows, claws and fangs bared, ready to finish off their enemies. But no one came.

They had to have heard the explosion, he thought. *They know where we're at and that we're hurt. So why—*

Because they weren't predators, he realized. They knew how to protect themselves, but when it came to killing, they were woefully inexperienced. A lucky break for Alan and his pack.

"Do your best to get the silver out," he said.

Using his claws, he dug into his wounds until he could feel the pieces of silver embedded in his flesh. He yanked them out one by one, making the wounds worse. But leaving the silver in wasn't an option. It wouldn't kill them—only a direct hit to the heart could do that—but the pain it caused was excruciating. If they didn't remove it, all they would be able to do was lie here writhing in agony. Eventually, the jakkals would realize they could kill the wounded werewolves while they were helpless, and that would be the end of Alan's pack, one that could trace its ancestry back to the Alpha himself. He would not allow such a hallowed line to end here. Not like this.

So they clawed, pried, pulled, and dislodged the silver shrapnel, burning their hands as they did so. They succeeded in removing most of the silver, but each of them was left with a few pieces that had buried themselves too deeply in the flesh to be taken out. At least not without the proper equipment to prevent blood loss.

Alan took a quick inventory of their injuries. Most were relatively minor. But as Spencer had indicated, his right leg was a mess. He could stand on it and likely walk as well, but he would do no running until it healed, and since the wounds had been caused by silver, they would repair slowly. Unless Spencer could feast on a fresh human heart to jump-start his healing powers, as his brother had done.

Sylvia's right arm had sustained the most damage, but she assured him it remained useable. As for Alan himself, his right knee had taken the worst hit from the barrage of silver. He was still fairly certain he could walk and even jump if he had to, but he didn't want to run on it until it was necessary. He wanted to avoid straining it too much in case it gave out on him in the battle to come.

The three werewolves looked at each other. It seemed the jakkals weren't going to be the easy prey that they'd imagined.

They started moving again, much more cautiously.

TWENTY-EIGHT

Dean heard what sounded like an explosion coming from deeper in the park. The three of them stopped running and listened.

"What was that?" Sam asked. "A grenade?"

"Maybe," Dean said.

They both turned to Garth.

"Don't look at me," he said, sharp teeth distorting his words. "I'm no explosives expert." Still, he cocked his head and listened. "Whatever made that noise, it wounded the sheriff and his family. I can hear them whining in pain."

"You think it was the jakkals?" Dean asked.

"Has to be," Sam said. "Who else is there?"

"Good point," Dean acknowledged. "Let's keep going. I want to get to Crowder before the jakkals finish him off." He smiled. "Can't let them have all the fun."

He started forward once more, but even as he took his first step, he knew something was wrong. He saw the tripwire—thin, barely visible, set up at the height of his shin—but not in time to avoid hitting it.

Before he could react, Garth's clawed hand grabbed his jacket and yanked him backward. He heard a series of *twangs* and three thin blurs shot through the space where he'd been standing a split second ago. He then heard the sound of metal embedding itself in wood—*thuk, thuk, thuk!*—and then the silence returned.

Garth pointed to a nearby game booth where a trio of crossbows were bolted to the counter. But instead of pointing inward toward a target, they pointed outward toward the path. The crossbows were empty. Dean looked around and saw the bolts sunk deep into the front of a food booth that, according to the faded sign above the counter, once sold "Tonions! The World's Largest Deep-Fried Onion Blossoms!"

"Want to bet those bolts were tipped with silver?" Sam said.

"Don't have to bet," Garth said. "I can smell the silver from here."

The three continued onward, but keeping a much closer watch on their surroundings. Where there was one trap—or two if you counted whatever had made the explosion they'd heard—there were bound to be more.

When Kayla heard the explosion, she jumped. She was holding Joshua, who'd been sleeping, but the sound—or more likely her sudden movement—woke him. He looked around, confused and frightened, and began to cry.

"Shush!" she said. But she spoke too loudly and instead of calming the baby, she only made him cry harder.

"Soothe the child," Muriel said.

What do you think I'm doing? Kayla thought. She would never say something so disrespectful to an Elder out loud, though, so she kept her mouth shut and tried rocking the baby back and forth. His cries turned to small whimpers. It seemed to be good enough for Muriel. She continued working, ignoring both Kayla and the baby.

They stood within the chamber of Anubis, and Muriel was making preparations. She was getting ready to conduct the Rite of Awakening, the spell that would restore Anubis to full consciousness. The preparations were primarily the same for the Rite of Renewal, but the elixir for the Awakening required a slightly different mix of ingredients, and of course different words had to be spoken. Muriel could conduct both rites smoothly, quickly, and precisely, without making even a minor mistake. She was the family's best chance to raise Anubis so the god might protect his chosen people.

Muriel would also be the one to offer herself as a vessel for Anubis. None of the family had ever done so before—not counting what had happened to Nathan earlier. This was the first time they'd ever purposely needed to rouse their god. Kayla knew serving as Anubis's vessel was supposed to be a great honor, but she was secretly glad her grandmother had volunteered. The idea of allowing the god to possess her frightened Kayla, and she was grateful she didn't have to experience this "honor."

"That sound," Kayla said. "It was the silver bomb we made, wasn't it?"

She knew she shouldn't speak lest she distract Muriel, but she couldn't help it. She had never experienced an attack like this before, and she was terrified.

Muriel didn't answer. She was adding various ingredients to the mixture bubbling in the brazier's copper bowl. The smell of spices filled the chamber with a cloying miasma that Kayla found oppressive. But the baby grew quiet and closed his eyes. Perhaps he found the stench comforting. He *was* an *iwiw* child. No surprise that foul odors would be pleasant to his kind.

Kayla resented being tasked with caring for the baby. He might be a child, but he was still *iwiw*. If it had been up to her, she would've made a small bed out of a blanket and left him on it.

Muriel spoke. "Try to keep calm, Kayla. Do not let your fear do the work of the *iwiw* for them."

Kayla didn't see how anyone could remain calm in a situation like this. Muriel, however, seemed to manage it. She finished putting ingredients in the elixir, then used the Blade of Life Everlasting to cut her palm and add her blood to the elixir. The elixir for the Awakening required twice as much jakkal blood as amaranthine, and Muriel had to cut her hand a second time when the first wound healed too soon. Then Muriel wiped the blade clean, returned it to its place on the shelves, and watched the elixir brew.

Kayla heard another noise then, much softer than the explosion. The *twang* of crossbows. The explosion came from the southeast corner of the park, but the sound of the crossbows came from the north: they were being attacked from two different directions.

"Grandmother—"

"I heard it, my child." Muriel didn't take her attention from the elixir as she spoke. "Trust your family to deal with the *iwiw*."

It wasn't her family she didn't trust. It was the werewolves, and the spy they had sent into their midst. The others might believe Morgan's story—even Erin—but Kayla didn't. She was certain Morgan would betray them when the right moment came. Why couldn't anyone else see this? How could they be so blind? And Greg was the blindest of them all. He was so besotted with the *iwiw* girl that Kayla wondered if he would turn on his family if Morgan asked him to. She didn't think he would. Greg could be stupid, but he loved his family as much as they loved him. But his feelings for Morgan—actually, make that his animal attraction to her—might cause him to hesitate at a crucial moment and get him killed. Maybe get them *all* killed. Anubis too, who would be unable to protect himself unless he was Awakened.

"I think we should wake Anubis now, Grandmother. We need his strength—before it's too late."

Muriel glanced at her granddaughter. "Our god expects his children to fend for themselves. It is one of the reasons he sleeps. He wants us to make our own way in the world as much as possible. He wishes us to be strong and independent. We call upon him when necessary, but only in the direst of circumstances. I admit that we are close to this point, but we are not yet there."

"The fighting has begun, Grandmother. You know that as well as I. What more do you want before you act? For one of our family to die at the claws of an *iwiw*?"

Anger twisted Muriel's features. They became even more distorted as she assumed jakkal form. Her clawed hands twitched, and for a moment Kayla thought Muriel might strike her. Muriel restrained herself though, and Kayla thought it was only because she held the baby.

Muriel became human once more.

"I will do what I believe is right, and I will do it *when* I believe the time is right. This is my last word on the subject. Question me no further."

Muriel returned her attention to the bubbling elixir. It had been an unappetizing brown color, but now it was edging toward red. A good sign.

Kayla gritted her teeth. It seemed that Greg wasn't the only willfully blind member of their pack. Kayla despaired of ever getting Muriel to see the truth, and she was desperately trying to think of an argument that might win her over when the shooting began.

TWENTY-NINE

Garth stopped running and motioned for Sam and Dean to wait. They stood between a carousel and a Ferris wheel, both in severe states of disrepair. He frowned, nose wrinkling.

"Another trap?" Sam asked.

Garth shook his head. "Something smells weird. I'm not sure what it is." He sniffed the air once more. "It's a mix of some kind of chemicals, but I can't identify them."

"Is it another bomb?" Dean asked.

Garth shrugged. "Could be, I suppose. But there's another smell blended in, kind of like spoiled meat." He whipped his head around, frowned, and said, "We got company."

Sam heard the sound of bare feet slapping on asphalt before he saw the two figures come running toward them from the direction of the Ferris wheel. At first he thought they were jakkals, but they didn't possess bestial features. They looked like human males, and while they moved rapidly, they did so with stiff, almost mechanical motions. Their eyes glowed with crimson light, and their faces were completely without expression. Sam judged both men were in their mid to late twenties. One was stocky, broad-shouldered, bearded, and covered with black body hair so thick he almost looked like a Hollywood version of a werewolf. The other man was tall and thin, with numerous tattoos and a scraggly brown goatee which matched his unruly hair. One more thing: they were both naked.

"Aw, man!" Dean said. "I do *not* need to see those things come flopping toward me."

Sam knew exactly how his brother felt. They'd never had to fight killer nudists before.

Neither brother bothered telling the naked men to stop or they'd shoot. Despite the creatures' stiff, jerky movements, they moved *fast*. Instead, Sam and Dean raised their guns and fired in unison.

The rounds struck the men in their chests, and the impact caused them to stagger back a couple of feet. Neither of them went down, nor did they cry out in pain when they were hit. Their expressions didn't change in the slightest. No blood came from the wounds, just small trickles of clear fluid.

"Oh," Dean said. "They're zombies."

That sounded to Sam as likely a theory as any other, and the brothers raised their guns a bit higher, aimed, and fired once more.

The zombies—if that's what they were—started forward once more. The bullets slammed into their foreheads and they went down.

Dean grinned. "Headshots take down zombies every time. I love it when the movies get something right for once."

Sam wasn't so sure it was that simple. What would zombies be doing here? They already had werewolves and jakkals to deal with. What was this, some kind of monster convention?

Sam stepped toward the bodies to get a closer look, making sure to keep his gun trained on them as he approached. Just because they looked dead—or dead again—didn't mean they were. The stocky one had rolled onto his side when he fell, but the thin man had landed on his stomach. Sam leaned in to get a better look at them while keeping out of grabbing range. Both men's arms were splayed out in front of them, and Sam could see what looked like bite marks on the underside of their right wrists. He frowned, trying to recall if he'd ever come across any lore describing undead beings with wounds on their wrists, but he came up empty. Whatever these things were, they were new to him.

And that's when the zombies pushed themselves off the ground and stood up, so fast that Sam was barely able to register it. One moment they were lying on the asphalt, then he blinked, and they were standing upright.

Sam raised his gun to fire again but thought better of it. He and Dean had already wasted a pair of silver bullets apiece trying to put down these zombies, or whatever the hell they were. No use throwing away any more ammo.

Dean rushed forward and as the zombies attacked, he swept his Colt through the air and struck the hairy man across the jaw with his weapon. He rammed the gold blade into the zombie's chest. He gave the blade a vicious twist as he pulled it free, releasing a gush of clear fluid that filled the air with an acrid smell.

Instead of going for the chest, Sam thrust the gold blade into one of the skinny zombie's crimson eyes and pushed it deep into the creature's brain. Sam hoped a more severe brain injury than a single bullet wound would take the thing out.

Both zombies shuddered as if their central nervous systems were short-circuiting, and then as before, they collapsed to their knees and fell forward. Sam and Dean quickly stepped back as they hit the asphalt face first. Still holding their weapons, the brothers stood looking down at the unmoving corpses.

"Twenty bucks says mine stays down and yours doesn't," Dean said.

"You're on," Sam said.

Several seconds passed, and then as before, both zombies swiftly rose to their feet.

"Crap," Dean muttered.

Before either brother could react, the zombies attacked. The hairy zombie slammed his arm into Dean's shoulder. The impact was so powerful that it knocked Dean off his feet and sent him sprawling. The thin zombie grabbed Sam beneath the arms and then threw him into the air. Sam collided with one of the carousel horses. The breath left him as he bounced off the horse and landed on the floor. He managed to keep his grip on both of his weapons—this wasn't the first time he'd gotten thrown through the air by a monster—but he was too stunned to get up right away.

He saw Dean lying motionless. He refused to entertain the thought that his brother might be dead. After everything they'd been through over the years, it seemed impossible that a single blow from a hairy naked zombie could take him out.

It walked toward Dean, obviously intending to finish the job. The skinny zombie was coming toward Sam, but he barely registered it. All his attention was focused on Dean and the creature that planned to kill him. Sam tried to shout *No!* but all that came out of his mouth was a wheeze.

Sam had almost forgotten about Garth. Their friend had hung back while the zombies attacked. But now Garth fell into a crouch and growled deep in his throat. Fury blazed in his feral eyes as he bared his teeth, raised his claws, and leaped toward the hairy zombie.

Sam knew their friend was a werewolf, but the reality of this didn't hit him until he saw Garth tear into the zombie. He moved so swiftly that he became a blur, his teeth and claws gouging out chunks of meat.

Sam sat up, but he made no move to help. He was too amazed to do anything more than sit and watch Garth destroy the zombie. Dean had started to come around by now. But even though he was closer to Garth, he didn't go to his aid either. Garth didn't need assistance.

Sam noticed that his zombie—the thin one—had stopped moving. He'd got within five feet of the carousel before freezing in place. Sam wasn't sure what had happened to it, and he didn't really care. Right now, he was too worried about Garth. Garth had torn off both of the zombie's arms, but instead of breaking off his attack, he continued taking the creature apart.

Garth rammed a hand into the zombie's abdomen, and a second later there was a loud *crack*. Garth had found the creature's spine and squeezed. Its spine broken, the hairy zombie fell backward, and hit the ground.

But even though the zombie was down for the count, still Garth didn't stop. He tore at what remained of the zombie's body, clawing at it furiously, almost as if there was something buried deep inside the zombie that he intended to get at.

The skinny zombie remained frozen, but Sam didn't care about him anymore. His only concern was for Garth. He hurried over to where Garth continued to ravage the zombie's corpse. Dean joined him and together they watched their friend—who was now covered in the awful-smelling clear liquid that had been inside the zombie's veins instead of blood—pull the zombie's heart from its ruin of a chest.

"That's not good," Dean said.

Garth drooled as he brought the heart toward his mouth, but then he stopped. His nostrils flared as he smelled the heart, and then with a snarl of disgust, he hurled the organ away.

"It's not a living heart," Sam said.

Then, as if the zombie's mutilated body could withstand no more, it fell away to a yellowish sand-like substance, and Sam knew that whatever kind of creature the thing had been, it was truly dead now.

Garth looked at the small piles of sand for a moment, and then he turned to face Sam and Dean. There was no sign of recognition in their friend's eyes. No sign that anything human remained inside him. His lips drew back from his teeth, and he began to growl, soft, low, and dangerous.

Sam and Dean still held their weapons—the gold blades, which were useless against a werewolf, and their guns, which were loaded with silver bullets. Garth was only a few feet away, and with his speed, he could be on them and tearing out their hearts in an instant. Sam knew they should fire. Garth was their friend, yes, but he was also a werewolf. He'd tried to keep his bestial side in check, but the Crowders had tried to force him to eat a piece of human heart. Melody's heart. Garth hadn't actually tasted it, but it seemed just smelling the meat—maybe combined with all the fighting—had caused him to turn all the way into a mindless, snarling savage. The man named Garth Fitzgerald IV was gone, and there was nothing left behind except an insane animal that needed killing.

But Sam didn't pull the trigger, and neither did Dean.

"Easy, buddy," Sam said in the calmest voice he could manage. "You know us."

Garth made no move to attack, but his growling grew louder.

"You're Garth Fitzgerald the Fourth," Sam continued. "Your wife's name is Bess. You live in Wisconsin with your pack. Your *peaceful* pack."

Garth stopped growling and rose to his feet.

Sam caught Dean's eye, and they exchanged a silent message. Sam slowly knelt and placed his weapon on the ground, and after a moment's hesitation, Dean did the same. When the brothers had straightened once more, Sam said, "See? We don't want to hurt you. We're friends."

Garth continued growling. He raised his claws and stepped forward, saliva dripping from his mouth.

Sam decided to try a Hail Mary.

"The way to inner peace is not always the straightest path," he said.

Garth stopped advancing and looked into Sam's eyes. From the expression on his face, Dean thought Sam had gone crazy.

Maybe I have, Sam thought, but he pressed on.

"Man and wolf must be in balance, like, uh…" Sam wracked his brain for an appropriate example. He went with the first thing that came to him. "A good salad. The ingredients must be perfectly balanced. Fresh, crisp lettuce. Cherry tomatoes, broccoli, cauliflower, carrots. Cheese, but not too much. Slices of hardboiled egg. And balsamic vinaigrette dressing, but you have to be careful not to use too much or you'll end up drowning your salad. And when you take that first perfect bite, you chew slowly, savoring the way all the ingredients work together in absolute harmony."

Garth had stopped growling halfway through Sam's speech. Now he lowered his hands, and his mouth, which had been twisted into a snarl, stretched into a smile.

"Now *that* was a good fangism!"

A wave of relief washed over Sam. "Good to have you back."

Dean clapped a hand on Garth's shoulder, and then he turned and looked at Sam. "Salad? Was that really the best you could come up with?"

"Hey, it worked," Sam said.

"Excuse me, but are you the gentlemen Morgan told us about?"

They turned in the direction of the newcomer's voice. An old man was standing in the middle of the path. He was flanked by the thin zombie and another zombie that they hadn't seen before, a middle-aged woman. Sam figured the man had been holding the other one in reserve, waiting to see how the first two did against them before sending her in. Smart strategy. Why risk losing all your weapons at once?

Garth inhaled, taking in the man's scent. "You're a jakkal," he said.

"Yes, I am. My name is Nathan, and I am an Elder in my pack. I was stationed here to protect my family from attack by the sheriff and his werewolf pack. His daughter Morgan told me that you three were good men, but she is still a child, and I couldn't be sure she was telling the truth. My apologies."

"What changed your mind?" Dean asked.

The old man nodded to Garth.

"When your friend turned wild you had the opportunity to kill him, but you chose to risk your own lives to bring him back to his senses. I'm not quite sure how you did it." He looked at Sam. "A salad recipe? But obviously the technique was successful."

Sam and Dean bent down to retrieve their weapons. Even though it appeared the old man wasn't going to sic his pet zombies on them again, Sam felt better once he was armed.

"I see you know something of my people," Nathan said. "You carry gold blades."

"Just in case your people turned out to be less than welcoming," Dean said.

"A wise precaution," Nathan said.

"I take it you control these…" Sam nodded toward the zombies.

"We call them *neteru*. It means guardians. And yes, they do my bidding. These two, at least, and the one you destroyed. I created them to help us against the werewolves. But it appears that they've chosen to enter the park from a different direction."

As if in response to Nathan's words, howling came from off

in the distance. They listened, but the werewolves made no further sound. Had it been a warning howl? An announcement of the werewolves' presence? Sam didn't know.

"That explosion we heard," Dean said, "and those crossbows…"

"Traps we set for our defense. We have more elsewhere in the park, along with more *neteru*. With any luck—"

Before Nathan could finish, a loud crashing sound filled the air.

"Another trap?" Garth asked.

"I fear not." Nathan's face was ashen. His features shifted until he became something that resembled a werewolf, except his ears were pointed and tufts of sandy-colored hair sprouted on his cheeks. He spun around and, moving incredibly fast, he ran in the direction the sound had come from. The two surviving *neteru* followed.

Sam, Dean, and Garth exchanged looks, and they started running too.

When Morgan saw her father, mother, and brother approach the area where she and Greg—along with his two *neteru*—were concealed, she experienced clashing emotions. She feared they would attack her the moment they saw her, but she was also glad to see they had survived the silver bomb the jakkals had planted, although from their wounds and the slow, painful way they walked, she knew they hadn't escaped entirely unscathed. But their injuries hadn't stopped them from continuing on, which meant there was more bloodshed to come. She wasn't surprised. Once her family had killing on their minds, they wouldn't stop until their prey lay dead at their feet.

Stuart's absence concerned her. Had he died in the explosion? Or had he taken a separate route from the rest of the family and was planning to come at the jakkals from a different direction? No. Her father would've wanted to assert his dominance over the remainder of his pack. He would've insisted they all attack the jakkals together. So Stuart was either gravely wounded or dead. The thought saddened her, but not as much as she expected it to. She'd never really felt close to her brothers. She did not share her brothers' love of the Hunt, nor did she have their cruel streak. She had so little in common with them that in many ways they'd been strangers throughout her entire life.

She expected her family to pick up her and Greg's scents as they drew near, but they didn't even seem to notice the reek of formaldehyde coming from Greg's *neteru*. *It's the silver,* she thought. Even if they'd managed to get every piece out of their bodies, the contact with the deadly metal would've dulled both their reflexes and senses. They were vulnerable.

Greg put his hand on her shoulder and gave it a light squeeze. He was asking if she was ready. She didn't think she would ever be fully prepared, but she nodded anyway.

Greg closed his eyes, brow furrowing as he concentrated. He could command the inhumanly strong *neteru* he'd created with his mind, and the two reanimated corpses—one male, one female—left their hiding places and ran toward Morgan's family, eyes blazing with crimson light.

Alan, Sylvia, and Spencer were caught off guard. They

barely managed to turn and look at the undead creatures before the *neteru* began swinging their weapons—lengths of sharpened steel rebar that Greg had salvaged from the park. They struck the werewolves with the steel rods, going for their heads first, then plunging the sharp ends into chests and necks. The werewolves howled in pain. The sound of her family's agony tore at her heart. She turned to Greg, intending to ask him to stop, but his eyes were still closed.

I wonder what father would think if he knew you were coordinating the attack? she thought. *Would he be surprised that a "carrion-eater" could fight so well?*

The werewolves fought back, biting and clawing, but they moved slowly and none of them caused any significant damage. Their wounds were healing more slowly than they should have, thanks to the silver shrapnel. Steel couldn't kill the werewolves, but while they couldn't heal it could do serious damage. Once they were down, the jakkals would restrain them and kill them later. The battle had barely begun, and already the jakkals were on the verge of winning.

Morgan was torn. She'd didn't want any harm to come to Greg and his family. But while she wished to leave her pack—and take Joshua with her—she took no pleasure from seeing her own father, mother, and brother get hurt like this. They were still her family.

She ran out from behind the ice-cream cart. She hurried to her father, covered with blood from the *neteru*'s assault, and pulled him away from the fighting. The female *neteru*—a woman in her thirties with long blond hair—regarded them for a moment. Morgan wondered if Greg was seeing her through the dead woman's eyes. She didn't know. The woman turned to Sylvia, who was trying to pull the male *neteru*—an overweight man in his twenties—off Spencer. The female *neteru* moved in to attack her.

"Dad!" Morgan cried.

Alan Crowder was still in werewolf form, but his face was swollen and his left eye had been destroyed. It was already growing back, and the swelling on his face was subsiding, but she doubted he would return to his full strength any time soon.

He focused his good eye on her, but he showed no sign of recognition. His skull had a large dent in the right side, and she feared he'd sustained brain damage. But then the haziness in his eye cleared.

"Morgan?" he said.

He slumped, and Morgan caught him beneath the arms. "Yes, Dad. It's me. Please stop this fight. The jakkals only want to be left in peace. Bridge Valley may be a small town, but it's big enough for two packs to co-exist. Give the command for Mom and Spencer to stand down, and the jakkals will stop fighting. I swear it!"

Alan didn't respond at first. *Maybe he really did have brain damage,* she thought. But then he made a snuffling sound, and it took her a moment to realize he was laughing.

"Werewolves don't surrender. We fight until we win or we die. You know this. Or you would, if you were *really* one of us instead of a traitor."

Alan moved faster than she thought him capable of. He grabbed hold of her and drew her close to his chest. He put a hand around her neck, his claws pricking her flesh.

"Make the zombies stop, or I'll tear her throat out!" Alan called. "She'll bleed to death."

Wounds that werewolves inflicted on each other took longer to heal—almost as long as those caused by silver. Morgan had no doubt her father would do as he said. She had turned her back on her people and thrown in her lot with their enemies. As far as Alan was concerned, she was no longer his daughter.

She looked toward the ice-cream cart.

"Don't listen to my dad!" she shouted to Greg. "Keep fighting!"

Alan increased the pressure of his grip, claws digging deeper into her neck until she could not speak, could not even cry out in pain.

The *neteru* suddenly froze, as if they were machines whose power had been abruptly disconnected. The male was crouched over Spencer, arm raised to bring his blood-smeared rebar rod down. The female had her hands around Sylvia's throat. The *neteru* was still now, and Sylvia pulled its hands away from her throat without resistance. Then she helped Spencer rise to his feet. Mother and son joined their leader and waited.

Greg rose and stepped from behind the ice-cream cart, hands up. "Don't hurt her," he said.

Morgan could tell from the tone of her father's voice that he was grinning. "Maybe I will, maybe I won't," Alan said. "But one thing's for sure. We're going to hurt *you*."

Sylvia and Spencer growled and started toward Greg. Greg continued to stand where he was, still in human form, eyes fixed on Morgan. He smiled, as if to tell her that regardless of whatever happened next, it would be all right.

Morgan shifted into werewolf form and fought to free herself from her father's grip. To hell with what he might do to her. She couldn't let Greg sacrifice himself for her. But Alan was too strong, and she couldn't break loose. All she could do was watch as Sylvia and Spencer closed on Greg.

Then a loud sound—almost like an explosion, but not quite—came from somewhere near the center of the park. *No,* Morgan thought. *From the jakkals' home.*

Sylvia and Spencer paused and looked back at Alan.

"What the hell was that?" he asked.

Thirty

Kayla shifted Joshua to her left arm and grabbed hold of Muriel's shoulder with her free hand. "You heard that, didn't you? The shooting? It had to be the hunters Morgan told us about!"

"I assume so," Muriel said.

Her calm tone was maddening. Didn't the old woman understand what was happening?

"They won't just kill the werewolves! They'll kill *all* of us! As far as they're concerned, we're all monsters. You have to wake Anubis—now, before we're all dead!"

Muriel's amber eyes flashed with fury. "I shall disturb our god's sleep only as a last resort, and I will be the judge of when that moment comes—not you, child!"

Kayla couldn't believe what she was hearing. She'd thought her family was done with running away, that this was the night they'd chosen to stand and fight. Now here was one of the Elders refusing to act even now, when their loved ones might be dying. Now was not the time to hold back.

Kayla's right hand became a claw, and she struck her grandmother across the face. Blood sprayed through the air as the left side of Muriel's face became strips of shredded meat. The impact of the blow sent Muriel sprawling. Her head hit the wall with a sickening *thunk* before she slipped to the floor, motionless.

Kayla was horrified. She'd never struck another member of her family, let alone an Elder. But she'd done what was necessary. Her parents, sister, and brother were out there, fighting werewolves. They needed all the help they could get.

Muriel moaned in pain, but she didn't rise. Her grandmother would heal quickly, but Kayla hoped she would stay down long enough for her to wake Anubis. Kayla hurried to a far corner of the room and put Joshua down gently. "Lie still. This won't take long," she whispered.

She hurried back to the elixir. It was still bubbling, but she saw several dark splotches on the surface of the liquid. Some of Muriel's blood had fallen into the bowl. She felt a stab of fear. The elixir had to be prepared with exact ingredients in precise proportions, in the proper order, or it would not work. Blood was part of the formula, yes, but was there now too much? Was this batch of Awakening elixir spoiled?

She heard howling. She thought of her family falling before the claws and fangs of the werewolves, their blood splashing onto the asphalt.

"Screw it," she said. She was still afraid to become Anubis's vessel, but she was more afraid of what the *iwiw* might do to her family.

She picked up the bowl, ignoring the hot metal burning

her fingers, and hurried to Anubis's side. Holding the edge of the bowl to the small space between the bandages around his mouth, she began to pour. As she did, she spoke the words of the rite as quickly as she could, rushing through the ancient Egyptian phrases.

"*Great Anubis, son of Nephthys and Set, Lord of the Sacred Land, Protector of the Dead, Guardian of Eternal Shadow. As we serve you, we now beg you to serve us. Rise from the never-ending darkness in which you dwell. Cast off the shackles of sleep, open your eyes, rejoin the land of the living, and let the world once more know your dread might.*"

She wasn't sure she got all the words right, but they were close enough. Some of the elixir spilled, soaking the bandages around Anubis's mouth, but she got most of it into him. She prayed it would be enough. She felt energy gathering in the room, the air crackling with power, like the atmosphere just before a huge thunderstorm broke.

Anubis drew in a deep breath and she could hear his heart begin to pound.

"Child, what have you done?"

Kayla opened her eyes and saw Muriel rise to her feet. She was unsteady, but her face was already healing, and she remained upright.

She shot Kayla a reproachful look before stepping to the table and addressing Anubis in ancient Egyptian. "*Mighty Anubis, I beg your forgiveness. In her fear, my granddaughter rushed the Rite of Awakening. Great Dark One, return to your slumber. All is—*"

Muriel's body went rigid, her features slack. She shifted

into jakkal form, and her eyes burned with crimson light. Anubis had possessed her.

Kayla stood face to face with her god, and in her shock, she dropped the bowl that had contained the elixir. It clanged as it hit the floor and the noise started Joshua crying. She barely noticed. She couldn't take her gaze off Muriel. She could feel the power emanating from her grandmother's body, and it was all she could do not to whimper in fear. She went to her knees and bowed low, forehead touching the floor, hands stretched out before her.

Despite her fear, she did her best to speak clearly and distinctly in Egyptian. "*My lord, thank you for answering our call. Your children have need of your strength and wisdom.*"

She waited for Anubis to respond in her grandmother's voice, but she said nothing. After a moment, Kayla cautiously lifted her head and looked up at Muriel. Her grandmother gazed down at her with crimson eyes, but her face remained devoid of expression. She sensed that something wasn't right, but she didn't know what it could be. She knew she'd made some mistakes while conducting the Rite of Awakening, but it had worked, hadn't it? Anubis had possessed Muriel instead of her, but he *had* awakened. He was here and ready to help. Maybe he was simply waiting to hear what needed to be done.

She rose up on her knees to address her god.

"*Our family is under attack by a pack of* iwiw. *You must kill them—kill them all!*"

Muriel continued looking at her without expression, and Kayla began to worry that something was wrong with Anubis's mind. Was the connection between his spirit and Muriel's body somehow faulty? But then Muriel smiled, revealing her sharp jakkal teeth, and she nodded once to show that she understood Kayla's words. Kayla felt a wave of great relief. Her family would be safe now. Anubis would see to it.

Muriel placed her right hand on top of Kayla's head as if bestowing a blessing upon her. At first Kayla smiled, and she placed her hands atop her grandmother's. Then Muriel's red eyes glowed and Kayla began to age rapidly.

Kayla realized then what she had done. *I said* Kill them all. *All—including me.*

Kayla's skin became dry as parchment, rough as lizard hide, and she lost weight, her body thinning until she was little more than a skeleton. Her clothing aged too, colors fading, edges fraying. She tried to scream, but all that came out of her mouth was a blast of dust. No, not dust, Kayla realized. *Sand.* And with that last thought, Kayla collapsed in upon herself, leaving nothing but a mound of sand.

Through Muriel's eyes, Anubis looked on the pile of sand that had been his vessel's granddaughter. He felt no sorrow over the girl's death. Her instructions had been clear: *Kill them all.* Anubis intended to do just that. He began to turn toward the chamber's door when he heard a baby crying. He stopped and turned in the direction of the sound. The child—an *iwiw* child, from its scent—lay on the floor in a corner of the room, face red, tiny hands balled into fists as it cried. Anubis could smell the child's frustration and fear. More than that, he could feel the life blazing strong and bright inside the child's small form.

Kill them all.

He took a step toward the child, then hesitated. The girl had said something else, hadn't she? He tried to remember, but it was difficult. His thoughts were chaotic, circling around in his head like a swarm of buzzing insects. She had said something about her family being under attack, hadn't she? By… *iwiw*. Yes, that was it. His children needed him, and the baby—while *iwiw*—was not the biggest threat. He would return for it later, when the others had been dealt with.

Kill them all.

Anubis turned and walked toward the wall. He raised fists now imbued with the strength of a god and smashed through as easily as if the wall was made of tissue paper. Plaster, wood, and brick burst outward and he stepped through the hole he had created into the night. He scented the air, and then he began running toward the southeast section of the park, where Greg and Morgan were stationed.

Dean, Sam, Garth, Nathan, and the two remaining zombies ran through the park. They were joined by three other jakkals—a man, and two women: one older, one younger. Members of Nathan's pack, of course. Nathan quickly introduced them, and the jakkals accepted their presence without question. Dean guessed that if Nathan—a pack Elder—ran with them, it was the same as vouching for them. Or maybe the other jakkals were too worried about the werewolves to care about the hunters.

Nathan slowed as they approached a round building with white brick walls and a black roof. A faded sign above the entrance said PARK ADMINISTRATION. He opened the door and hurried inside, the zombies and jakkals following close behind.

Dean turned to Sam as they entered the building. "Remind me not to run behind a pair of naked zombies again," he said. "Too much jiggling."

Everyone followed Nathan into a room containing a long table, shelves stocked with stone jars, a burning brazier, and a very large hole in the wall. Lying on the table was an honest-to-Chuck mummy, eight feet tall, with pointed ears and a pronounced snout. *A dog-mummy,* Dean thought. *Now there's something you don't see every day.*

Garth nodded towards the hole. "Now we know where the sound came from," he said.

"Anyone want to tell us what busted through this wall?" Dean asked. He pointed at the mummy. "We know it wasn't this guy. Unless he decided to take a nap when he was finished."

Dean's words cut through the jakkals' grief. Nathan turned to look at him.

"For untold generations it has been my pack's duty and privilege to guard our god, the great Anubis." He gestured toward the mummy. "To keep him slumbering when times are good, and to call upon his strength when times are bad."

"Like when a pack of less-than-neighborly werewolves decides to pay a visit," Dean said.

Nathan nodded. "My wife Muriel has become Anubis's vessel, and he has gone forth to do battle with the *iwiw*. I assume my granddaughter Kayla accompanied her, but I don't know why she left Morgan's brother behind. Perhaps to keep him away from the fighting."

Marta went over to pick up Joshua, but then she inhaled deeply and frowned.

"Something's wrong," she said.

The other jakkals began scenting the air, as did Garth. The other granddaughter, Erin, was the first to speak.

"Kayla," she said. She pointed to a pile of what looked like sand lying on the floor.

"No," Marta said, looking at the sand with a horrified expression. Her husband Efren went to her and put an arm around her shoulder, just as upset as she was.

"I don't understand," Dean said.

Garth nodded to the pile of sand. "That's what's left of Nathan's other granddaughter."

Dean and Sam regarded the sand, and Dean realized what had happened.

"Anubis did that to her," he said.

"Yes," Nathan said, his voice filled with sorrow.

"I thought Anubis was supposed to protect you," Sam said.

"He is," Nathan said. "I don't understand what happened. Perhaps something went wrong with the Rite of Awakening, and Anubis isn't thinking clearly."

Dean turned to Sam. "This case started out simple, but now we have to stop an ancient Egyptian god who isn't picky about who he kills." He looked at Nathan. "Does Anubis have any specific weaknesses? A special way to kill him?"

The jakkals, although all in human form, started growling.

"Anubis may have killed my child, but he is still my god," Marta said. "He is eternal and cannot be killed."

That's what they all say, Dean thought. He looked at Sam. "You know any lore about Anubis?"

"Not much. I'll see what I can find online."

Sam took out his phone and began typing. He scanned the results of his Internet search for a few minutes. When he was finished, he looked up. "I didn't find anything useful. I posted on a few mythology message boards asking about any weaknesses Anubis might have, and I set up automatic alerts if I get any replies." Sam slipped his phone back in his pocket. "Until then, we'll just have to improvise."

"What else is new?" Dean said. "Let's saddle up. Looks like we're going god hunting."

"Your favorite sport," Sam said.

Dean made a sour face. He *hated* fighting gods. As far as he was concerned, they were nothing but another kind of monster, only with delusions of grandeur. They pretended to be something they weren't so they could take advantage of their worshippers. They were the con artists of the supernatural world.

Dean and Sam ran toward the damaged wall and jumped through the hole. Garth was right on their heels, and the three friends started running southeast.

A moment later, the jakkals followed.

Greg feared what the loud crash might mean, but he couldn't afford to worry about that now. Morgan's mother and brother had stopped advancing when they heard the sound, and he needed to strike while they were distracted. He ran forward, slashed Sylvia's shoulder, then lunged toward Spencer and bit into his bicep.

Alan's grip on Morgan's throat had slackened. Not a lot, but enough. Morgan slammed her head back into his face. Alan's nose broke with a crunch and she pulled herself free. She landed on all fours and sprinted toward Greg. She had several dots of blood on her neck from her father's claws, but the wounds were minor.

When Morgan reached him, Greg sent a mental command to the motionless *neteru*, ordering them to attack the werewolves. They didn't respond. His grandfather had said he needed to be able to clear his mind to control the ambulatory corpses, and his mind was anything but clear right now. He was too afraid for Morgan's safety. He wanted to grab her hand and lead her away from here as fast as he could. Once they'd put some distance between them and the werewolves, they could join with the other members of his family, and then they could all bring the fight to the werewolves.

But the werewolves were too fast. They blocked off Greg and Morgan's escape in a triangle formation. Greg and Morgan weren't exactly surrounded, but he knew that if they tried to escape, one of the werewolves would get their claws on them, and then the others would join in on the fun. They were trapped.

He turned to Morgan to tell her he was sorry. But before he could speak, she looked past him, eyes widening in confusion and fear.

Greg turned to see his grandmother coming toward them. She was in her jakkal form, but something was wrong with her. Her eyes blazed like twin fires, and her features were twisted into a mask of savagery.

"Grandmother?" he said.

Muriel smiled, displaying sharp teeth, and slowly shook her head. Greg then understood what had happened.

Anubis had risen.

THIRTY-ONE

When Sam, Dean, Garth, and the jakkals saw the werewolves confronting the ancient god, it was Dean who spoke first.

"So Anubis's vessel is a grandmother. Like that's not weird."

Sam couldn't argue with his brother. They knew that the outward appearance of a vessel didn't reflect the nature of the entity inside, but this small, older woman didn't look anything like an Egyptian deity—even if she did have fangs and claws. But Sam could feel power emanating from the woman, rolling off her in pulsing waves.

Crowder, Sylvia, and Spencer surrounded Anubis, snarling and snapping their teeth at the god, but keeping out of his—her?—reach. Morgan and a teenage boy Sam assumed was Greg stood back, watching, as if unsure what to do. Two other *neteru* stood close by, unmoving. Sam assumed they were under Greg's control, but the boy was too preoccupied to command the corpses.

Anubis lunged and swiped at the werewolves, but they managed to avoid being struck by her claws. They were wounded, but fast as they were, their injuries still slowed them down. So when Spencer leaped away from one of Anubis's strikes, he was a split second too slow. The god's claws sank into his right shoulder and Spencer howled in pain. Anubis lifted him into the air with ease. Spencer—stuck on the god's claws like a worm on a fishhook—grabbed Anubis's wrist and tried to free himself, but his efforts were useless.

Alan ran forward to attack Anubis. But the god swung his other arm in a vicious backhand swipe and struck Alan so hard that bones cracked like shotgun blasts. The sheriff flew through the air. Sylvia jumped toward her husband, trying to catch him, but Alan was flying too fast. He hit her, and they both fell to the asphalt.

Now that Anubis had dealt with those annoyances, he turned his crimson gaze back to Spencer. He dug his claws deeper into Spencer's shoulder, and the werewolf screamed. Blood poured from Spencer's flesh like a waterfall.

Greg—who was holding Morgan's hand, Sam noted—seemed to see the rest of them for the first time. "Anubis has possessed Grandmother!" he shouted. "We have to help her!"

The other jakkals didn't respond. Instead they stared at Anubis in awe. Sam wouldn't have been surprised if they fell to their knees and started praying. But even if they weren't overwhelmed by Anubis's presence, the jakkals had no reason to interfere. After all, he was still dealing with their enemies, wasn't he?

Spencer screamed in pain. The crimson light in Anubis's eyes blazed brighter, and Spencer began to rapidly age. He began to fall apart, flesh and blood transforming into sand, which drifted to the ground until nothing of the werewolf remained.

Sam looked at Dean. "Anubis is a bigger threat than the Crowders."

Dean scowled. "Yeah, I know. Too bad we can't just hang back and let them kill each other."

Dean, Sam, and Garth drew their guns and fired at Anubis. The god staggered as the silver rounds slammed into Muriel's body, but he didn't go down. A second later, his wounds healed, and he trained his crimson-eyed gaze on the Winchesters.

"Well, we know silver bullets don't work on him," Dean said.

Alan and Sylvia stared at Spencer's remains in horror. Sylvia let out a mournful cry that was half human voice and half wolf howl. She rose to her feet, eyes filled with hate. But as she ran toward Anubis, the god's eyes blazed bright again. The eyes of Greg's *neteru* glowed crimson and hurled their rebar spikes at Sylvia. All four of the makeshift weapons slammed into her. She fell to the ground, screaming in agony. Alan ran to her side and began pulling out the spikes, and she cried out even louder.

"Anubis possessed those *neteru*," Sam said.

"Not just them," Dean said.

The two corpses attacked the closest people: Efren and Erin. The *neteru* grabbed each of them by the throat and began to squeeze.

Greg's *neteru* were heading towards him and Morgan. The teens picked up the ice-cream cart and hurled it at the *neteru* coming for them. It struck the two possessed corpses and exploded in a shower of splintered wooden fragments. Sam heard bones break and both *neteru* went down. The crimson light faded from their eyes, and they collapsed into piles of sand.

Marta placed Joshua on the ground, and then she and

Nathan attacked the two remaining *neteru*, clawing their hands and forearms down to the bone. Their tendons destroyed, the zombies could no longer maintain their hold on Erin and Efren. Sam and Dean brought the zombies down with gunshots to the head, and Garth raced forward and tore the corpses apart. As they died, they too collapsed into piles of sand.

Anubis roared. Alan had finished removing the rebar spikes from Sylvia and helped her stand. The god strode toward them, eager for more destruction.

Anubis tried to grab Alan and Sylvia. They dodged, rolled and came up on their feet. Sylvia was unsteady on hers, but she remained standing.

Alan and Sylvia stiffened then, and their yellow werewolf eyes became a fiery crimson.

Morgan stood next to Greg, watching her parents. She shook her head and cried, "No! Please, don't!"

But her parents' minds were no longer their own. They snarled and came running toward Sam and Dean, their injuries forgotten.

It seemed that Anubis's ability to control others wasn't limited to *neteru*. Sam knew the Crowders weren't attacking of their own volition. But he also knew they were responsible for the deaths of Clay Fuller, Amos Boyd, Melody Diaz, and many more people whose names he would never know. So when he and Dean shot them both through the heart with silver bullets, his conscience was clear.

The werewolves fell to the ground. They returned to human form, all light, crimson or otherwise, gone from their eyes.

Morgan let out a sob. Greg wrapped his arms around her as she cried.

Dean turned to Nathan. "You got any spells up your sleeve for sending Anubis back to beddy-bye?"

"No," the old jakkal said. "When the Rite of Awakening is performed properly, it has a time limit of six hours. After that, Anubis departs his vessel and returns to his slumber on his own. But now…" He shrugged.

"So he might conk out in a few hours, or he might keep chugging along for years," Dean said.

"Or centuries," Sam added.

"Fantastic," Dean said.

"Something has gone wrong with the transference of Anubis's spirit," Nathan said. "Our god isn't in his right mind. He seems confused, animalistic…"

"You mean there's a bad connection between the dog-mummy's brain and your wife's?" Dean said.

"Yes," Nathan confirmed. "It's as if Anubis is only partially awake, as if he's in a dream state and lashing out at everyone—not just the *iwiw*—as if they're enemies. If the connection between Anubis and Muriel is shaky, then there's a chance I can break it. If I can get through to her."

Nathan started walking toward Anubis.

"Grandfather, don't!" Greg shouted.

Nathan didn't take his gaze off Anubis as he approached the god.

"It's all right, Greg. I know what I'm doing."

Dean doubted that, but all he could do, all any of them could, was watch and hope.

Nathan reassumed human form as he drew near Anubis, and he held his hands out to his sides, palms outward in a universal gesture that said *I mean you no harm.*

"Muriel? It's me. Nathan."

She looked at him without recognition and began to growl softly.

Not a good start, Dean thought.

Nathan stopped when he was within six feet of his wife.

"You performed the Rite of Awakening, but something went wrong. I don't know what, but the connection between you and Anubis is faulty. Our god is out of control, killing indiscriminately. You need to break the link between you before—"

Anubis roared with fury and crossed the distance between them in the blink of an eye. He fastened a clawed hand around Nathan's throat and the god's eyes glowed brightly. Nathan shifted into jakkal form and grabbed Anubis's arm, intending to break his grip, but before he could begin, his body withered, skin becoming parchment-dry, cheeks sinking inward as the flesh of his face drew tight to his skull. He managed to gasp a final word that might have been his wife's name, and then his body lost all cohesion and he fell to the ground as sand.

"No!" Marta shouted. She started to run toward Anubis, but Greg grabbed her shoulders and held her back.

Anubis gazed upon the remains of his vessel's husband. Was there a hint of sorrow in his expression? If so, it was quickly gone. He fixed his crimson-lit eyes on Sam, Dean, and Garth and began growling.

"Any word from the boards yet?" Dean asked Sam.

Sam shook his head.

"All right," Dean said. "Let's go kill us a god."

Dean didn't want to hurt Muriel. She was only a vessel—Anubis was the threat. But Dean knew from long experience that sometimes vessels died in the fight against the supernatural, and while they tried to save people like Muriel, sometimes there was nothing they could do, especially if the entity possessing a vessel was a danger to others.

Dean, Sam, and Garth started walking toward Anubis, armed and ready.

The three hunters spread out as they drew close to Anubis. Their plan was simple—they would attack Anubis, trying different techniques to see if any had an effect on the god. If they managed to discover a weakness, then they'd exploit it.

"Be careful," Dean said. "We don't want to let Anubis turn us into more of his red-eyed puppets."

Dean felt the god's consciousness already beginning to probe the outer layers of his mind, but both he and Sam had been psychically and spiritually attacked numerous times over the years, and they knew a thing or two about resisting mental assaults. And Garth was experienced in resisting the animal side of his nature. After that, resisting Anubis's influence was a piece of cake.

Round one to us, Dean thought.

Dean raised his Colt. They'd already tried silver bullets on Anubis, but those had been quick shots. He wanted to try more precise ones. He fired two shots—one to the head, one to the heart, but all that did was piss the god off. Anubis roared, and Dean fired one more round into his mouth to be thorough, but it had no more effect than the others.

"He's not even bleeding," Garth called out.

"I'm going to try the eyes!" Sam shouted.

Good idea, Dean thought. When Anubis possessed someone, their eyes glowed red—could be those eyes were the source of his power.

Sam squeezed off two rounds. Each found their target, and Anubis's burning-coals eyes went dark. The god roared again, much louder this time, and Dean felt the asphalt beneath his feet vibrate.

Now he's really mad, Dean thought.

The god clawed at Muriel's dead eye sockets. Dean hoped Sam's idea would work. But then Anubis lowered his hands. The light in his blazing red eyes had been rekindled.

"Worth a try," Dean said.

Time for another experiment. If silver didn't do the job, maybe gold would. The metal was deadly to jakkals, and Muriel was a jakkal. Maybe gold would work against the god possessing her body too. Dean edged around and hurled the gold dagger at Anubis's back. It struck the god between the shoulder blades with a satisfying *thunk* and sank all the way to the hilt.

Anubis cried out in pain again, but this time the sound that came out of his mouth was far beyond a simple roar. The scream was so high-pitched and intense that Dean and Sam dropped their weapons and clapped their hands to their ears. It was worse for Garth and the jakkals, with their far more powerful hearing. They moaned in pain and fell to the ground, blood trickling from their ears.

Gotcha! Dean thought. Maybe gold couldn't kill Muriel so long as Anubis's spirit inhabited her body, but it sure as hell could hurt the god.

Anubis stopped screaming. The god remained standing, but he was unsteady on his feet. One strike with a gold weapon hadn't brought him down. Time to take things up a notch.

"You and me, Sammy! It's acupuncture time! Garth, try to keep him distracted! And don't let him touch you—you saw what happened to Nathan!"

Sam and Garth nodded.

Dean snatched up his Colt, Sam retrieved his weapons and together they ran toward Anubis. Dean yanked his gold blade from the creature's back, and ducked in time to avoid getting sliced when the god swiped his claws at him. The Winchester brothers avoided Anubis's blows, ducking, dodging, and weaving as they plunged their gold daggers again and again into Muriel's flesh. Garth shouted taunts at Anubis as he took swipes at the god's arms, legs, chest, and back, doing his best to draw Anubis's attention away from the Winchesters. Anubis tried to catch hold of Garth, but the god was beginning to slow down, and he couldn't manage to land a claw on him.

Anubis stopped trying to kill them. He went down on one knee, slumped forward, and lowered his head. The god wasn't dead yet, but he *was* weakened. Still, they needed to stop him—but how?

Sam felt his phone buzz in his pocket. He took it out and looked at the screen.

"I got a reply on one of the mythology boards. It's from an Egyptology professor. She says 'Burn Anubis's body. That will destroy the god and free the vessel. Hopefully.'"

"I don't like the hopefully part," Dean said.

Sam turned to Garth. "Do you remember back in the room where the jakkals kept Anubis? There was a brazier there." Garth looked at him blankly, and Sam said, "A fire."

Garth gave Sam a fang-filled grin.

"I get it," Dean said. "It'll be just like those old-time movies. The heroes always burn the mummy in the end."

"You're the fastest of us," Sam said to Garth. "Run back to the building and—"

Anubis raised his head. His red eyes began to glow more intensely. Dean thought the god was trying to take over their minds again, but he didn't feel anything. Then he realized that the three of them weren't the only people around.

He turned. Greg, Marta, and Efren—as well as Morgan— had stiffened. Their eyes began to glow with crimson light, and as one they turned their attention to the hunters. Joshua, still lying on the ground, shrieked with anger. The child was possessed too.

"—hurry!" Sam finished.

Garth glanced at the possessed jakkals and took off running. They swiped at him as he passed, but they missed. The jakkals then came running toward Dean and Sam, claws out and red eyes blazing.

Dean and Sam stood back to back as the jakkals came at them. The brothers struck out with their gold blades, slicing hands and arms. The jakkals hissed in pain and withdrew, only to attack again a few seconds later. Since Anubis was using the jakkals as weapons against their will, Sam and Dean tried to avoid dealing any serious blows. Dean didn't know how long they could keep that up though. Eventually, the brothers would be forced to kill them. At least all Joshua did was lie on his back, scream with anger, and thrash his arms and legs. No way in hell Dean wanted to kill a baby.

There was one servant of Anubis who did not fear gold though.

Morgan hung back at first. But then the jakkals parted to let her through, and she raced toward the brothers.

"Sorry about this," Dean said. He still held his Colt and he shot Morgan twice, putting a round in each leg. She went down bleeding, but the red light faded from her eyes.

She spoke through pain-gritted teeth, hands pressed to her wounds. "Thanks for not killing me."

"No problem," Dean said.

The possessed jakkals attacked once more. Out of the corner of his eye, Dean saw Anubis rise to his feet. The god was recovering from his wounds, and if they didn't do something soon, he'd be back to full strength. And if that happened, the Winchesters would either end up ripped to pieces by jakkals or turned into piles of sand by their god. Neither fate sounded appealing.

Come on, Garth! he thought.

Garth entered Anubis's chamber through the large hole in the wall. The god lay on the table, just as he had before, and Garth could hear his inhuman heart beating and his lungs working. The god was alive and awake, or at least his body was. His mind currently inhabited Muriel's body, and Garth hoped it would stay there long enough for him to do his job.

The room was filled with mystic energy. Garth could almost hear it crackle in the air like electricity. The hair on the back of his neck rose, and his animal instincts warned him that this was a bad place—*very* bad—and he should leave immediately. But he didn't need supernatural instincts to tell him what he was doing was dangerous. He was a hunter—danger came with the territory.

He hurried to the shelves and grabbed a large stone container. He knew by its scent that the chemical inside was plain old kerosene. He removed the lid and tossed it away, then dashed to Anubis's side. He splashed kerosene over Anubis's body from head to toe until the container was empty. He threw it aside and ran to the burning brazier, lifted it, and returned to Anubis.

"Flame on," he said and touched the brazier's flame to Anubis's kerosene-soaked wrappings.

Efren lunged at Dean, fangs bared. His teeth were only inches from Dean's neck when Dean rammed the gold blade into his heart. Efren gasped, the crimson light faded from his eyes, and he fell to the ground, dead. Erin came close to tearing Sam's throat out with her claws, and Sam put her down with a thrust of his gold dagger.

Greg and Marta were the only two jakkals left, and Dean feared he and Sam would be forced to kill them too, when they suddenly froze in place. Anubis shrieked in agony, and the Winchesters watched as flames spread across Muriel's body until she was wreathed in fire. Anubis staggered back and forth, screaming in agony as his vessel's body burned. Anubis collapsed to the ground, and lay there, unmoving, as the flames finished their work. Greg and Marta's eyes cleared and Marta rushed to her mother's side. Everyone stood watching the last of the fire burn, Marta kneeling next to Muriel's body and crying while Greg tended to Morgan. Sam picked up Joshua, who had returned to normal after Anubis's death.

"Garth did it," Dean said.

"Yeah."

Dean didn't feel any sense of a triumph though, and he knew Sam didn't either. They'd stopped Anubis, but despite what the Egyptology prof had said, they hadn't been able to save Muriel. When you were a hunter, sometimes—too many times—you lost even when you won.

THIRTY-TWO

They took Alan, Sylvia, Erin, Efren and Muriel's bodies to the woods near the park and buried them. No one spoke any words over their graves, but many tears were shed.

Then they returned to the park, Marta carrying Joshua, Morgan leaning on Greg while her wounds healed. Dean had pried the bullets out of her legs and field dressed her injuries. He figured she'd be fully recovered before too long.

Dean, Sam, and Garth went to the Impala, and Morgan went with them. Greg came too, as well as Marta, who still tended to Joshua. Dean drove them to the newspaper office where Garth had left his car—a Ford Ranchero Squire with a personalized plate that read WULF. Garth followed them back to Morgan's house.

They buried Stuart in the woods. Morgan didn't cry, and they returned to the house without conducting a ceremony or leaving a marker of any kind.

Afterward, they got cleaned up and changed into fresh clothes. Then they sat around the dining table, talking.

"It won't be long before someone realizes the sheriff is missing and comes out here to look for him," Dean said to Morgan. "If you still want to go with Garth, you should pack up and hit the road ASAP."

Joshua was sleeping in her arms, and she gazed down at her little brother with a sad smile.

"Okay." She didn't sound enthused to be leaving. Dean couldn't blame her. This wasn't exactly a happy occasion.

"I've already called Bess and told her you were coming," Garth said. "There'll be a room prepared for you and your brother by the time we get there."

She gave Garth a grateful smile. Then she turned toward Greg, who was sitting next to her. She gave him a questioning look.

He smiled and took her hand. "I want to go with you," he said. He turned to his mother. "Come with us."

"Yes," Garth said. "My pack would be glad to have you."

Marta looked uncomfortable at the idea, but then she smiled wearily.

"Thank you," she said.

And that settled that.

"But we should shake a leg," Garth said. "Dean was right about us needing to get out of here, and it's a long drive to Wisconsin."

Morgan quickly packed a few bags for her and Joshua, and then everyone went outside. Morgan looked back at her house one last time, and Dean wondered what sort of memories she'd be taking with her. He hoped at least some of them would be good ones.

The Winchesters said goodbye to Morgan, Greg, Marta, and

Joshua, and watched as they climbed into Garth's Wulfmobile.

Dean, Sam, and Garth stood together one last time.

"You think the kids will be okay?" Dean asked Garth.

"Yeah," Garth said. "Like it says in *The Way of the Fang*, 'Family don't end in blood.'"

Dean looked at Sam, but neither of them said anything.

Garth gave the brothers a bear hug, and then he stepped back. "It was good working with you guys again. You take care of each other now."

Sam smiled. "We always do. Give our love to Bess."

Garth nodded. He got in his car, started the engine, and backed down the driveway.

Before leaving the Crowders' home, Sam reported Amos's and Melody's deaths to the sheriff's department. Anonymously, of course. Then he and Dean hit the road. Before long they were cruising along Route 65 on the way back to the Bunker in Kansas.

No, Sam thought. *Back home.*

They drove without speaking for some time, classic rock playing on the radio. Eventually Sam said, "Do you remember that old werewolf movie we watched when we were kids? *Night of the Blood Moon?*"

"Sure," Dean said. "Why?"

"I was thinking it might be fun to watch it again. Get a chance to see it from an adult perspective, you know?"

Dean gave Sam a look. "'Adult perspective?'" he said dubiously.

"I've never really understood why you like horror movies. Don't we get enough horror in our lives as it is? But after what we just went through, I think it would be comforting to only have to deal with pretend horrors for a change. Maybe we can find the movie online when we get home."

Dean grinned and turned his attention back to the road. "No need. I got that bad boy on Blu-Ray. And after we finish that one, I'll show you one of my favorites: *All Saints' Day*."

Sam settled back in his seat and looked out of the window, watching the Indiana countryside go by.

"Sounds perfect," he said.

ACKNOWLEDGMENTS

As always, thanks to my agent, Cherry Weiner, for her guidance, advice, and friendship. Extra-special thanks to my editor, Joanna Harwood. The book you're holding in your hands is far better because of her efforts. Thanks for making me look good, Joanna!

ABOUT THE AUTHOR

Tim Waggoner writes original dark fantasy, horror, and media tie-ins including *Supernatural*, *Kingsman*, and *Resident Evil*. In 2017 he received the Bram Stoker Award for Superior Achievement in Long Fiction, he's been a finalist for the Shirley Jackson and the Scribe awards, and his fiction has received numerous honorable mentions in volumes of *Best Horror of the Year*. Tim teaches creative writing and composition at Sinclair College in Dayton, Ohio.

For more fantastic fiction, author events,
competitions, limited editions and more

VISIT OUR WEBSITE
titanbooks.com

LIKE US ON FACEBOOK
facebook.com/titanbooks

FOLLOW US ON TWITTER
@TitanBooks

EMAIL US
readerfeedback@titanemail.com